THE OTHER SIDE OF REALITY

BOOK TWO

THE CONQUEST OF SAPIENT CASTLE

DEDICATION

To my two eldest grandsons, Gavin and Eathan Russell, and my granddaughter and youngest grandson Kaia Grace and Ian Ryan Durham; and to all the grandchildren everywhere, young and old, whom the Living One so deeply loves.

∞————————————————————————————————∞

This Trilogy is also dedicated to the memory and impact of Charlie Kirk whose gracious and staunch love of the truth helped so many to find the light leading to *the other side of reality*.

ABOUT THIS TRILOGY

This Trilogy is what C. S Lewis would have called "a supposal."
It is a story using *likening*—comparing different aspects of reality to
what it is *not* for the purpose of revealing more of what it is—to pull
the reader into an other-worldly adventure from which he or she may
look back on this world with an enhanced objectivity and clarity.

The haunting awareness—clear to some and vague to others—
that this world is pointing beyond itself, that it is even sometimes a
poor mirror giving us fleeting, tantalizing glimpses of another world,
or an echo that dies away before the beauty of some majestic melody
can be fully heard, often awakens us to deliciously painful longings.
The Other Side of Reality seeks to bring the objects of these longings
into sharper focus for the reader, and perhaps, for some, to awaken
the experience of such longings for the first time.

These longings point to more than desire. They leave an
imprint on the soul like an ocean wave leaves on a beach. The imprint
testifies to the reality of the wave. When we properly contemplate the
imprints left on our souls by the invisible waves often washing over
us uninvited, we are startled by an involuntary spring of hope rising
within us. It is a hope crying for life to have a meaning and purpose
that comes from beyond this world and will outlive this world.

In this sense, this Trilogy is an attempt to give perspective:
a perspective much needed in a culture where reductionism has
shriveled the organ of meaning—our imaginations—by dehydrating

the significance of life and everything it contains. If, *"this is only that"* is the ultimate pathway to reality, then the only possible conclusion is unrelenting despair.

But that despair, itself, raises the question: Why do we despair? Why do we hope for more? If there isn't any more, why do we long for it? Why do we pine? If we are mere accidents between two cosmic voids, why do the desires for meaning and purpose, identity and security tug so relentlessly at our souls? Are there truths beyond our senses to which this hunger and thirst point?

The Other Side of Reality, by means of a fascinating story, seeks to raise and focus these questions in the form of a *supposal*. *Suppose* someone were taken to the other side of reality and could see not only the material world but the world lying beyond and behind it. *Suppose* they were also taken out of their time and dropped into the flow of our world's first history. *Suppose* there was a critical reason for them to be there and the meaning and purpose of all future life would hang on their willingly engaging a dangerous journey, and so forth. By means of such a story, it is my belief this kind of *likening* can silhouette the answers—the *objects* for which we hunger and thirst— and resurrect the true passion of living.

I make no apologies for believing there is another side to reality and that it can be known because *Someone* is seeking to reveal it. What is more, I believe the other side of reality has a very definite character and nature; it is filled both with risk, danger and possible tragedy as well as adventure, love and possible triumph; and you will determine which it will be for you by how you engage these unseen actualities.

Welcome to *The Other Side of Reality!*

— *Gary L. Durham, June 14, 2025*

PREFACE

Dr. Gary L. Durham is a fascinating man—scholar, science buff, theologian, counselor, teacher, musician, even a bit of a daredevil. He's one of those guys who keep surprising you with new facets of his personality that you didn't know were there. He's the only man I know who writes patents for fun on his "day off" and thinks zip-lining less than 100 feet off the ground is boring. Among his many other talents, I've discovered that Gary is an incredibly creative storyteller. I'm honored to call him my friend.

The Other Side of Reality is an imaginative adventure born in Gary's heart many years ago and is finally making its way to the printed and digital page. It's the tale of a young woman who is pulled into a daring quest in which the future of humanity is at stake. The quest takes place on The Other Side of Reality, the realm in which both material and spiritual realities are seen and interacted with in ways that reveal the Creator's grand Story more clearly than most of us have ever imagined. She fights intense battles, confronts many faces of evil, learns to love and trust, and is forever changed by her encounters with *the real world* like you've never seen it. The story entertains, inspires and teaches, all with one stroke. Editing this work has been a labor of love.

Congratulations on discovering *The Other Side of Reality*. This tale will enrich your life!

— Don White, Editor

ACKNOWLEDGEMENTS

In undertaking any endeavor and bringing it to completion, I doubt any of us can fully comprehend the extent to which we owe gratitude for the contributions of others. From our first breath until our last we are continually being formed and re-formed by the influence of other people either for good or ill.

At this stage in my life, I have come to acknowledge and appreciate that whatever successes I can claim are owed more to the competent generosity of others as they have impacted my life. By sharing their knowledge, skill, friendship and gifts with me they have determined the outcome more than any autonomous efforts of my own. In deciding and executing the writing of this Trilogy, I have found it to be a journey continually highlighting and reenforcing this truth.

In one sense, in writing a supposal with historical truths interlaced and undergirding the whole novel story, with the addition of theo-philosophical and apologetic applications embedded, I was in my element. However, I soon realized my many years of academic research and theological writing had trained me to a style of writing inappropriate to the new audience I was seeking to reach. And it was the many contributions of my colleagues and friends lovingly seeking to assist me, which confirmed this realization.

They loved the story. They loved its many impacts on the worldview of the reader. Yet, they ever-so-patiently kept suggesting I needed to use a very different style of writing to communicate it.

My primary editor, Don White, was the first to suffer through seeking to redirect my writing style to one more appropriate to the content and its intended audience. To state Don is a good friend who has the patience of Job is no overstatement. His kind, yet unyielding editorial skill and work continually confronted me with the need to stop and seek to learn another way of writing.

To the extent I succeeded remains to be assessed by you the reader. To the extent attained it is due to the generous, skillful, loving and persistent help of numerous literary friends God has brought into my life.

That being said, I must express my heartfelt, though abbreviated, appreciation to the following colleagues, friends and family members:

To Joshua "Gavin" Russell, my grandson, whose brilliant, creative and imaginative mind added untold value in getting me beyond some stop points when once I took the story, begun many years before, off the shelf to be finished. Gavin, Papa will always be more grateful than you could possibly know! I will always treasure our times of reading and discussing the books on our *Man Trips*. There are many ways in which this is your story, too.

To my editorial reading group, many of which are very talented and successful authors in their own right, the Red Inklings: thank you for the many hours of reading, discussions, corrections and suggestions. To Hugh Vickery (who has two excellent books just becoming available for which the Red Inklings provided editorial feedback), Diane Rudd, Rose Arndt, Jeannine Voisinet, Rose Rohloff (whose red pen was merciless but effective), Anthony DeSantis (whom I want to congratulate on his New York Times best seller, *The Stowaway In First Class*, which the Red Inklings helped to edit), and Rick Walker.

Also, a few years back as the books were taking form, I want to thank my accountability reading circle, which at that time included Gary & Irene Merritt and Diane Rudd. They held me to the task and provided much-appreciated feedback week after week.

To my dear friend and ministry partner, Gary Merritt, whose loyal and effective ministry as Executive Pastor has enabled me to give myself more fully to the teaching and writing I am called to do.

To my general editor, Don White (mentioned above), whose skillful and creative massaging and rephrasing of my early manuscripts has made this work much more readable and attainable to a broader audience than my own academic and sometimes-verbose writing style could have accomplished.

To a good friend, who has since unexpectedly gone Home to be with our Lord, Darren Currin, who took several vacation days from his ministry at Life Church in Oklahoma City, to go through the books with me as a content editor. I will always be thankful for your contributions.

To my C. S. Lewis reading group at New Hope, which took several weeks away from our normal diet to read through some of the early material for the Trilogy. Thanks for being willing to descend from the joyous, intoxicating heights of *Jack* to the lowlands of Gary.

To several precious friends who have been willing to read the manuscripts and give sage feedback. Among them my lifelong best friend and brother, Rev. Larry Ryan, and another precious longtime friend, Dr. Steven Fletcher, and a longtime colleague and partner in ministry, Rev. Alan Scott. Also, Dr. Stan Toler, Dr. Pat and Mark McNab, and Lois Fazier (Lois read some of the first chapters written over 30 years ago when the dream of this Trilogy was first given birth). Thanks to all of you for letting me impose *my* dream on *you*.

To my wonderful New Hope family who are a constant encouragement to me and my ministry. No pastor/teacher could have a more positive atmosphere of love and support in which to serve.

To Tony and Judy DeSantis, Gary and Jan Motley and Larry and Gayla Ryan for making unsolicited financial investments in seeing this dream become reality. Your generosity has been a blessed confirmation for me to finish strong.

To my precious, loving and supportive family. My son-in-law, David, my daughter, Janet, my grandsons, Gavin and Ethan (and Gavin's new wife Kayla), for your example of sacrificial ministry and commitment to excellence as missionaries in Tanzania, Africa and now in the counseling ministry here in the states after your return. To my son, Ryan, who has served many years in ministry as Worship Pastor, many of which has been here at New Hope, and his wife, Colleen. Thanks for being such dedicated, loving parents to my two grandchildren, Kaia Grace and Ian Ryan. Ryan, your creative gift of music and composition shared in both worship settings and through your albums, is a constant source of inspiration. Every week you lead in creating a Spirit-anointed atmosphere of worship in which I can preach and teach.

To my dearest friend and loving wife, Sheryl, who has been my partner in many different ministry assignments from missionary, pastor, teacher, counselor, musician, etc. Your own mastery of music and your use of it to serve our Lord and even teach hundreds of students is beyond expression. Several years ago, the Living One used Sheryl to confirm I was indeed to finish this project. Sheryl, you are God's gift of so much beauty and grace to me and our family. I am indeed blessed to journey this life with you!

Above all others, my thanks goes to the Living One, Himself, King Jesus, who kept stimulating and sanctifying my imagination and efforts to His purpose through the long and sometime-tedious hours of writing, rewriting, editing and revising. All the while, His Presence never left my side, giving me direction and clarity and the self-control I needed to keep this hyperactive Type-A personality focused on such a long task.

Repeatedly I have looked back after writing a chapter and realized He had written something through me I could never have conceived of on my own. All the good is from Him. All the flaws are from me.

I have grown as I have struggled to find new ways of communicating the old, unchangeable, ever-new realities of His beauty and glory. And in those months of emersion, I really did have the privilege of being sometimes on *The Other Side of Reality!*

— *Gary L. Durham, June 14, 2025*

TABLE OF CONTENTS

Hole in the World

Valley of Son

El River

Hi

N e k u s

Sapient Castle

Upper Great
Meadow

Sapient River

The Great Meadow

Nekus River

Map of
Severed Lands

The Great Chasm

f EL

Beast of Paranoia

Thanatos' Domain

ateau

Nekus Canyon

Rock Bridge

Altar

ellicose's
Domain

Valley

Lavon's Savanna

The
Garden

Dorogon Ridge

Mist Forest

Ruins of Dorogon Castle

Mist Mountain

Hill of Voices

Tree Bridge

Dry Stream Bed

IMPORTANT NAMES AND MEANINGS

Diakrina (Dia-KREE-na): The prefix, Dia, is to be pronounced Anglicized as in, *Diaphragm*

Strateia (Strah-TEE-ah—Anglicized from the true Greek pronunciation, Strah-TAY-ah): Warfare, to make war, a great host or army, thus as applied to one person: A Great Warrior

Anomos Poneros (AH-no-mos Po-NAY-ros)

Heylel (Hay-LEL): Morning Star; one who shines brightly

Scepter Of Kabod (Kah-BAHD)

Kingdom Of Parad (Paw-RAHD)

Tuphoo (Too-FAH-oh)

Thanatos (THAN-ah-tos): Fallen angel of death, lord over the realms of the dead

Nekus (Neh-koos): The canyon of Thanatos, which name means corpse

BOOK TWO
THE QUEST CONTINUES

Chapter One

THE GREAT MEADOW

Strateia led Diakrina from the Spring of Longings and out through the mouth of the cave into the sunlight of a perfect day. The birds were busy at their chattering songs. Walking over and resuming his place on the wide stone in the grassy area alongside the stream, he motioned for Diakrina to find a seat.

Diakrina, who preferred the soft green carpet of grass, laid her sword, shield and the crystal container, along with the Atheos, on the rock beside Strateia. She then turned and settled down cross-legged in the grass in front of him. Strateia's face expressed solemn intensity as he began to outline what lay ahead of them.

"As yet, Diakrina, you have not been allowed to go among your ancient progenitors, but soon you must. However, first we must make our way to Sapient Castle. Within its walls you will obtain an important form of light—a source of illumination and power, a transcended weapon—you will need to engage the next phase of your quest. Only then will you be fully prepared for this next phase where you will also need the help of Lord Mazzaroth and his warriors."

"Who is this Lord Mazzaroth?" interrupted Diakrina.

"He is the third son of Adam, your Great Father who fell from the Great Dance. You would know him as Seth. He is first in importance after Adam, for Adam's firstborn son, Cain, invalidated himself by committing the first murder when he killed his younger brother, Abel, in a jealous rage."

Strateia then recounted to Diakrina an ancient story of her earliest ancestors and how most of Cain's descendants are deceived by Anomos and are in league with his purposes.

"They are in league with the fallen elohim, known as the two hundred—who have broken with the Living One's law of creation and have taken women from Cains lineage and mated with them to create a polluted and corrupt race of beings—hybrid humans. These children of the fallen elohim are called the Nephilim."

"Nephilim? I have heard the term used. Isn't it in the first book of the Great Book?" asked Diakrina.

"Yes, it is. And it there describes how the Nephilim came to be. They are the result of these fallen elohim—gods that once were part of the Living One's Divine Counsel—conspiring to pollute mankind by intermarriage with human women. They were very high-ranking beings. But they were among those led into the great Fall by Heylel.

"These Nephilim are the hybrid humans they gave birth to. They are great in statue—giants—and will come to be remembered in later days as, 'men of renown' in the myths of many pagan stories. They are causing much bloodshed in these times, and they are terrorizing, enslaving and oppressing many people groups."

Strateia also informed Diakrina that many of the descendants of Lord Mazzaroth were beginning to be corrupted as well and were succumbing to the Cainite culture of hostility toward the Living One.

"What is more, Diakrina," continued Strateia, "you need to know these Nephilim are in the land. You will do well to avoid them when possible."

As you can see, Anomos has more than one plan aimed at trying to remove mankind as a weapon in the Living One's hands."

"These Nephilim, can they also intermarry with humans?"

"Yes, they can. And the result is a constant endangering of the human race."

Diakrina thought for a moment. "So, is there some way to stop this?"

"Yes, it will demand being dealt with soon enough. The Nephilim are so wicked and so large and powerful, they are causing bloodshed and violence to become the norm all over the inhabited planet. They are not only corrupt they are on a course to corrupting all humanity.

Already, as a form of early judgment the Living one is causing the various clans of the Nephilim to be at war with each other. This will result in their near extinction in a few hundred years.

"So, what will the Living One do to bring a full end to them and preserve the human raced?" asked Diakrina, suddenly aware of how serious such a situation could be.

"Think back to the place in the Great Book where the Nephilim are mentioned. Do you remember the next event in the history of earth?"

Diakrina thought for a moment and then it came to her. "It's the Great Flood."

"Yes," confirmed Strateia, "and it will greatly grieve the heart of the Living One that such a remedy will become necessary. But it will be. If He had not dealt with the problem so decisively, there would have been no hope for your race to ever come Home. The Promised-One to come, the One who crushes Anomos' head—destroying the power of his lying accusations against the Living One and mankind forever—could never have been born from a Nephilim-polluted gene-pool.

"When the Great Book stated, 'Noah found grace in the eyes of the Living One,' it was not just because he and his family were still faithful to Him, but also because their family-line was, as yet, unpolluted by the Nephilim bloodlines. For it further states, 'Noah was a righteous man, blameless in his generations …' Notice that, generations, is plural. It is not merely talking about Noah being upright within his time—generation—but that his generations—bloodline was blameless—unpolluted. This was one of the important characteristics qualifying him and his sons and their wives to carry the Seed forward beyond the flood."

"So, you are saying," interjected Diakrina, "from my vantage point looking back at history from—A.D. the 21st century—Anomos almost succeeded in destroying all hope for mankind to be restored during this time prior to the Flood. And this is why the Living One had to deal with it so radically?"

Strateia nodded to the affirmative.

"So … my quest is another of the same kind. Right?"

"Yes and no, Little One. You see this is just as dangerous a plot, but the Living One's decision was to crush it in the bud, so to speak, and never let it produce fruit of any kind. This plan was devised before mankind's fall into bondage to Anomos, and no humans have yet cooperated with it in any way; they simply don't know about the plot or the danger it poses. So, the Living One is going to stop it before it can happen."

"So," interjected Diakrina with wide-eyed hope, "that means I will succeed!"

"Well, again, yes and no," answered Strateia with blunt candor. "It means someone will succeed. And it can be you," he quickly added. "Already the Living One has brought several others here before you to engage this quest. Unfortunately, all before you failed. In fact, Diakrina, none ever made it this far. They never conquered Nekus Canyon or retrieved the Atheos. They all failed the test of trust."

This bit of information left Diakrina stunned. She sat there for several moments, likely with her mouth open in astonishment, while hundreds of what ifs flooded her mind. Strateia did not wait until she regained her voice.

"The test of trusting is always the hinge-point of the quest. The Living One will not stop until this vile plot is undone. And He is with you to see to it you have everything you need to succeed. I am one of those provisions. But in the end, it will be your faith in the Living One, or the lack of it, deciding the outcome for you and the present quest to eliminate this dreadful danger."

Diakrina tried to speak, but no words would form. Her mind seemed to be like an overloaded computer trying to play a movie yet is stuck buffering.

Strateia seem to understand. And his solution was to change

the subject back to his original reason for mentioning the Nephilim.

"Diakrina, you will have to deal with the Nephilim. They are very dangerous. Many of them are over 12 feet tall and extremely massive and strong. But you must not think because they are large and massive they will be slow and lumbering hulks. Most are as quick and agile as a cat. And they are three to four-times as strong as the average human. None of them serve the Living One. All of them are His sworn enemy.

"But your trust in the Living One, and the power of your Kingdom sword, will give you the edge. Remember the Beasts of Paranoia—face all fears head-on in faith."

All Diakrina could say was, "I will do my best, Strateia." But a dread was now looming on the horizon of her mind.

"You must be aware of the Nephilim, so you are not caught off-guard. But they will not be your only obstacle. There will be many others. This is why you will need the help of Lord Mazzaroth and his warriors."

They sat together for several seconds in silence. Then Strateia broke the silence.

"I need to continue with my information concerning Lord Mazzaroth and the Sons of El. For they are the last remnant in the Severed Lands that can provide us help. Many of them are still very committed to the Living One because of the Promise.

"As I have told you, the Living One gave Adam, your great parent, wonderful promises as to how He would undo the work of Anomos and restore mankind, even though it would cost the Living One a great sacrifice of Himself. To preserve these wonderful promises, Adam and Seth—Lord Mazzaroth—have written the elements of the story revealed to them on the stars. They did this by associating certain constellations of stars with different parts of the story with images they laid over the constellations. Each image is designed to depict one key aspect of the unfolding story."

However, Strateia then warned her that in her day the language of the stars would have become so terribly distorted and corrupted it would no longer be useful except by those who knew the original story and meaning of the constellations and who could, then, show how it perfectly depicted how the story actually unfolded in the history of the Great Book. He said the corrupted and commonly taught meaning of the constellations would, in her time, lead people to completely misinterpret the symbols and their messages and claim to read absurd stories and missives in the skies and ascribe false power to them giving them life-altering influence.

"It will be a corrupt foundation for false worship and religions—complete deception. It will be propagated down through history by the spirits of Babel which seeks to collect mankind in hostility to the Living One's creation order and plan. The spirit of Babel, later know as Babylon, will resist the New Creation renewal plan all through the ages down to the very end.

"Anomos always seeks to corrupt any means of communicating truth and to replace it with falsehoods," added Strateia. "It will be mostly only false religions that will use the messages of the stars in your time—and those will be corrupted, false messages."

Diakrina sat for over an hour enraptured by the vivid history of her race, as Strateia braided story upon story together. She would gladly have sat there all morning and listened to him relate more and more, but Strateia's mind turned to other things.

"Diakrina," he said after a brief pause from his ancient tales, "we must now turn our attention on more urgent matters. We will eventually sojourn through the Land of Lord Mazzaroth, but first we must go to Sapient Castle."

Strateia stood and motioned for Diakrina to gather her things and make ready for their journey.

"What is this Sapient Castle, Strateia, and why must I go there? Something about light?" Diakrina asked as she fastened her sword belt around her waist.

"Sapient Castle holds a treasure you will need if you are ever to get back to the Tree Bridge with the Atheon and then be able to cross back over. The Castle is designed into the realms of the metaphysical to allow you to walk, as it were, through your own spiritual being and through things the Living One needs to show you and do for you.

What is more, it will awaken your understanding so you can accept His help—grace—to experience needed transformations.

"Sapient Castle, as its name indicates, means a place of great wisdom and sagacity. It holds many treasures generally neglected by your race in its present spiritual bondage. However, the Living one intends to awaken within you many of these spiritual sources of wisdom so you will be prepared to succeed on the rest of the quest.

"The treasure you need most from within the Castle is called the Lantern of Logos, with which you must rekindle an ancient Altar deep within the Castle. The Castle has been haunted for some time by the spirits of ignorance, lies and fears—the primary weapons of Anomos chaining and binding your race. They have created a kind of stupor over the Castle which you must undo in regard to yourself. This Altar, which has become darkened, must burn again in order for you to succeed. By means of it being rekindled within you, and together with the Lantern of Logos, you will be given an inner light vital for you. Without its light, you could not succeed.

"What is more, Diakrina, when you leave the Castle you must pass back through the Mist Forest. You traversed only its very edge before you entered the cave just beyond the Tree Bridge. But this time you must pass through the Forest carrying the Atheos, and you will likely be fleeing with all your strength from Anomos' hordes."

"Can we use the cave to pass through the mountain again?" asked Diakrina hopefully.

"No. Now that you carry the Atheos, you must avoid all underground, dark places. There are creatures controlled by Anomos moving though earth as easily as you move through air. They would use the underground riverbed as a place to trap you. There would be no escape. No, you must keep above ground while you carry the Atheos, and this will mean passing through the Mist Forest back toward the Tree Bridge."

Diakrina felt a new dread rising within her at the mention of the terrible Mist Forest. She wanted nothing to do with that dripping, dead, illusion-spinning place. Strateia felt her reluctance.

"Diakrina, it is imperative we make it to Sapient Castle soon.

Anomos will have his spies everywhere. And once he realizes we are headed to the Castle he will likely try to ambush us before we get there or while we are there. You must have time to pass through and rekindle the Light within your spirit, and awaken the Rose Red Stone Altar, before Anomos can hem us in."

Diakrina started to ask about the altar but Strateia interrupted her before she could speak. "There will be time to speak about these things later. For now we must only speak while we act, as time is short."

Diakrina felt a sense of urgency descend on her. And it is likely this is the very effect Strateia desired his words to have on her.

She rose and quickly completed her dressing so they could leave. As she finished putting her last pieces of gear in place, Strateia walked close to her and turned her around toward him.

"Diakrina, we will soon go into the land of the Antediluvians after we leave Sapient Castle. They do not speak your language and you do not speak theirs. Yet, it is necessary they understand you, and you understand them. They speak the first language—the original tongue. Though it has been diminished by the Fall, it is still a near perfect version of the language given to Adam by the Living One, Himself. It is the mother tongue of mankind and their many languages. But this original language is itself lost to the world in your time."

"Then how am I to understand them and they me?" asked Diakrina, looking rather bewildered.

Strateia lifted her chin with his giant hands so that she looked straight up into his eyes.

"I have been given a gift for you, Little One. And this is as good a time as any to give it to you. Look in my eyes, Diakrina."

Diakrina looked deeply into Strateia's clear eyes with their subtle hint of blue. There she saw such strength, such knowledge and such peace she was overcome with wonder. But before she could think more about it, a golden light, with swirling blue and white light within it, came from Strateia's eyes and floated slowly down toward hers. She gazed, astonished, into the beauty of the swirling circles of light as they drifted toward her and came to rest on her own eyes; and then, ever so slowly, they sank inside her.

Diakrina came to herself suddenly. "Strateia, that was incredible . . ." She stopped in mid-sentence for something felt strange. Then she realized she had indeed communicated the phrase, "Strateia, that was incredible," but she had said it in a different language; one she had never spoken or heard before.

Shock covered her face, and then she started speaking again. "I am speaking a different language which I . . ." she meant to continue by saying, ". . . have never spoken before." But instead, she stopped again in mid-sentence because the music of this ancient language amazed her as it came from her mouth. She understood exactly what she was saying, but the sounds were new and wonderful.

When Strateia responded, he spoke the ancient language, also. "Now you speak more beautifully than ever before," he said with a smile.

Diakrina was enraptured by the words Strateia spoke. Not only were the sound and meter wonderful to hear, but she understood them perfectly and the language had marvelous powers of expression—greater power of expression than she had ever known.

"Come, Little One," said Strateia in the new tongue. "It is time we were on our way."

Diakrina fell in behind Strateia as they made their way toward the wooden bridge. As they walked, she couldn't help saying to Strateia, "This language which we are speaking is beautiful to the ear," for she wanted to hear her own or Strateia's voice using it.

"You are speaking the language the Living One gave to your first parents. It is an exquisite and complex language: one not only of expression, but also of thought. It provides a structure by which the mind can organize and communicate thoughts that would otherwise be impossible even to think. All language does this to some extent, but none as fully as this original tongue."

"Do all the languages come from this one?" asked Diakrina.

"There is a little of it in all the languages that have ever been spoken," answered Strateia. "A few languages have retained more of it than others. But none is but a poor caricature of its eloquent power."

They walked along the stream until they reached the small wooden bridge and then turned left and crossed over it to the opposite bank. As they set foot on the other side of the stream, Strateia suddenly froze in his tracks. He lifted his left hand in a gesture for Diakrina to stop as he turned and fixed his eyes on her. "Don't move," he whispered as he leaned down until his face was close to her right ear. "We have company."

Diakrina stiffened and nodded her understanding of his warning. As yet she could hear nothing even though her every sense was on full alert. But she knew to trust Strateia's perception. She had come to realize his senses were many times greater than any human.

He listened intently for a moment and then motioned for Diakrina to softly retreat back across the bridge. This she began doing with steps as stealthy as she could manage while Strateia followed her walking backward with his sword and face still looking up the hill and the path leading over its top to the gate through which Diakrina had come when she arrived at the Spring the day before.

When they reached the other side of the stream he turned and motioned for Diakrina to follow him. He made for a large tree not far from the bridge and they positioned themselves around behind it and waited. As yet, Diakrina had still heard nothing.

Then she heard it. It was the sound of marching feet. They were coming from the south and were clearly on the path at the top of the hill. They were marching uphill headed back the way Diakrina had come the day before, which meant they would turn east toward the western branch of Nekus canyon if they continued the path as it passed the gate.

"Stay here and don't move until I return," whispered Strateia. And with that he disappeared into the sky.

Diakrina could now hear the marching feet much clearer as they were getting increasingly closer. Then she heard a deep, thick, inhuman voice bark a command.

"Increase the pace, you swamp rats. Double-time this turn. I don't like this area. It smells of longings." Then came a vile curse—

which Diakrina would not repeat—as the inhuman voice grumbled rather loudly, "!#$^&*! this Hole in the World. It is no end of trouble for us. I wish it could be sealed off and dammed up." The marching cadence nearly doubled as the soldiers quickly responded.

As the voice finished its' cursing, suddenly Strateia was back beside Diakrina. "It is a unit of about 31 of Anomos' soldiers. Most are Nephilim. There are 30 on foot, marching in formation 3 abreast and 10 deep. The captain is mounted," whispered Strateia. "They are on patrol and I don't doubt you are the reason."

"It doesn't sound like they are coming down here," responded Diakrina in a low whisper. "Not likely," whispered Strateia. "This spring is a place that makes them feel ill if they spend too much time near it. They feel about this place like you would feel about a haunted forest. There is too much of a scent of life here. That captain will not have to urge them very much to get them to quicken their pace. They will do it on their own."

Then they heard the rumbling voice speaking again. "Keep moving you marsh toads. Hopefully that little vermin of a human is still caged in by the beasts. If so, we will have her before she can get free into these forest and mountains."

There was no doubt now. They were clearly looking for Diakrina.

Diakrina could tell by the sound of the marching they had now made the turn in the path and were marching away from them toward the east and the western branch of Nekus.

Strateia went down on one knee behind the tree and replaced his sword. "We will be fine for the moment. We will let them get a few hundred yards to the east and then make our way up to the path. We are going south, and it will be some time before they will discover you have already escaped the Beasts of Paranoia.

The sound of the marching feet and the growling commands of the captain slowly died away as the unit moved up the hill away from them and over the rise toward Nekus.

"Let's go," said Strateia suddenly standing to his full height. They made their way back across the bridge. Then together they walked back up the path leading to the wooden gate.

Strateia reached it first and opened it, as it made a slight creaking sound. He held it open as Diakrina passed through. Then passing through himself, he let it slap shut with that homey sound, which the day before had reminded Diakrina of her childhood.

She paused in the path looking back at the gate.

"For some reason you like that sound, don't you?" said Strateia as he eyed her expression.

"Yes, it reminds me of childhood summer days on my grandfather's farm; days filled with play and exciting adventures with my cousins. We had the run of the farm, and it was a wonderful place full of hills, forest, streams and fields in which kids could create their own imaginary world."

Strateia studied her face for a moment and then said, "Such memories are precious. Cherish them."

"I do, Strateia . . . I do."

Strateia made one last glance around the curve of the path toward the east, and seeing all was clear they stepped out and quickly headed downhill to the south. As they traveled south they were descending toward a green, forested valley spread out ahead of them. A tree-covered path wound down between two wooded, winding hillsides, toward the valley floor.

Always to their right was the sound of the tumbling stream from the Spring of Longings also making the short hike into the landscape below them. The songs of the morning birds, the gurgling of the stream and the occasional scamper of a squirrel or rabbit out from among the bushes and flowers lining the path gave the morning a storybook quality to Diakrina. This helped Diakrina take her mind off the soldiers behind them. But the aggressive pace Strateia was setting made the need to put as much distance between themselves and the soldiers as possible, unforgotten.

In about an hour they came to a level, grassy place where their path forked. The right-hand fork turned toward a small wooden bridge spanning the flowing water and connecting, on the far side of the stream, to another path continuing westward up a hillside.

Diakrina pointed to the small wooden bridge, "Are we to go that way?"

"No. Though that path does lead up to the hilltop and over to Sapient Valley and the Castle, it is a long and winding way and passes too close to one of Anomos' outpost. We would likely encounter another patrol if we took that path. No, we will continue south with the river into the Great Meadow. A few miles into the Meadow we will turn back west—to the right—and make our way up on top of this ridge. We will then transverse along its top coming back north for a way. On the ridge's top is another path going along the hills and then down and over the west side into Sapient Valley. Sapient Castle lies on the slopes of the far side of that valley."

Strateia motioned toward the path continuing south along the east bank of the stream, then set out in his usual warrior's stride. Diakrina hurried to keep pace.

Except for the passage though the mountain, this was the first hard march they had undertaken since Diakrina had come through the Door of the Rose. While she had to trot at a brisk pace to keep up with the striding Strateia, she soon realized, after several minutes of this fast pace, she was not experiencing the fatigue she would expect. It would be some time before she would learn the reason for this newfound stamina, but it made it possible for her to speak to Strateia even while she trotted beside him.

"Strateia, you mentioned the people of this time live much longer lives," said Diakrina referring back to the lengthy stories he had told her earlier that day. "They must grow quite wise over time, since they live so long."

"Yes, they have that opportunity, and some become immensely knowledgeable. Yet, there are others who only use their time to compound their foolishness and become more cunning in evil."

"I think I understand something of what it would be like to live so long, Strateia," said Diakrina. "In the vision at the Spring of Longings, I lived for thousands upon thousands of years as an immortal. Much of it was wonderful at first, quite beyond anything I have ever imagined. But toward the end, the whole of the cosmos seemed to be closing in on me. Why was that so?"

"The Living One has put eternity in your soul, Little One. Only He can fill your yearnings. The longer you lived in your vision, the more inadequate all other things became. Once you experienced it all, apart from Him, there was no more to be had. A limited, finite universe soon becomes a prison to a soul with boundless hungers and thirsts. You are a limited being, but you bear the image of the infinite Living One and He has created you to know Him and need Him. He has welcomed you into His own Life in amazing ways. In your vision, you were condemned: eternally severed from any possibility of knowing and partaking of His infinite Life.

"By choosing immortality only within the context of this dying creation, you—by 'you' of course I mean the Diakrina of the vision—were doomed to suffer death with it. Your immortality was confined in a dying material world. All things, apart from the Life-giving presence of the Living One, will ultimately implode, leaving even immortal souls in a context of complete nothingness, left only with an insatiable hunger for what can no longer be attained. Immortal existence severed from Life is the most horrifying of curses. It is the darkest and emptiest of hells."

Diakrina shuddered as she recalled the terrors of her vision and processed Strateia's last words aloud. "So . . . immortality apart from a relationship with the Living One would only be a slowly emerging hell?"

"Yes, Diakrina. This is why your mission is so crucial. It is this the Living One is determined to save you and your race from ever knowing. In your time Anomos makes fools of many with the idea science will give them a way to abolish death. It cannot, for death is more than a physical reality. It is such a powerful curse only the Living One can overwhelm it.

"But even if science could abolish physical death, and even if it could give you perfect health, it could not give you a life worth living. Everything would soon close in on you. You need more than unending existence. You need a new kind of life—His Life—and no science could ever give that to your race. Humans and the cosmos are dying together. Both need rebirth."

They soon began to descend at a steep rate as they made

their way toward a wide valley stretching out before them to the far horizon. As the valley and its inhabitants came increasingly clear, Diakrina was shocked at the world emerging before them. This valley, full of rolling hills, flourished with trees and vegetation looking otherworldly to Diakrina.

Trees over 300 and even 400 feet tall filled the landscape. But these were not slender, towering trunks with branches only at their upper-most top. They were massive oaks, gigantic elms and colossal maples larger than the renowned redwoods Diakrina had seen in her time. Each tree was so immense it appeared to create its own biosphere where villages of small creatures and birds set up an almost discrete world of interaction and subsistence.

As they descended into the trees, a strange sensation came over Diakrina. She had a strong intuition the trees were aware of her, observing her every action. She tried to dismiss it as mere nerves. It was too foolish to be taken seriously. After all, she told herself, she was rather keyed up about meeting these distant relatives, and the world emerging around her was so gigantic and beautiful she could not help but feel strange about it all.

But try as she would, she could not keep from being unnerved by the growing sense of being watched by the gnarled, leafy titans all around them. Yet, it was not malevolent.

This keen attention—whatever its source—seemed without purposes or schemes. It merely wanted to watch. It feared nothing, wished nothing and intended nothing other than informing its own curiosity.

Diakrina was not sure how she knew any of this, or if indeed she only imagined it. But the farther they walked, and the more the trees dominated the landscape, the more haunted she became by this sense of steady, unblinking attention.

Their descent was soon steep enough to force small waterfalls in the stream every few hundred yards. The great forest grew thick with venerable, massive branches. The signs of life multiplied, as hundreds of butterflies—with foot-long wingspans—floated toward them on the sunlit breeze. Honeybees buzzed busily all around them, harvesting spacious mats of wild and beautiful flowers covering the ground not claimed by the gigantic trees. Diakrina silently absorbed the dance of life erupting all around her. The fragrance of the flowers and trees filled her senses with delight.

As they came into the valley itself the river turned slightly away from them to the right to circumvent a small hill ahead and the dale widened to both the east and west. The valley floor, though level overall, was still filled with rolling, tree-draped hills.

As the hikers topped the small rise, the trees thinned, giving way to a spectacular panoramic view. A vast meadow opened below them, which appeared to stretch for over 50 miles in every direction like a great savanna.

Diakrina stopped in her tracks, her eyes wide with astonishment. What met her gaze took her breath away. A Jurassic landscape spread out before her, filled with animals seemingly too enormous to be real.

A great herd of elephants gathered off to the right around a watering hole where the river Strateia and Diakrina had been following widened out and flowed into the meadow. But these were like no elephants Diakrina had ever seen. The larger of them stood four stories tall. Their imposing tusks protruded out from under the root of their trunks and curled down, out and back up again, ending in upturned daggers. Even the pictures she had seen of prehistoric Mammoths failed to do justice to the enormity of these creatures. They were not hairy, but were exactly like gigantically proportioned African elephants with their grey, wrinkled skin and large, fan-like ears.

She stared mesmerized by the elephantine herd until a peripheral flicker of movement snapped her gaze to the left. There, just beyond some shorter trees, a long slender neck rose into the air. Her eyes went from wide to bulging as the great neck, topped by an oval-shaped head, rose higher and higher into the sky. She took two steps backward to put Strateia, who was standing on her left, between the creature and herself.

It was a dinosaur!

Before she could speak a word, a second head and neck

rose above the trees beside the first. Both continued chewing on mouthfuls of oversized leaves as they looked in Strateia and Diakrina's direction. Then they slowly lowered their heads back into the tops of the trees. Then again, with replenished mouths, they lifted their heads and renewed their sizing up of the two strangers on the hilltop. Or were they looking only at her?

If this weren't enough, just then, from about 100 feet in front and below Strateia and Diakrina, strode a great cat, which had stepped confidently out from behind a clump of green foliage and was moving toward the towering elephants. Even in its somewhat crouched trot, its shoulders matched the height of a large Belgian horse and its stride was considerably longer. It wore the colors of a lion—a light yellow-brown—but it had no mane. Immense saber-like teeth curved down and backward from the two corners of its mouth.

Diakrina instinctively froze in place, but her silhouette interrupted the natural contour of the hillside and alerted the ever-watchful feline senses. The creature paused and turned its gaze directly at her. Its tongue flicked up to its nose a couple of times and its eyes narrowed as they squinted hard in her direction. Then, deepening its crouch slightly, it turned fully toward her and began a stalking, creeping motion in her direction.

"We are going to have company," said Strateia in a matter of fact way as he pointed toward the approaching mountain of a cat.

With a quivering voice, which she was trying hard to control, Diakrina stammered, "What is it?"

"It is a Chisel-tooth cat, or Smilodon. You likely know it by the name saber-toothed tiger. But it is no tiger. It is closer to the lion than the tiger."

"I don't like it," said Diakrina moving so as to put Strateia between her and the approaching beast. "It reminds me of those creatures I had to fight in the cave of Nekus Canyon."

"I can see why it would remind you of them," responded Strateia, "but it is nothing like those beast, I assure you."

While this conversation was going on, the cat inched closer and closer up the rise toward them with its ears pulled back slightly and its pinched gaze fixed on the trespassing biped.

"It is definitely coming up here, Strateia! What do we do?"

"Well, first, I should inform you that it does not see me. It sees only you, and assumes you are alone. I must say, you do look remarkably like a small, slow meal for a hungry cat."

Ignoring what seemed an abominably inappropriate remark under the circumstance, Diakrina pleaded, "Well, just because it doesn't see you doesn't mean you can't stop it, does it?"

"No," said Strateia, calmly rubbing his chin. Then turning toward Diakrina, "But I think it would be best if you took care of it yourself."

By this time the gigantic cat was within 30 feet of Diakrina. It crouched down even closer to the ground and bared a mouthful of sizeable teeth with a vicious snarl.

"What do I do, Strateia? What do I do?"

She peered out around the warrior's imposing frame, still hoping he would do something. Surely Strateia wouldn't stand by and let her be eaten by this brute.

"I would suggest, quite simply," he said, "that you take out your sword and stretch it out in front of you, move confidently toward the kitty and give it a good whack on the nose."

Diakrina was flabbergasted. "You have got to be kidding, Strateia! Look at the size of that thing! Look at those teeth! Look at those claws! Whack the kitty on the nose? Are you serious?"

"It will respect your sword once it gets a taste of it. And the more aggressive you are with it, the more it will believe you are in charge."

"But I'm not in charge!"

"I think you had better draw your sword, Diakrina, and take charge. These Smilodons have a habit of springing on their prey from several feet away. You don't have much choice about meeting him. The question is who will be in charge when you do."

Diakrina had heard enough. Strateia was clearly not pulling his sword and the cat was now within 20 feet. Unsheathing her sword, she hesitated only a split second before stepping around Strateia and holding the blade up toward the face of the giant cat. Even in its crouched position, it stood eye to eye with her. The sword pulsed bright crimson red, sending a wave of courage through Diakrina's body.

"Don't wait long, Diakrina, or he will pounce. Step forward quickly and slap him with the side of your blade. Don't use the edge or you will severely wound him."

"The side of my . . .?" but she never got out the word blade. The cat suddenly sprang forward with snarling teeth. Diakrina jumped sideways and came down with the flat of her blade in the direction of the roaring beast. She missed his nose and hit him forcibly on the top of his head.

In an explosion of crimson light the cat fell flat on its stomach with all four legs spread out in different directions. It lay perfectly still on the ground with its sandpapery tongue hanging slightly out of its mouth.

The force of its charge hitting her sword sent Diakrina stumbling backwards. Strateia nimbly caught her just before she hit the ground.

Diakrina struggled to regain her feet under her. "Did I kill it?" she finally asked looking back at Strateia while keeping a nervous eye on the limp creature.

Strateia looked downright amused. Anyone else might have tried to hide it, but beings like Strateia are so transparent it never occurred to him to make a pretense of sobriety.

Smiling broadly he answered, "No, he is only stunned. He will soon wake up with a sizeable headache and go on about his business."

By this time Diakrina was starting to regain her composure and found Strateia's attitude somewhat offensive. "That cat could have killed me, Strateia. Why are you smiling like that? I don't think there is anything amusing about this."

Strateia's face went straight for only a moment, but the smile could not be suppressed and immediately broke out again under his dancing eyes. "Let's just say I found a certain pleasure in your sword work. Remind me to give you a few lessons."

"Why didn't you think of that before this cat showed up?" Diakrina snapped back even as an unintended smile broke through onto her own countenance. She giggled a little at herself, as much out of relief as anything else, as she returned the object of Strateia's amusement to its sheath.

"We had better go before your Smilodon friend wakes up. Unless of course, you would like to get in some more sword work?"

"No thanks. I'll wait until school is in session."

Strateia led Diakrina around the unconscious cat and they began their trek down the slope of the hill toward the meadow. Once again Diakrina was amazed as she looked over the valley and saw animals that, like the elephants, were familiar except for their incredible size. Towering giraffes raised their heads at least six stories high, while herds of oxen the size of Paul Bunyan's Babe roamed the meadows.

Strateia motioned toward the oxen and said, "Definitely stay out of their way. They are reem: a terrible and fierce ox with immense strength and two razor-sharp and powerful horns. They are wild beyond any man's power to tame, and they don't like to be bothered. Reem are one of the most feared beasts of this time. But if you leave them alone, they will not bother you."

After circumventing the knot of elephants, whose overwhelming size left Diakrina breathless, Strateia guided her along the river. Before long she spotted, ahead on their right, a forest of the huge oaks, elms and maples stretching up a hillside from the opposite shore of the river.

"It will not be long now," said Strateia. "Up ahead where the path goes between those two towering rocks is the boundary of Lord Mazzaroth's land."

Diakrina looked ahead to where Strateia pointed. Close to the river two immense rock pillars had formed what almost looked like a gate, though there was nothing to close it. As they walked closer, Diakrina caught sight of a bridge-like structure crossing the river just beyond the pillars. Strateia led her through the soaring would-be gate and toward the bridge.

"We will cross the river here. The path over the hill to Sapient Valley is just beyond it. Once we enter the valley itself, things will change drastically. Sapient Castle is just across the valley, beyond Lord Mazzaroth's realm. Lamech, of Cain's line, rules in that area, and Anomos is quite free to operate in the open.

"By the time this river reaches Sapient Castle it will have mixed with many different streams from the Severed Lands and its life-giving powers will be much diluted. But it will still accomplish the purpose for which it exists."

They crossed the bridge and climbed a winding and steep westward path up into the forest. The path was washed out in many places, exposing massive tree roots and rocky outcroppings to be navigated like carelessly strewn steps ascending the hillside.

The forest grew more rugged and wild as they climbed, with increasingly larger and closer-set trees forming a dense brown and green canopy giving the bright, sunny day an overcast aura. Near the summit of the hill, they came to large rocky outcroppings forming bluffs about 80-feet high and rimming the top of the hill in both directions. Strateia turned right at the base of the cliffs and traversed the hill for a few yards through the dark woods and then, finding a boulder-littered landslide between two cliffs, turned back left and climbed up a small gorge.

Diakrina fell in behind Strateia and tried to keep pace with the agile warrior as they picked their way up the boulders and rock piles. The farther up the cut they ascended the surface of the stones became increasingly covered with a mossy, moist film, making the boulders treacherously slick. Diakrina nearly fell several times. When they were close to the top, Diakrina could see the trunks of the trees were also covered in moss where the forest continued beyond the cliffs.

When finally they reached the top, she stood and peered into the dense forest beyond. The trees were thickly draped in what she knew as Spanish moss, making the forest decidedly dark and oppressive.

Where they topped the cliffs, no path was visible anywhere through the dense forest. Strateia stayed near the cliffs and, turning right, continued alongside them until they intersected a trail winding off into the forest to the west.

This newfound trail was rough and rutted as it meandered through the tangled roots of moss-hung trees. At first it cut a level, though somewhat zigzagged track, but after about 15 minutes of navigating gnarled roots, Diakrina began to notice a subtle downward grade. The gently sloping terrain and the rare speckles of sunlight squinting through the trees ahead hinted of an open valley below them, and Diakrina wondered at the incredible view they might have if the trees were not so thick. As it was, they could see little more than the shadowy brown and grey tree-scape immediately around them and the craggy trail at their feet.

Soon, however, their trek veered gently southward, and the elevation gradually rose to the right of the trail and slumped off to the left, until it became obvious, they were skirting the northwestward side of a hill. The pitch of their descent increased as they continued.

After several minutes, all pretense of a forest path surrendered to a blatant stone-cut ledge of a trail, as the hill grew steep to their right and on the left plummeted sharply toward the valley. Trees still stood thick and high from the slopes below and to the left, blocking the view of what lay in the valley.

Presently, however, the terrain to the left of the trail dropped steeply away and a few of the treetops could not reach as high, allowing Strateia and Diakrina a glimpse out over the valley to the north. The first thing Diakrina notices was there was mist over the valley.

It wasn't the writhing serpentine Mist she had encountered at the edge of the great Mist Forest, but a subtle fog laying over Sapient Valley like someone took a dull grey pencil and drew the flat surface of a milky lake beneath the blue sky.

On the far side of the valley, halfway up the other side, sat an enormous Castle with two imposing towers, one on each end. The left tower was slightly taller than the right and its top protruded a few feet above the fog like a fist jabbing at the sky from out of a misty lake. It seemed to have a crystal-like dome, or something, on its top, but Diakrina could not be sure of much from this distance.

Strateia turned and pointed toward the Castle. "We must go there, Little One. It is time we cross the valley and climb the other side up to Sapient Castle."

Chapter Two

SAPIENT FORDS

Strateia found a place where they could leave the path and begin descending west directly toward the Castle. They had not gone far before the sunlight capitulated to the thin layer of pervasive fog covering the valley floor. Here the trees grew larger and the forest denser, leaving Strateia and Diakrina to the sword-wielding task of trailblazing their way through the underbrush that stubbornly claimed any ground not already owned by massive hardwoods.

Even though this fog was not the malevolent Mist she loathed from her ordeal on the hillside and long night in the cave, a sense of oppression closed in on Diakrina as she descended into the valley floor. She had to flex her resolve to brush away the taunting faces and hissing voices of her memories. She comforted herself with the assurance of Strateia's protective presence and followed closely behind him as they cut their way through the forest for more than an hour.

Soon they came out at the riverbank. High above them on the hillside of the opposite shore—somewhat upstream to their left— loomed Sapient Castle. Strateia had navigated them slightly past the northern end of the Castle, where the lower of the two towers stood.

The ruins of four stone pylons, two in the midst of the river and one on each bank, equally spaced in a straight line across the river, told of an ancient three-span bridge that once stretched from one bank to the other. Nothing of the spans remained, and the torrent rushed deep and swift as it rolled and splashed against the forlorn pillars. Clearly the waters of the Spring of Longings had been joined by other tributaries along the way multiplying the force and volume of the river.

Where the former bridge had once joined the opposite bank, the remains of a road turned left and ascended along the ridge toward the Castle. The ridge was so steep the road formed two long switchbacks before it leveled and widened near the center of the eastern wall of the Castle, high above and to the left of the bridge ruins.

Having studied the road, Diakrina turned her attention to the Castle wall, itself. The two ends of the Castle—north to south—appeared to be made of two distinctively different materials, and odd streaks stretched horizontally across the wall between the two ends. The Castle was still some distance away however, and she could not determine much else about it from her vantage point.

Strateia's voice suddenly brought her back to the moment. "As you can see, the bridge no longer exists and the water is deep and swift. But there is a tree here on the bank tall enough to reach across the river if it were felled. Cut properly, it would catch on the upstream side of the pylons and form a makeshift bridge."

Diakrina looked over her left shoulder and down the bank to a large tree which ascended from the river bank to high above them on the bank where they stood near the top of the near-shore pylon. The tree was indeed big, with a 10-foot diameter trunk and roots burying themselves in the soil of the bank right up to the water's edge. Its lowest limb protruded about 25 feet up the trunk, and Diakrina judged the top to be some 175 feet in the air. If it fell straight across the river, it should stretch to the far bank.

"How will we fell it, Strateia?"

Even as she voiced the question, she remembered how he had handled trimming the much larger tree falling across the great Chasm. But Strateia did not seem to take much notice of her stuttering when she tried to correct herself by saying, "I guess . . . I mean . . . of course you can handle it." He simply walked past the nearest bridge pylon and toward the base of the tree, motioning for Diakrina to follow him.

They walked down the rise toward the river bank. Once they got to the level of the riverbank Diakrina was surprised when Strateia walked a few steps beyond the tree, then backed up the rise behind it several feet, and sat down.

"The honor is yours, Diakrina. You must fell this tree and create this new access. Use your sword."

For a moment Diakrina stood there looking wide-eyed at Strateia. Then she looked up at the tree and back at Strateia. "You mean I must cut down this giant by myself?"

"Yes, it is required you provide the way across to Sapient Castle."

Diakrina wanted to ask "Why?" but the question stuck in her throat. Her expression communicated the question well enough.

Strateia pointed toward the base of the shore pylon they had passed and said, "Walk back and look at the message carved on the large stone about head-high in the center of that pylon."

Diakrina retraced her steps. There in the middle of the structure was a rectangular stone about four feet long and two feet high. In letters worn and ancient looking, about one-inch high, were strange words unknown to Diakrina. But somehow she was able to begin understanding them. (This happened quite often while Diakrina was on the other side of reality.) The translation into English was as follows:

Who may enter?
The Living One formed the man from the dust of the ground and breathed into his nostrils the spirit of life, and the man became a living soul.

Who may accompany?
The invited.

"That, Diakrina, is the law of Sapient Castle, decreed by the Living One at the beginning. There are those who violate this law, but we will not be among them. They do so to their own ultimate harm. You are allowed to enter, and you must answer the call yourself."

"Then I guess I had better get busy taking down that tree," said Diakrina.

"You will find the spiritual reality infused into the essence of your sword more than a match for this physical tree, Little One," interjected Strateia.

She walked over to the tree, laying down her shield and the crystal container on a rock close to Strateia, and then pulled her sword. Just as she was pulling her sword a breeze picked up a wonderful … no, glorious, fragrance. She immediately knew it was the fragrance of the Immortal Fruit.

She was shocked and began to wonder if something had happened to the crystal container. She turned to lift the container to examine it. When once again the fragrance hit her it so reoriented Diakrina's attention suddenly Strateia and the tree were forgotten as her arm went limp and her sword tip rested slightly on the ground. She stared at the glorious swirling light within the beautiful orb of the Fruit and felt as if she were being taken on a journey into its very essence. She was about to lift the crystal container up to her face to examine it closer—and to get closer to the Fruit—when suddenly the right hand of Strateia was laid down over the surface of the container, pushing gently downward and away, while his left hand was on her shoulder turning her slightly toward him.

"The container is just fine," Diakrina. The fruit is just starting to saturate the crystal a little."

His firm hand on her and the disappearance of the Fruit below his other large hand broke the spell. Diakrina blinked once or twice, then slowing shaking her head in submission, bent over and laid the crystal container back on the ground.

"Let's get back to the project at hand," said Strateia returning to his former place seated on the bank. He instructed her to make a V-cut on the side of the trunk toward the Castle slightly lower than she would cut the trunk on the backside of the tree. Standing just to the left of the trunk, with her feet nearly in the water, she put both hands on the sword handle and took a line of sight over her right shoulder to make sure she was putting the cut in the right place. She then swung the sword blade into the tree, expecting a shoulder-jarring thud that never came. Her blade sliced right through a major portion of the trunk.

"Wow! Like a hot knife through butter!" she muttered to herself.

With just a few more swings of the sword she completed a large V-shaped notch in the side of the trunk nearest the river. Then moving to the backside of the tree she took several full swings until the blade had burned its way through a major part of the trunk. She was about to take another swing when the trunk shuddered with a loud cracking sound.

"Step back, Diakrina," instructed Strateia, "It is about to fall."

Diakrina scrambled up the bank beside Strateia as several more wood-shattering pops came from inside the tree. Slowly the tree leaned toward the river and then, with one more louder cracking sound, fell toward the far bank. It landed with a crash, taking several limbs from some smaller trees on the opposite shore down with it.

The water immediately began pushing the tree downstream. But as Strateia predicted, it was only carried a few yards before it slammed into the stone pylons and wedged into place.

"There's your bridge Diakrina," said Strateia with a smile. "Good job!"

Trying to suppress a gleeful grin, Diakrina picked up some grass and wiped the blade of her sword, and then sheathing it, picked up the crystal container and her shield and scampered over to the tree trunk and climb up onto the top of the tree. She was about to begin her crossing when she looked back and found Strateia was not behind her.

"Coming?" she said from the topside of the trunk.

"If I am invited, most surely," responded Strateia.

Diakrina was about to question his meaning when she remembered the inscription on the stone pylon. "Of course, Strateia, I extend an earnest invitation for you to accompany me to Sapient

Castle."

Diakrina did this with a twinkle in her eye and mock formality in her voice, but both she and Strateia knew she was dead-serious. Before she could turn around, Strateia gave a quick hop and leaped up and then over Diakrina and landed on the trunk beyond her.

"I don't think you need this bridge of mine," said Diakrina, eyeing him with admiration.

"I think it will serve us both well," retorted Strateia as he stepped aside and motioned for Diakrina to lead the way across.

Diakrina strode quickly along the makeshift bridge until she was about a fourth of the way across the river. Here her progress slowed as she navigated around thick branches and leaves. Reaching the far bank, she climbed up to where the bridge formerly joined the old road.

From here the steep switchback ascent led left, then right, then left again up the canyon wall to where the Castle stood embedded into the hillside. The closer they came to the Castle the more Diakrina could discern the strange characteristics she had noticed before.

Reaching the top placed them at the base of the foundation, about 50-feet away from the north tower and the main structure. Diakrina could now see along the whole length of the Castle.

While the north tower, which was closest to them, was of grey stone, the south tower appeared to be made of a semi-transparent dull yellow or gold substance. It reminded her of a dark brown glass that might be brilliant yellow or gold if a light were placed behind it. But with no light shining through it, it appeared opaque and brown except for an occasional golden glint catching her eye and then vanishing.

Dry, brittle ivy covered the lower portion of the entire Castle wall between the two towers. The wall itself was indeed streaked horizontally of both the brownish-gold substance and the grey stone. The south end was dominantly dull gold with only a hint of grey stone, while the north end revealed the opposite composition, with the wall being nearly entirely grey stone streaked with faint traces of golden brown. Moving toward the center of the wall between the two towers, the materials merged into equal parts grey and dark gold streaks.

Something else about the Castle seemed odd, though it took a few moments for Diakrina to identify it. "Oh," she said half aloud when the realization came to her: from her vantage point, no windows or doors could be seen in the Castle wall. Only at the top—among something like battlements—could she detect any break in the flat wall. The only windows visible were high up around the circumference of the towers.

Diakrina began to wonder if she were looking at the backside of the Castle. Perhaps the door would be around the other side. She spotted what looked like a small door nestled at the base of the north tower, but it looked more like a servant's entrance or a work exit. It certainly did not present itself as the main entrance to such a structure. In addition, the remains of the road they were following led toward the south end of the Castle, so the main entrance would likely be there.

"What do you think, Strateia? Should we follow this old road to the other end?"

"Yes, we should. It is where we must enter," answered Strateia. Then he added, "But move slowly and carefully, Little One."

Reading Strateia's demeanor, Diakrina understood she must take the point, so she stepped out to lead the way along the foundation of the Castle wall. Though nothing looked amiss or dangerous, she picked up on Strateia's cue and pulled her sword from its sheath for reassurance.

She walked about 100-feet along the old road, which slowly brought them closer and closer to the Castle wall. Here, in the near center of the structure, the wall of the Castle loomed impressively overhead. She paused to look up at the battlements for only a moment and then resumed her pace.

Diakrina had taken only about four steps, which placed her exactly center of the Castle, when suddenly—SPLASH!—she was standing knee deep in marshy water. She was so startled she tried to jump backwards. Her feet, ankle deep in warm mud, did not come free soon enough for her to keep her balance. She stumbled backward and fell onto the bare dry earth behind her.

"Where did that come from?" she muttered to Strateia as she jumped up to get a look at the water. But she saw no water! Stretching out before her, all the way to the south tower and beyond, the ground appeared to be solid and dry.

As Diakrina stood there trying to understand what had just happened, other sensations came flooding back. At the moment she had stepped into the water, she had also been suddenly aware of slithering life forms. As she jumped backward, her peripheral vision had caught strange hovering beings with dark countenances. And the mud, she recalled now, had been warm. In fact, the air itself, in those quick moments, had seemed hot and damp with a slight, stinging acidity. For a few strange seconds she had been in another place: a dark swamp. Was she going mad? The ground before her revealed nothing but bare, dry earth.

Strateia quickly placed his hand on her shoulder and pulled her back a few steps. Diakrina could tell by the firmness of his grip he was on full alert. She backed up close to him and asked in a breathy tone, "What just happened, Strateia?"

At that moment Diakrina realized she had dropped her sword. Looking down in front of her she saw the crimson handle glowing, but there seemed to be no blade. She stepped forward cautiously and, reaching down, took the handle in her hand. As she stood up, the blade reappeared as if it were growing out of the handle, no . . . as if it were emerging from a sheath: a sheath of . . . invisibility.

This realization froze Diakrina. And in her freeze-frame stance the blade was still only half visible. She stared at it for a moment trying to take in what was happening. Slowly she pulled the sword handle toward her and slowly the complete blade reappeared. She reached out her left hand where the sword had come out but found nothing unusual. Little by little she pushed the sword in front of her again and its blade gradually disappeared, as if it were being inserted into an unseen curtain.

"Strateia, what on earth is this?" asked Diakrina as she pulled the sword back toward her to see the full blade reappear.

"I think," said Strateia in a firm, but quiet voice, "you have found the passage to the other side of Sapient Castle's deeper reality. The sword reveals the passage."

Diakrina thrust her sword into the earth beside her and, leaving it there, walked carefully forward to the spot where the sword had been disappearing and where she had fallen into the warm swamp. Nothing. Only dry bare earth spreading all the way to the far tower.

She retreated to Strateia and took her sword back in hand. Strateia could see in her eyes what she had in mind and he nodded a slow approval, which communicated a wordless caution to take care.

Diakrina stepped forward warily. The sword blade slowly disappeared again, then the handle and then . . . HER HAND! And instantly she felt hot, damp air. She stepped slowly forward and her arm disappeared before her as the hot dampness slid up past her wrist and then her elbow. She inched forward until her face was against the precise plane where her right arm was disappearing—against some unseen curtain. She moved ever so slightly forward and felt warmth on the end of her nose. She drew back her face for only a moment, but then leaned determinedly into the warmth, keeping her feet firmly planted on the north side of the curtain.

Suddenly visible were her sword and arm, and … the swamp! The acidic air stung her nose and eyes as her sight adjusted to the darkness. It was night on the other side of this barrier.

When finally her eyes adjusted, and she looked down at the water, she was puzzled for a moment. Yes, there was water, but there was also earth—bare earth—but translucent not opaque. It lay over the water in the place it had been before she put her head through this curtain. But it was changed—or was it? She looked back at her feet and saw she was standing on this bare earth, which overlaid the swamp. Then it hit her: from this side of the curtain she could see both sides at once. Instinctively she pulled back her head to see if the swamp could be seen from her former vantage point, but she could see nothing but bare earth.

"Strateia, a strange transition is happening here."

"Yes, Little One. I suspect the division, corruption and

infestation of human nature are reflected in the composition and condition of this Castle and its grounds. But we must continue. I cannot lead the way or I would. You must venture forward. But be extremely careful. I will be as close behind you as possible."

Diakrina loathed what she sensed was about to happen, but knew she had no alternative. If she had, she trusted Strateia would have mentioned it to her.

Gathering her nerve for a moment, she took a deep breath and let it out slowly. Then leading with her sword she pushed her head back through the curtain intent on studying this transition in more detail.

Bright red eyes, hideous countenances and hovering wings greeted her. They stood suspended in the air in a semicircle around Diakrina about 20-feet away. Startled, she jumped backward and found herself once more looking at bare earth.

"I don't want to go there, Strateia," she said turning to him with a face drained of all color. "There are awful creatures there!"

Strateia looked beyond her with eyes focused on things she could not see. "You are already there, Diakrina. The change you are experiencing is in your perception, not in reality."

This statement by Strateia sent shivers up and down Diakrina's spine. "Do you mean what I saw over there, is also around us here?" she asked with her eyes darting in every direction.

"Yes, Little One. And the only question for you is whether you wish to face the danger sighted or blind."

"Are my perceptions that impaired?" shot back Diakrina in a tone too argumentative. Fear was rising in her.

"Are you a daughter of your Great Parents?" asked Strateia in calm rebuttal.

"Yes . . . of course I am," answered Diakrina with a downturn in her voice.

"Diakrina, the spiritual and material realms are not discrete realities. The material realm is produced by, and exists within, the spiritual realm. Only a sword of truth can reveal the deeper realities to one with impaired spiritual perception. I suspect," added Strateia, "this change-point has something to do with the composition and structure of the Castle which is designed to depicted human nature. Here we are at the center of the north-south span of the wall and the material of its construction is more than half changed from the grey stone of the north end. The far side of the Castle must take its essence from the dimension of spirit. For you to interact safely and properly with the dual nature of Sapient Castle, the sword of truth must awaken your perception to the deeper, denser realities of the spiritual dimension as represented by the very construction of this Castle.

"In a sense, Diakrina, this is a small replication and illustration of what happened to you when you came through the Door of the Rose to this side of reality. However, the Door of the Rose brought you to unblemished spiritual reality and unblemished material reality. But here, in the Severed Lands, the deeper reality of Sapient Castle will reveal the degeneration and infestation of the spiritual realms once under your Great Parents' rule, but are now ruled by Anomos and his minions."

Standing there with the growing realization the evil eyes and creatures could still see her, but she could not see them, caused a wave of panic to roll over Diakrina. Just a moment before, she had wanted never to pass through this change-point, as Strateia had called it, but she now found herself eager to pass quickly through and assess what she was facing. It felt a little like what she had experienced in Nekus Canyon when the oppressive darkness smothered every other sensation. But here she could do something about it.

Strateia could see all this registering on her face and realized she was about to step quickly through the change-point. He placed his hand on her shoulder to hold her back long enough to say, "Diakrina, when you pass through, not only will you be given perception, but they—the corrupt creatures and beings you glimpsed—will gain a greater perception of you, and thus greater access to you. Be prepared to fight!"

This thought of needing to fight gave Diakrina pause. Using her sword in battle was not yet something she had actually done.

The closest she had come was her encounter with the beast she had decapitated as she ran for her life after acquiring the Immortal Fruit. But in that case, she had been told exactly what to do and shown how to do it. Her apparently feeble attempts to fight off the enormous cat in the Meadow had just hours ago amused Strateia.

Her tumbling thoughts were interrupted by Strateia once again. "Be sure to keep the crystal container with the Immortal Fruit secure under your shield."

Diakrina put her hand on the strap and followed it down and around to where the container hung slightly behind her on her left side. Lowering the shield with her left hand, she covered the container somewhat from the front. She took a deep breath, and with the sword held out in front of her and with a glance to be certain Strateia was behind her, she pushed through the change-point.

Chapter Three

BEYOND THE CURTAIN

Splash! Swamp water and mud swallowed Diakrina's feet and ankles. Night reigned on this side of the curtain and Diakrina found her first few moments quite frightening as she strained her eyes trying to adjust to the darkness. Fear came over her and she instinctively turned to her right looking behind to confirm Strateia had followed. He had.

Then, in an instant, he disappeared! At the same moment she heard the ring of a fast moving sword blade in the air near her left ear, felt the sharp report of the air from the blade on the side of her face and then heard a loud thud as the blade struck something large and hard. Startled, Diakrina jumped to her right as she turned back around just in time to see Strateia's sword had lobbed off the head of an anaconda-sized serpent. The head careened through the air as the headless body flailed at her feet.

"Pull the crystal container under your shield!" Strateia ordered. "They are after the Atheos!"

Diakrina had inadvertently uncovered the container when she turned to look back for Strateia. Evidently the serpent had seen this as an opportunity to strike at the strap and tear the container from her shoulder. Diakrina quickly pulled the shield, which was now blazing with white, gold and blue flames, over the container and its strap just as the head of a second serpent struck with violent force sending Diakrina stumbling backward. Strateia's sword took off its head at almost the same instant it hit the shield while the shield also exploded with white, gold and blue rays of light sending the serpent's body careening out into the darkness as many severed pieces.

Strateia was now in front of her and his sword sang through the air in a flaming crimson-red figure-eight pattern. Diakrina saw a third serpent's head pull up short and retreat back into the darkness.

As her eyes adjusted and the light from her shield penetrated the darkness around her, Diakrina was stunned at what she could now see. Reptilian-like creatures were everywhere. Some took familiar forms, such as snakes and lizards, and some appeared more hideous and unknown. The eyes staring at her were strange and uncanny. Some blinked like mammals. Some were unblinking and cold, like reptiles.

These were not the eyes of mere beasts. They were self-conscious, perceptive eyes transmitting an attitude Diakrina could only interpret as intelligently vicious and savage. They were unsettling to say the least.

The more her sight adjusted, the more of these eyes she could see peering at them from the branches of mossy damp trees. And among these eyes, here and there, were certain eyes bothering her more than the others. They were not only self-conscious but filled with self-allegiance, pride and hatred. They shone red with a pale, greenish glint. Nauseous green light flashed from the eyes when they moved.

These arrogant, hateful stares unnerved Diakrina. They reminded her of a rabid wolf snarling with bared teeth. Yet this insane rage and savagery made a wolf seem timid by comparison. A creature such as a wolf could not produce such defiant, self-obsessed stares. They might become the channel through which something like this might project itself, but she knew, as she starred into these eyes, a mere beast could never be the source of such malignant intelligence.

Diakrina wondered if all the manifestations of hatred and pride she had ever seen had somehow been only a channeling of the insane rage she now felt crouching in the dank bog just beyond the reach of Strateia's sword. She detested this damnable swamp.

Strateia suddenly stopped but continued to hold the sword out in front of him. He then motioned with his head toward the Castle while he continued to put himself between Diakrina and the circle of eyes. "There is a raised area with more of the old road just a few steps toward the Castle. It will get us out of this muck. Move close to me!"

Diakrina waded up close to Strateia's back. Then Strateia sidestepped toward the road and Diakrina walked with him being sure to keep the shield over the container. In a few steps they came to a bank of earth that rose above the water level. Stepping onto it, they continued up the bank as it climbed about three feet above the swamp. At its top were the remains of the old road continuing toward the south end of the Castle. Diakrina was glad for the chance to get out of the dark water.

"What is this place?" asked Diakrina with fearful disgust.

"It is the Dead Swamp, and it is enemy-occupied territory," answered Strateia, not taking his eyes off the dark horizon.

"Dead? It may be full of things one could wish were dead, but it seems to teem with disgusting life!"

Strateia used his sword to point at one of the closer pair of evil, red eyes. "What you see here is but a remnant of life. This is only animated existence in the grip of ever-increasing decay."

Diakrina's thoughts rushed eagerly back to the beauty and glory of the Garden and the playful animals. The contrast of this swamp with the former splendor made Diakrina shudder and feel nauseous.

Then it hit her Strateia had used the phrase, "a remnant of life." Could there be a former connection between this place and the Garden? She looked up and was about to distill her thoughts into a verbal question, when she caught Strateia's eyes and knew he was well aware of her thoughts.

Strateia spoke first. "Yes, Little One, the Living One never made anything to be originally like this. This is a state of death."

"But didn't He have to allow death to cause this?"

"Your question is not quite correct, Little One. Death cannot do or cause anything. It is the result of what someone does. It is a consequence. The Living One did allow for death's possibility for good reason, but He did not allow for its necessity. He provided everything needed for its prevention."

"I'm not sure I understand why He would allow for its possibility while providing for its prevention. Why did He not simply make it impossible to do the thing which causes this state of death?"

"Because," answered Strateia, "the possibility provides one thing and the making it preventable provides another—both of profound importance. For in a moral world the possibility of the one is the possibility of the other. Both good and evil had to be possible."

"So," interrupted Diakrina, "doesn't that mean evil is actually necessary and, therefore, there can be no possible world where there is goodness unless there is also evil?"

"No! Absolutely not true!" responded Strateia with such force it startled Diakrina. "This is part of Anomos' lie. Possibility and necessity are not the same thing."

"But, Strateia, if evil must always be possible, isn't it true there will never be a time or place when we are secured against it?"

"No, Little One. But before I explain to you how evil will one day be completely defeated and we will be forever beyond its threat while still living in a world of free persons, we must put ourselves in a more secure position. These creatures are not going to stay at bay for long."

The words were hardly out of his mouth when his sword flashed crimson and sang a shrill tune over Diakrina's head. "Your sword, Little One!"

Diakrina turned to see the black swamp filling with red, hovering eyes glinting pale green. She froze in her tracks, seized with instant terror. Strateia's sword circled overhead in crimson patterns and penetrated the air with a piercing, high-pitched whistle, interrupted every few seconds by excruciating screams as his weapon found its mark.

"Your sword, Diakrina! Use your sword!"

But she was frozen.

Suddenly out of the darkness, about the level of Diakrina's knees, appeared the charging head and body of an enormous serpent. It thrust its head between Diakrina's feet and began entwining itself around both of her shins.

"Strateia! Strateia!" screamed Diakrina trying to dance out of its coils to no avail. "Strateia!"

His sword whirled and whirred in front of her and pieces of serpent went in all directions. With surgical precision, Strateia sliced every coil of the serpent encircling Diakrina's legs, but never as much as touched her skin.

"Your sword, Diakrina!" came the stern command as he raised his protective song back over their heads. This time Diakrina obeyed like a frightened soldier reacting to the shouts of her commanding officer. Her sword glowed crimson in the darkness as she lifted it for action.

Two sets of red eyes quickly appeared and raced toward her and became the heads of two serpents such as the one Strateia had just dismembered. For a split second she was sure she could not move, frozen in the grip of pure terror. But Strateia had seen the serpents before she had and anticipated her possible reaction. His silver battle cry was in her ear as the sinister heads raced for her legs: "Swing, Diakrina! Swing, NOW!"

She swung the flaming blade at the malignant forms and felt the terror break like thin ice from around her now animated body. The sword struck its mark and passed through the reptilian frames without noticing their mass—though their density would have been like that of solid spring steel in our world. Two gaping heads left their writhing bodies and disappeared into the darkness to Diakrina's left to splash into the black muck with a thud.

Diakrina had no time to congratulate herself on victory, for as she heard the splash of the dismembered heads to her left, an evil countenance appeared close to her right. She jumped back to see four hideous creatures, three of which were engaging Strateia while the fourth rushed toward her using the other three as a shield to avoid Strateia's sword. Instead of walking or crawling, the creature flew.

It looked horribly deformed. Patches of bronze skin clung to its body here and there, but most of it was blistered with black, scaly skin, twisting itself into hideous, cancerous looking growths. It looked like something once noble but was now covered with horrible filth and festering sores. The contrast was shocking.

In its left hand the creature carried a sword with a serpentine blade made of a dimly glowing material, the color of which Diakrina described as pale death-green. It was the same sickening color of green emanating from the sword of Thanatos in the valley of Nekus. The evil in its eyes made the serpents she had just dismembered look like innocent children at play.

As Diakrina raised her sword to meet the attack, the creature looked suddenly surprised and, if Diakrina was not mistaken—for you could not read much else but hatred in its countenance—alarmed. Evidently it had not yet realized Diakrina was also brandishing a sword.

Whatever the creature's emotion, it pulled up and hesitated. Diakrina never lessened her resolve to strike and had already begun the first motions of her attacking swing when the creature charged her with savage rage. Her unhesitating resolve had won her a slight advantage in the clash and she struck the beast's sword hand at the wrist before it could land a blow. Both sword and scaly hand cart-wheeled like a propeller through the air into the black swamp. The creature screamed hatefully, exposing fangs of the same pale green color as the sword, and retreated into the blackness.

With a moment's reprieve, Diakrina looked up at Strateia. His clear eyes flashed with golden fire. His singing sword formed a literal roof of crimson protection over their heads. The air was filled with pale greenish teeth and red hateful eyes as the death-green swords flashed from all directions. The hideous creatures darted in and out, each trying to thrust its sword at Diakrina while Strateia was dealing with one of the others.

Without the least hesitation in his movements, Strateia commanded, "Diakrina, call to the Living One for help!"

Eager to obey, Diakrina raised her voice. "Living One! Help!"

Instantly, a shaft of blazing light surrounded them for nearly 100-yards in all directions, setting the Dead Swamp on fire with golden light. Diakrina gasped at what she saw. The horrible army surrounding them numbered in the hundreds. Just as suddenly as this revelation came, every foul creature within the circumference of the golden light began to vaporize, their screams fading into distant echoes as their liquefying, then evaporating forms were sucked into a cavernous abyss somewhere over the horizon. Within five seconds nothing but quiet, motionless swamp lay under the circle of golden light.

Strateia raised his crimson sword to the light and bowed on one knee. Diakrina did the same, looking up into the blazing glory. A crystal atmosphere of purity and sparkling light drenched her in unimaginable joy. She saw something like the mountains to the east of the Garden, only she could now see further up than ever before. Up, up her perception soared until she saw a City on a vast mountain, higher than any mountain could be in our world. Yet all was lush and warm, covered with the blazing glory of brilliant flowers in all directions. The City itself was crystal clear as purest glass and reflected every color of the rainbow and then some, all bathed in the most glorious light.

Slowly the golden light faded and Diakrina's eyes rimmed with tears of longing. What she had seen took all irreverence out of her. She could not speak, but only close her eyes with a soaring hope rising within her. Then she felt the ample, strong hand of Strateia softly on her head.

"Look, Little One," he said quietly.

Diakrina lowered her head and opened her tear-rimmed eyes. Though night had once again fallen, a rainbow of colors glowed in front of her. In the circle where the golden light had shone, the whole swamp had disappeared and the earth had lifted above the water level to the same height as the path where they stood. Green turf sparkled with living light, and flowers of every description glowed in the darkness. Yet beyond this circle of life the swamp still lay dark and unchanged.

Diakrina rose and walked out into the middle of the circle of life. Falling on her knees in the soft green grass, she took a tulip in her hands. Its petals, colorless and transparent, sparkled like highly polished crystal, yet they were soft and silky to the touch. A faint golden glow radiated from within the flower: from where the petals connected to the stem.

"Where did these flowers come from?" asked Diakrina raising one knee and turning to look back at Strateia.

"They were already here waiting for the light. Their life is locked up in potential until the condition of death here is banished. Then this whole Dead Swamp will cease to be and the original beauty will return."

"How did this place become dead? Can a place like this somehow take itself out of the Great Dance?"

"No, Little One," said Strateia, as he walked over and knelt on one knee beside her, leaning his right elbow on his right knee. His massive sword, still in his right hand, resting on the ground in front of him while he stroked a beautiful flower with his left. "It was the masters of this place that left the Great Dance and took this place with them."

"Was it these masters we were fighting just now?"

"No. They are the minions of Anomos who have invaded and occupy this place now that the original masters have lost the power to withstand him."

"You are referring to my Great Parents, aren't you?"

"Yes."

"You have told me the story of Anomos' rebellion and madness. And you told me of the mighty host whom he deceived into following him. But where did these creatures, the last ones we were fighting, come from?"

"They are part of the fallen host," answered Strateia turning toward Diakrina while still on one knee.

"Did they always . . . look like they do now?" questioned Diakrina as she groped for words.

"They once were like me," answered Strateia with a sense of

mastered loss in his voice. "The ones I once knew are dead—they have Life no longer. But they exist as you see, locked into an eternal degeneration. They possess nothing but pride-induced insanity and blind rage. This is the gift, the wage of their independence. They inherit nothing: darkness, emptiness, a bottomless abyss.

"They have become moral and spiritual parasites, feeding only a growing, insane, insatiable hunger driving their murderous carnage. They feed on all whom they master and make them dead like themselves. Then they curse their victim's emptiness."

"I find it nearly impossible to believe they were ever like you," said Diakrina, as she compared the magnificence of this noble warrior to the hideous features of the beings they had just encountered. "Their shape, their features, their malignant appearance; how could they change so?"

"Because Little One, in this real world of spirit, all things are seen as they are. They have become dead, separated from all Life both directly or indirectly, except by means of murderously devouring helpless life—if they can find it. What you see is the decaying remnant of their former self, which they can no longer properly sustain."

"Will they ever die? I mean, cease to exist?"

"They are already dead. And as to their ceasing to exist, it is not possible."

"But why not? Will they not decay or degenerate finally into nothing?"

"No, Diakrina. Not in the sense you are thinking. In one sense, they are already nothing. But in another sense, they yet possess a characteristic given them by the Living One at their creation that cannot be lost or taken away. That characteristic is moral potential.

"All moral beings have been given a special gift. This gift is the potential to reflect increasingly the highest and most beautiful aspects of the Living One. We can forever grow more and more like Him Who can never be equaled. This gift is a finite reflection of His infinite beauty. We can never be fully like Him, for we are forever finite, while He is innascible," then Strateia added quickly, "eternal and without origin," to define the word innascible for her. "Yet we can become increasingly like Him, for from the time of our creation we are eternally becoming.

"These were once becoming like Him, and this could have gone on forever. After they left the Great Dance, they are still becoming—that cannot cease. But now they are becoming increasingly unlike Him. The former was eternal conformity. The latter is eternal contrast. The first is eternally increasing beauty, the second, eternally increasing deformity.

"As you cannot now comprehend eternal increase, Diakrina, so you will not be able to comprehend eternally increasing deformity. But you must remember the standard of comparison in both cases is the Infinite One, Himself. This moral potential He has given us is created to work by means of an eternal comparison through an eternal becoming."

Diakrina's forehead furrowed as she tried to keep up with these thoughts. "I know I cannot understand eternal increase or decrease," responded Diakrina thoughtfully. "Neither can I understand their opposites: an absolute destination or absolute nothing. I know if I try to imagine an absolute height or an absolute depth, I always end up asking, 'But must there not be something above or below this?' If something is large, can there not be something larger or no matter how small, can it not be divided again?"

"Diakrina, this inability to imagine an end to anything is a subconscious awareness of reality," interrupted Strateia. "It is because one part of you lives in the original reality of the spiritual, which is endless, and the other part of you lives in the realm of the material and limited. So, you experience a paradox: trying to conceive and explain the limitlessness of one realm in the perception and language of the limited realm.

"Before you were brought through the Door of the Rose, like all your race, you were blind to the spiritual realm. You had direct perception only of the limited material realm. Even then, however, you found it hard to reconcile and confine your conclusions about life and reality to the limited answers provided by only the material. That constant, insistent voice on the inside, which you often ignored or misunderstood, keeps interrupting with the whisper, 'There must be more.'

"Diakrina, you will never be able to describe with your mind what you sense in your spirit. You were created for eternity, and eternity is in you. This forever draws you back to the greatest fact of all existence—The Living One's innascible—uncreated—presence."

Diakrina's intense concentration, which had been narrowed fully on Strateia's golden face, slowly widened. A kind of inner seeing began to come into focus. She realized she was in a most wonderful sanctuary of peace and reasonableness in the middle of chaotic insanity. Strateia was setting a banquet of truth before her, which her spirit devoured hungrily. She felt inner strength surge through her. She now knew true strength did not come from within but was placed within by the Presence of the Living One.

"Perhaps it is time we finished the conversation we left undone," said Strateia as he stood to his feet.

"Please, let's do," responded Diakrina getting up herself and walking toward him. "I am yet troubled about how the possibility of evil is necessary but will not always threaten us."

Strateia took a deep breath as if he were thinking long and hard about how to help her understand. "Let me begin by stating a fact and then following it with explanations." Then fixing and holding her gaze he said, "Diakrina, your world is the best possible world, leading to a better possible world."

Strateia paused to give Diakrina a few moments to think.

"Now, I know that sounds impossible, but it isn't if you understand what I mean when I say, your world is the best possible world. The prime directive of all creation is created beings exist to reflect the Creator; and to do so, moral beings must respond to the Creator on a relational level, and ultimately by love. This necessitates freedom. The will, or freedom to choose, is a fundamental ingredient of a moral capacity. The most important things are impossible without it."

"But must we have moral capacity?" interrupted Diakrina.

"We must if we would experience meaningful relationship with the Living One and respond to His Higher Love. We cannot know meaningful relationships of any kind without some measure of freedom to choose. And what we choose, in regard to the Living One and in regard to each other, is either moral or immoral, proper or improper, good or evil."

"So, without freedom we would be incapable of love?"

"Correct. Your eyes are growing clearer. Can you imagine forced love, Diakrina?"

Diakrina thought for a moment. "No . . . it is a contradiction. By its definition, love cannot be coerced."

"Again, correct. And what is a contradiction is impossible even to God. He can do all things, Diakrina, but a contradiction is not a possible thing. It is intrinsically impossible—it carries its impossibility within itself, and therefore cannot be—cannot become. A contradiction forever cancels the possibility of its own existence.

"This impossibility is not due to some limitation of God's power. It is the very expression of His power; for His power is according to His nature. And His nature is logical and reasonable. It is beauty, glory and design. His nature forbids contradictions and He cannot—He will not, you can say it either way—cause that which is illogical: to do so would contradict His own nature. He cannot be what He is not.

"The rules of logic are not something external to God, to which He pays homage. They flow from Him—they are one expression of who He is. The more we adhere to the rules of proper reason the more we conform to His image.

"Nonsense is still nonsense, even in Heaven. And God can no more create a being capable of love without moral freedom than you or I can both exist and not exist in the same moment and in the same way. Love, by definition, requires freedom. God has made love the prime directive of His creative purpose—it is His deep will—and He works all things according to His will; and that is for His glory. Do you see this, Diakrina?"

"Yes, it makes sense."

"Good! However, Diakrina, remember while love requires freedom, it does not require absolute freedom. If it did, only God could love for only He is free in that sense.

"The freedom we possess as limited beings is not, and never could be, absolute. We have been given a finite, yet profoundly real, freedom. We can choose between real alternatives with real consequences flowing from the choices we make. But never forget the Living One is Sovereign over all consequences. He has already predetermined the consequences of our choices—He has determined the nature of reality, is another way to say it. He has done this by creating all reality in accordance with His own nature. Thus, in the end, He still controls the flow of history and the ultimate outcome even while He allows for real freedom within it. Because He has made all freedom consequential, all creatures will answer to Him for the use they make of their freedom."

"So," said Diakrina, as Strateia paused, "God took a real risk in creating us so we could love?"

"Yes and no," responded Strateia. "It is no risk to Him. It does not force anything upon Him or endangers Him in any way. It is only a risk to Him in as far as He wills to embrace such a risk for the sake of love. In the end, He will determine the final outcome. So the outcome He has determined is not at risk. However, that outcome can only be reached through the freedom He has sovereignly bestowed upon His creatures. In other words, His sovereign will defines, and contains, the freedom He has given.

"By His infinite wisdom working through freedom, He sovereignly controls a complex world of morally free beings. He is not sovereign by revoking freedom. He demands love and, therefore, will never revoke love as the prime directive of creation. Each creature is approved or condemned on the basis of love, for in the end all are questioned about love."

"Wow! Strateia, the more you tell me of the Living One, the greater I see Him to be. I never imagined One who could rule such a complex creation with such complex possibilities!"

"Yes, His rule is complex, not simple. He is truly the Almighty in every way. To be in control, He does not need to micromanage a predetermined, puppet-like world. This is the best possible world because it is a world making love possible, and it is designed to give birth to another creation immune to evil. The world that shall be—

the world immune to evil—will still be free, but that freedom will be brought, lovingly and patiently, to full health and sanity for those who have chosen His love. Evil will be defeated and seen for what it is. Once this happens, no rational creature will be drawn to evil ever again after having been saved out of it and given perfect insight and understanding regarding it.

"On that day the battle with evil will be over. The Living One, in your time, has already crushed the head of the awful serpent, Anomos, and removed the power of his slanderous accusation. The heart of God was put on display before all creation when the Living One poured out His blood as the blood of the covenant to heal the creation Anomos had led into rebellion against Him.

"Anomos doomed his own appeal and put the failure of evil on display when he attacked the Living One, who had embraced the full depths of mankind's weakness. Anomos has no more appeals left and the time will soon come for his sentence to be carried out. And when it is, Diakrina, we will all be there, before the Living One's Throne.

"The life of every person of your Great Parents' race will be reviewed before the whole creation. Every choice—every thought, emotion, desire, attitude, motive and action—will be exposed. Every weakness, and every subconscious and unconscious cause will be seen and understood. Every relationship, with all its influences extending down through all of time and reaching beyond that relationship, will be explored and explained. The influence evil spirits and fallen beings have had over mankind by the power of their evil schemes will be uncovered. Everyone will understand the full and true effect of evil. The mask will be pulled from evil's twisted face: and the universe will gasp in irrevocable horror.

"And when the books are closed, the Living One will be adored. His perfect wisdom, mercy, grace and love—played out in perfect patience on the stage the size of the whole universe—will stand forever vindicated beyond all accusation. Evil and its ultimate incarnation, Anomos, will be condemned beyond refutation. The power of the truth will be so complete that every knee will bow, and every tongue will confess, the Living One is Lord. And among those bowing under the weight and power of truth will be the fallen host of

Anomos. Even Anomos, himself, will bow. None will dissent, even to their own condemnation and destruction.

"Now, imagine, if you can, Diakrina, what those of you cured from evil, or those like me, untainted by evil, will do in regard to evil, having finally seen its twisted face unmasked, and seeing its ultimate and only possible outcome. Or imagine those of your race, having been saved from the horrors of its insanity and unending darkness, who have been redeemed to utter joy and indestructible life and wisdom; imagine what they will freely do with the power of their now unblemished life and sanity. Will we not all, immortal human and immortal spirit alike, willingly and lovingly elect for God to seal forever the door to evil and bolt it so fast that none can enter it?"

With this question hanging in the air, Strateia rose to his full height with both his hands lifted to the sky in an obvious act of passionate worship, and continued.

"And the bolting and double bolting firmly securing that door will be nothing other than our perfect knowledge and undeceived wills ruled by a glorious gratitude to Him who is and was and is to come! Amen!"

Diakrina's eyes widened in astonishment as these words filled the air around her. Her mouth dropped open as she heard coming from over the horizon the sound of thousands upon thousands of voices in unison, greater even than the roaring voice of Thanatos through Nekus Falls. The sound reverberated as if the oceans had gathered themselves and spoken with perfect unison, "SO SHALL IT BE! AMEN AND AMEN FOREVER!"

Diakrina thrust her sword into the ground and, clinging to its handle, fell to her knees with her head bowed low. Then she heard Strateia whisper words seeming to carry far off into the distance: "Amen! My brothers, Amen! Forever!"

A beautiful silence followed. Diakrina stood up and looked into Strateia's countenance. His face was radiant with pure satisfaction. Strateia walked slowly over to her and took her face in his giant, powerful hands and, smiling down at her, dried her tears with his thumbs, like a parent with a child.

Finally, Diakrina composed herself enough to break the silence with what was inside of her. She took a deep breath, closed her eyes, and whispered a reverent, "Amen."

Strateia turned and motioned for Diakrina to follow him toward the south end of the castle.

∞———————————————————————————————∞

For those of you who are interested in this line of inquiry and insight into Strateia and Diakrina's discussion, you can turn to, **Chapter Three B** in the Appendix. It records the final part of this conversion Diakrina had with Strateia about the meaning of the Fall and how it has impacted God's creation. It fits here in the story and will dovetail into Chapter Four. However, you are free to skip it and move immediately to **Chapter Four** with no loss to the story of Diakrina's experiences.

∞———————————————————————————————∞

Chapter Four

THE PORTICOS

Diakrina followed obediently, in deep thought. Within her grew a heavy sense of responsibility for the death she saw around her. The question rose in her mind, "Had she not broken with the Great Dance, too, and danced the dance of death?" Yes, it was the Couple who broke with the Dance, yet, somehow, she knew deep inside, while she was not directly culpable, she could not shift the blame entirely onto her ancient ancestors. Many times she had validated their betrayal of the Living One by her own actions.

Strateia gave her several glances indicating he understood her thoughts, but he said nothing as they made their way toward the dark gold-brown tower. The path followed the curve of the structure's round base. Soon they had made a complete 90-degree turn to the right and were on the south end of the Castle. Light was breaking over the eastern horizon behind her, but the dim, grey morning seemed reluctant and weary.

Strateia stopped. As she walked up beside him, her eyes began taking in what his formidable presence in front of her had hidden for the few moments they had rounded the corner. There before them loomed an immense double portico—one towering over the other. The smaller of the two—a hexastyle portico, attached to the wall of the Castle—protruded southward out under the enormous span of a much larger, indeed colossal, heptastyle portico, which stood detached from the Castle wall.

Seven massive and extraordinarily beautiful columns held

aloft the larger freestanding portico. They were arranged in a precise figure V, or a triangle, with the point of the triangle facing south, away from the Castle, or left from where Diakrina stood. This southernmost column, which formed the point of the triangle, was even more massive than the others and served as the front of the Great Portico, as she came to call it.

The roof of the Great Portico, instead of triangular, was a perfect square. This left the two front corners visibly unsupported, though they definitely appeared to be so solidly in place one could easily imagine the corners being upheld by something invisible yet very dense.

The columns were of a beautiful material Diakrina had never seen. It looked like crystal yet did not appear breakable like crystal or glass. It gave one the impression of something impenetrable, like marble or steel.

Each column, though semitransparent, had a deep and distinct color, with the two closest to the Castle, and farthest apart, appearing identical. Those two were crimson red. The next column out from the Castle, on the far side of the Great Portico, was green—almost a living green, like that of a plant. Its counterpart on the near side was of brilliant sparkling yellow. The next two columns, outward toward the point, were a gorgeous royal purple on the far side, and a beautiful sky blue on the side closest to Diakrina. At the point of the triangle, the largest of the seven columns was of a color difficult to describe. It appeared almost colorlessly transparent, yet the shimmering clearness itself was somehow a color, though Diakrina could never quite explain what she meant by this. The entire roof of the Great Portico was of this same colorless color.

The columns rose a full 300 feet into the air and were so beautiful in design and balance a deep sense of awe hushed Diakrina into silence as she gazed at their stately presence and towering height. The translucent roof was massive and imposing, and though almost crystal-clear, the dark clouds of the sky could not be seen through its enormous thickness.

Diakrina had never seen a structure so magnificent. "Or had she?" she thought. "Of course, the City!" She had only seen it from a distance, yet she was sure this was unmistakably like the architecture she had seen there.

Two things about the Great Portico struck Diakrina as strange. First, its material did not surge with the living Light she had seen in the City. Second, though it did not possess the living Light, it was still obviously untouched by the Dead Swamp. No ivy or moss grew on its surface. It stood noble, clean and impressive—yet, lifeless.

Diakrina turned her attention to the Small Portico, as she named it, although it was, itself, a huge edifice and would be considered a great architectural wonder in the world of men. It could be called "small" only in comparison to the Great Portico which loomed above and around it.

This Small Portico and its six columns were covered with hanging ivy and moss, which had crept out from where it attached to the Castle wall. The columns had been erected in two parallel rows of three, stretching southward from the Castle, supporting a long, narrow rectangular roof that ran perpendicular to the Castle wall and extended up under the roof of the Great Portico. The columns were spaced in perfect east-to-west alignment with the larger columns of the Great Portico. This effect gave almost the impression of a long, narrow covered aisle running from the Castle out under, and extending nearly the entire depth of, the Great Portico.

The color of each column, though partially shrouded beneath the ivy and moss, corresponded to that of its respective larger column of the Great Portico. No center column stood in front, however, and the roof of the Small Portico was crimson red, not the clear color of the massive roof overshadowing it.

The Small Portico itself had profound and untiring beauty. Looking only at it, one could become enraptured in studying its balanced symmetry, which at the same time was offset by surprising features that normally would not have been expected in a symmetrical design. But staying focused on its splendors proved difficult in light of the awe-inspiring glories of the Great Portico above it, like a giant redwood towering over a sapling.

"Oh! OHHHH!" was the best expression Diakrina could manage, as she stood mesmerized by the enormity and beauty of the two structures. Strateia motioned for her to follow him and they began covering the 150 yards or so between them and the near side of the

Great Portico.

The nearer their approach, the wider Diakrina's eyes became. It started slowly, but she was soon keenly aware of two intense emotions rising up inside her. One was a sense of holy hush, as if she were walking into the presence of hallowed antiquity. The second was contrary to this and could only be described as an immense sense of loss, as if one were looking on the ruins of some great but vanished civilization.

Instead of walking directly toward the Porticos, Strateia veered left and led Diakrina to the south end, or front, of the Great Portico. Its floor lay about nine feet above ground level and could only be reached by three massive steps, each about three feet high, which lined the entire perimeter of the edifice. As Strateia approached the steps, he mounted them as one normally walks up steps, though he obviously was stretching even his legs to do so.

Diakrina, instead, had to scramble up each step as if it were a tabletop. She thought it strange Strateia did not offer to help her master the imposing stairs. Instead he reached the top and turned to wait on her as she clambered up each step in turn.

Strateia looked down on her and answered her unspoken question. "You will understand better someday why you must mount these steps yourself. For now I will only say it once was a law you must do so, and it would be a law still if the living Light were here. For now you may consider it respect given to the past and faith given to the future fact of the living Light's return."

Having spoken, Strateia then turned and walked toward the Great Column, which looked like a 30-story cut diamond. Diakrina had never before been able to think of Strateia as small, but beside the mass of the Great Column he indeed looked like an ant. Diakrina could only imagine how she must look.

The floor of the Great Portico was a color Diakrina could not describe. She said the closest color she had seen to it—and it was not actually that close at all—was once when she had flown in an airplane over the Caribbean Islands. She remembered noting the islands were only the tops of huge underwater mountains, and often a mountain rose near the surface of the water for several miles before it broke above the surface as an island. In these places the white sand of the beaches reached out into the shallow water, sometimes for miles. As the bright sun hit the crystal clear water of the Caribbean over these submerged white-sand beaches, the most beautiful light-green aqua color surrounded the whole island, like a single-color rainbow with edges slowly fading into the deep blue of the ocean. "If you have seen this," she would say, "then you have seen the closest thing I know in this world to the color of the Great Portico's floor."

They walked to the right of the Great Column. Just beyond it lay the Small Portico, also with three steps circumventing its perimeter. These steps too were of a considerable scale, but closer to the size of steps Diakrina was accustomed to seeing.

The Small Portico had no center column and Strateia mounted the steps at its middle and proceeded down the aisle between the six columns. Diakrina followed, stretching to master the steps upright. The floor of the Small Portico was crimson in color, like the color of its roof and the two columns out in front of them closest to the Castle wall.

Proceeding forward, they passed the first set of columns, the purple on the left and the blue on the right. Diakrina briefly noticed the larger columns of the Great Portico beyond and in line with the columns of the Small Portico. They were of the same color, purple on the left and blue on the right.

Coming to the second pair, the green and yellow, on the left and right respectively, and Diakrina had a sense of lessening spaciousness—as if the space around them had somehow narrowed. She looked at the nearest green and yellow columns and noted they were the same distance apart as the purple and blue. This sense of narrowing space was due—as best she could determine—to the widening distance between the larger green and yellow columns of the Great Portico. As one ventured further into the increased spacing of the larger columns, the scale became greater and the aisle between the columns of the Small Portico seemed to narrow, though it did not.

This sense of narrowing space became even more pronounced as they approached the last two columns of the Small Portico. This dimensional contrast made the path between the two smaller crimson-red columns feel somewhat like a doorway.

Strateia walked between the crimson columns and toward an oversized door, which was straight ahead of them in the side of the Castle wall. As Diakrina came closer she saw just in front of the door spread a wide, depressed landing in the floor of the Small Portico, with a set of three steps descending into the landing from all sides. The door was even larger than it had at first appeared, for from a distance she had only seen its upper two-thirds.

Strateia did not descend the stairs but suddenly stopped in front of the steps as if he were alerted by something. His right hand went slowly to the crimson handle of his sword. He backed up and motioned for Diakrina to do the same. He never took his eyes off the door but kept backing up at an ever-greater pace until Diakrina had to run backwards to keep up with him. When they were back between the two crimson columns, Strateia pulled his sword and motioned for Diakrina to follow his example. As she did so, she heard noises coming from the direction of the door. Then she noticed—though she is not quite clear as to why she noticed it just then—the door had no handle on the outside but simply a pull rope for closing it from the outside near the top of the door.

"Little One," whispered Strateia, "go behind that column," he pointed to the crimson one on the right, "and do only what you see me do. Stay hidden unless I do otherwise." With that said, he moved swiftly behind the column on the left and Diakrina made her way behind the one on the right. The moment she had done so, a sound reached her ears of something like the links of a heavy chain clanging on a hard surface, followed immediately by the faint creak of what had to be the large door opening.

She moved so she could see just around the inside edge of the column and observe the door and Strateia at the same time. The door, which swung inward, suddenly disappeared into the blackness of the opening.

"I don't agree!" came a coarse and angry voice from the lightless opening.

A pale greenish glow emanated from the doorway, followed by its source: a lanky frame, about eight feet tall, came striding out onto the landing and up the steps. He stopped there, turned back toward the door and continued talking.

"I think it is too dangerous. They might learn too much and then all would be undone."

The speaker looked like a blend between Strateia and the creatures Diakrina had seen in front of the Castle. He had bronze colored skin like Strateia, but he did not have the same golden glow about him. Rather there was a sickening, pale greenish glow Diakrina would forever associate with her memories of Thanatos. Like the creatures of the swamp, his skin was beginning to erupt with black scaly patches appearing to be tumors. He was much less deformed than the others, but deterioration was clearly at work in him.

He had no white tunic of light like Strateia's, but was clothed in what reminded Diakrina of pictures she had seen of ancient warriors in battledress. His simple, bullet-shaped helmet was made of some cold, grey material. A sleeveless, armored vest covered his upper torso. Two spikes on each side of the vest protruded upward from his shoulders and outward over the arms. Around his waist he wore a heavy black chain belt, from which hung slightly smaller black chains cut into lengths reaching to just above his knees. These were attached all the way around, forming a steel (or something much harder) loin skirt. Diakrina surmised these were the chains she had heard. A sword—the size of Strateia's, with a pale greenish, death-colored, glowing handle—also hung from the chain belt. His shoes appeared to be metal, with two imposing horns protruding from the toe of each. He also had shin guards, strapped in place by chains just below his knees at the top and just above his ankles at the bottom, protected his lower legs.

A cruel face hung out from under the bullet-shaped helmet and was the source of the angry voice. "I'd rather keep them chained and ignorant than bring them here and chance their figuring something out."

"You worry too much about that, Desmos," came a calm but sinister voice.

This second speaker walked through the doorway. He resembled the first, except for his dress. His attire resembled that of a 15th century monk: a simple black skullcap, and a grey, almost black robe wrapped at the waist with a heavy chain belt, much like that of Desmos. The belt, however, had various kinds of emblems hanging from it, which looked to Diakrina like pagan religious symbols. The monk, as Diakrina thought of him, wore no sword, but carried a small black book in one hand. The book emitted a pale greenish glow from the edges of its pages where one might expect to see gold or silver gilding.

Draped around his neck hung a decorative chain with a large charm Diakrina recognized. It was a circle with a bar down the middle. About two thirds of the way down the bar, two arms extending outward and down and connected with the lower arch of the circle. Diakrina had heard it called a "peace symbol," but remembered being warned that in some strange cults it was designated an upside-down, broken cross—a symbol of rebellion against the Living One used in occult practices. She had not given much notice to the warning merely thinking it odd such a symbol could have two very different meanings. But now, seeing it around the monk's neck, she knew it must have a significance more sinister than merely a symbol of peace.

"I agree with Hairesis," came a third voice from the doorway as Diakrina heard steps on the stairs and a third cruel giant appeared pulling the door closed behind him with a tug on the rope. "These fools are much too blind to figure anything out. They can't see the Porticos even when they are out here. And even if they could—and I remind you, they can't—I think we could always keep them in the dark as to their real purpose. And if we can do that, we can accomplish more in a day by bringing them here than we could keeping them locked up for a year of conditioning."

"Sarx," retorted Desmos angrily, "you and Hairesis are too overconfident. You work well together. But you have the same weakness."

"And what might that be?" asked the monk, Hairesis, in a cold, steady, cutting voice making Diakrina feel ill inside.

"You play too close to the line. You try to help our cause by manipulating certain traits in these fools. I find that dangerous. You awaken too much in them. And once awakened, you sometimes lose control of them. I prefer to manipulate nothing but to enslave everything. I do not awaken them. Rather I drug them and numb them. I forge chains of their coarser appetites and use those chains to bind cloaks of illusion tightly around their minds. My lies drive them to despair as they chase the wind seeking satisfaction for their illusive, unquenchable thirsts. I create endless discontentment!"

Diakrina shuddered as Desmos boastfully shouted his tactics, his red eyes flaming with cruel contempt. She noted Strateia stood calmly behind the crimson pillar and made no motion.

"You're a fool, Desmos," snarled the monk. "You say you play it safe, but you lose as many as we do! You drive them to raging thirst and hunger through your tortures. Even the simplest of them sometimes realize these awakened desires—which you have made unbearably obvious—must spring from some actual reality. For thirst they reason there must be water, and for hunger they reason there must be bread. The less fearful ones then become susceptible to our Adversary's message of—and here the monk used a harsh mocking sing-song fashion as he chanted—'living water and living bread' ... and you lose them."

Desmos' hand slid toward his sword in determined, seething rage. The monk raised his book just as determinedly and shook it slowly in the air with glaring evil eyes, radiating that greenish color of death. Desmos seemed to fear the black book more than the monk did his sword, and his hand relaxed returning to his side.

"You would do well to listen, Desmos," interrupted Sarx. "What we are after is more beneficial to our cause. Yes, it is satisfying to torture His likeness in them, to imprison His 'children,' as He calls them. But what we do is better. We turn them more fully against Him. We do not merely imprison His likeness; we use it to curse Him. They shake their fists in His face with contempt when we are through with them. That cuts deeper!"

"Do you think," retorted Desmos, "that none of mine ever curse Him? I make them believe He is the source of their pain and despair or else, He is indifferent to it. They ..."

"And it is highly satisfying, as Sarx has said," interrupted the snarling monk. "But who wouldn't curse under such circumstances? We get them to curse Him in their pleasures. They raise a defiant fist and demand their independence while drinking the wine of His provision with their other hand."

A short—and for Diakrina, terrifying—pause followed.

Then, "I think both approaches are needed," offered Sarx, stepping between the other two. "I find there are those I must deliver to you, Desmos, if I am to keep the ground I have gained. And there are those which I must deliver to you, Hairesis, if they are not to be lost. Sometimes when one of you is losing one, I can derail them from going to our Adversary by redirecting them from one of you to the other.

"But, Desmos, Hairesis' way is the shortest road to what we are really after. In the past, most would do better under you. But now, we have succeeded so well in our conditioning of these fools we can lead them like cattle. So, it is best to take as many as possible straight to Hairesis. In the end, even these will not be lost to you.

"We are enjoying considerable progress in making them so blind they will embrace you both and not see through either of the illusions. You will find, Desmos, their arrogance makes a less visible chain, but it is in reality more effective and cruel. It is embedded in their will, mind and emotions on a deeper level. The slightest twist can bring more pain, with resulting subservience, than your cruelest tortures."

"You see," interjected the monk, "if you will follow my plan we shall all have greater success. Our crowning achievement will be to make these blind pneumasomas into both magicians and materialist at the same time."

Diakrina recognized the Greek construction of the word pneumasomas and understood it to mean spirit/body beings. The monk's tone obviously intended it as a term of ridicule, and his last comment formed a pun soliciting a vile sneer and chuckle from the three.

"And" added the monk, obviously pressing this small victory in the debate, "they are becoming so brain-dead they will not notice being a materialist and believing in magic at the same time is utter nonsense, sheer foolishness. And if some of them do begin to think about the contradiction, we already have intellectuals (he said this last term with a contemptuous sneer) who will explain to them it is "not a contradiction at all" (he mimicked a sing-song, placating voice), because the spiritual realm really doesn't exist; however, there are forces and energies within nature that seem magical and can give them amazing power and ability if they learn to tap into them. And that is where we will be waiting. They will think they are tapping into forces they can control. What they will get is us and the actual spiritual realm; and we will invade and slowly but surely take control!"

Desmos seemed to be clearly inspired by this description of possible events and was obviously considering the arguments presented by his cruel companion before replying.

"Now you put it this way, I think it could work. But we must not forget the dangers of bringing them into interaction with this other dimension of the real world. They may be blind and ignorant of it, yet they were created originally to have as much perception as any one of us of the spiritual. When you bring that to life, you must be sure you have prepared them well or they might discover things which will make them unmanageable."

"It is a point well taken," said the monk with surprising pleasantness. Diakrina could hear the manipulative undertones in his voice as he baited Desmos into submission. "But our leader has demanded we move along this path. These fools are to be made over into his image and he will not be appeased until they are. So in fact, it matters little what any of us think. This is the plan. But I confess, I like it."

"If it ends as you say, so will I," snarled Desmos. "However, do not think our Adversary will not be up to something." He paused before continuing. "We will bring them here and I will work with you. But if it fails, remember my warnings!"

"For now," began the monk, obviously wishing to change the subject, "we had better make our report to the leader. The council convenes shortly. It would not do to be late."

This last comment seemed to bring them, for the first time, into total agreement, and the threesome began walking together toward the Great Column at the south end of the porticos from where Strateia and Diakrina had just come.

Diakrina stealthily edged around the outer side of the crimson column, keeping the column between the evil trio and herself. A sudden panic began to rise inside her. She could see the distorted reflections of the three through the semi-translucent column. Well …

surely … they could see her!

Her questioning eyes turned to Strateia across the aisle and found a grave and stern rebuke on his face. She knew instantly he recognized her fear, and he was troubled by it. Just then, she heard the threatening rattle of Desmos' chains as three sets of heavy footfalls came to an abrupt stop. Strateia held her eye with authoritative urgency. She could read his noble face like a well-written book: "Do not fear! It is dangerous for you to fear! Do not move! Be calm!"

Diakrina knew she must obey. She must master her fear. Why fear was particularly dangerous at this moment she did not know, but she trusted Strateia and would do all in her power to obey him. Determined to only look at Strateia, she studied his fixed gaze, to lose herself in the sense of security she always felt flowing from him.

"For a moment, I thought I detected the scent of human fear in the air," spoke the dark voice of Desmos.

"So did I," agreed Sarx.

"I can always identify the strong drink of fear," continued Desmos.

Except for the sound of their shoes turning on the portico floor and the slight clinking of Desmos' chains, a searching silence fell for a few seconds. Diakrina did not allow herself to think of anything except the steady gaze of Strateia. She knew she mustn't. The peace and calm in Strateia's eyes washed over her like cooling waves on a hot summer day. Somehow, she knew it would be alright.

"I detect no scent of fear," came the analytical voice of the monk after a moment.

"It was there, you can be sure," came the slow, studied response of Desmos. "But you are right. I sense nothing now."

"There must be an open window in your torture chamber, Desmos," said Sarx with a chuckle.

There followed a short, pregnant silence. Then Sarx spoke again. "I sense nothing. We must go or risk the pain of our leader's displeasure. But," he added with another chuckle, "if my troops opened a window you would have a fine scent to enjoy, indeed. Nothing like senseless lust and burning, selfish passion and ambition to make my day."

Desmos snarled something like a laugh. "You can keep your lust and passion, though I confess it makes a fine dessert. I'll keep to the strong meat of bloody terror and maddening panic for my fare."

"You would both do well to develop a taste for the more basic and important attributes," offered the smug voice of the monk. "A hardened pride drawn out to an arrogant independence blended with a defensive and ignorant certainty makes a tasty stew indeed."

As they turned and continued down the aisle and off the steps of the Small Portico, Diakrina could hear the fading voice of the monk drone on: "You, with your spicy appetite, Desmos, and you, Sarx, with your love of the sweetened forms. You both would do well to remember . . ."

His voice faded into the distance.

Chapter Five

THE STAIRS

Strateia smiled at Diakrina and sheathed his sword. "You did well, Little One. You mastered your fear."

"I nearly gave us up. It was all I could do to control my panic." Then with a soft smile of gratitude she added, "I am glad you are here with me."

"You are not yet ready to engage these three. In time, you will be ready, but it is still to come."

"I would rather not!" responded Diakrina with a shudder.

Then she remembered the question bringing on the fear that almost conquered her. "Strateia, why did they not see us? The columns, though crimson, are nearly transparent and I know our forms must have been visible in the play of light within them. They should have seen us."

"You are correct in observing that we could be seen through the crimson columns. But there is a reason why we were perfectly safe from detection. These fallen ones will not look straight at or into the crimson columns. They know they are there, but will not—and it may be, cannot—look straight at them. It is one of their blind spots."

"Is there some good reason for this blind spot?"

"Yes, an exceptionally good reason, indeed. However, that it another lesson, better learned at its appointed time. For now, you will do well simply to remember the fact."

Strateia started toward the Castle door and motioned with his head for Diakrina to follow. Reaching the landing at the base of the stairs, he stopped and turned toward her.

"You must open the door and invite me to follow you if you wish for me to come with you." Strateia pointed to the door. There, in its surface, were the same carved words Diakrina had seen on the stone of the bridge pylons:

Who may enter?
The Living One formed the man from the dust of the ground and breathed into his nostrils the spirit of life, and the man became a living soul.
Who may accompany?
The invited.

"This is the Castle of your race, mankind," said Strateia as Diakrina stood looking at the carved letters, "constructed to reveal the inner nature of your souls. This end of the Castle represents your spirit. These Porticos represent what once was the place of fellowship and worship with the Living One. The spiritual, the foundation of all, is the realm of true worship. The Living One has forever existed as Spirit."

Diakrina followed his gaze as Strateia turned and looked back along the columns to the Great Column at the south end.

"The crystal of this place was once bursting with glorious Light. A whirling rainbow of dancing splendor moved within the Great Column, painting scenes of beauty no creature can describe or reproduce. It told stories from eternity so beautiful and ancient, filled with adventure and meaning, it made one's heart burst with longing and delight.

"Here your Great Parents walked and talked with the Living One before He became one of your race. They walked among these columns, which pulsed with light so intense the crystal you now see disappeared into pure Light: living green, royal purple, sky blue, blazing yellow and wine-red crimson . . . ringing and resonating with glorious music—singing colors—beautiful beyond imagination.

"The aquamarine of the Great Portico floor would come alive— living water to walk upon, filled with joyous creatures jumping and playing at their feet. The crimson floor of the Small Portico remained, however, a beautiful wine-red swirling with a beckoning mystery, refusing to give up its great secret.

"I know this will be hard for you to understand, Diakrina, but the living Light of these columns would produce fruit all over their inner surface: fruit so beautiful and perfect, seeing it and eating it brought immeasurable pleasure. Your Great Parents had only to reach into one of the columns and their hands would be filled.

"Each column produced fruit in keeping with its character. The living green column produced fruit of the untarnished earth. The royal purple column produced kingly fruit. Fruit from the heavenly realms grew from the sky-blue column, and from the brilliant yellow came fruit causing joyous dancing and celebration.

"But the two crimson columns produced the most delicious fruit of all. Within each was the fruit of love. To taste it was to taste the infinite depths of His love for His children, whom He created out of his passion and joy. Each bite infused the partaker with identity, security, meaning, purpose, belonging and joyous, unending adventure.

"Yet, at the same time, through this fruit's wonderful gifts ran a dark, pungent and mysterious tang. And somehow, though bitter, it— mixed with its indescribably wonderful nectar—was, in its place, the sweetest and most delicious strain of all."

As Strateia spoke a kind of glorious haunting came over Diakrina. For those few moments Diakrina saw the things Strateia described. The vision was faint and far away. Even so, it was overwhelming.

The columns seemed to burst to life, the glorious fruit visible within them. The swirling, mysterious wine-red of the immediate floor around them, and beyond that, the living, moving aquamarine surface from which jumped beautiful fish and creatures in unrestrained celebration, all became visible. In the center, the Great

Column filled with scenes too beautiful to comprehend, yet telling stories so soul-moving Diakrina longed to leap into the Column, itself, to live the unfolding stories. As this longing grew within her, Strateia finished with these words:

"And the Great Column revealed stories inviting you to come live within, and in so doing, truth would be learned by experience as well as related facts."

Though Strateia had finished speaking, the vision held for a few moments. Suddenly, He was there in the midst of the porticos. His glory made the glory of the porticos vanish by comparison. Diakrina gasped in a long breath, so transfixed she could not breathe out. She wanted to run to Him, to fall into His arms. He smiled at her and her soul was drenched in joy and quivered with transfixed delight. Then . . . the vision faded.

Diakrina holding her breath stared in the direction of the Great Column when Strateia softly placed his hand on her shoulder. She came to herself with a start and began to breathe deeply.

"Someday, Diakrina, someday soon, the Light will return with Him, and all will be well."

Strateia gave her a moment to compose herself and then he lifted an eyebrow toward the door.

"You must enter Sapient Castle, the Castle of Humanity. You must travel through the levels of its spirit—which will be your own spirit—in order to obtain the Lantern of Logos. Only by its light will you be able to find your way back to the Tree Bridge to take the Atheos beyond the reach of Anomos. Your passage through Sapient Castle will be both a quest and a means of your own transformation. It will be a journey of life and becoming.

"As the castle's name also suggest, this journey through the castle will be an adventure to engage knowledge and wisdom as well. They are weapons no warrior should be without.

"While we are within, you will be able to interact freely with all those inside. I, however, will be obscure to most. You will be, so to speak, primarily without my help."

"But you will not leave me?"

"No, I will stay with you and help guard you and the Atheos. There is too much at stake for failure."

Diakrina smiled. "Good. I will feel much more secure with you near." Then, turning toward the door, she asked, "How do I open it? There is no handle or knob to turn."

"Simply push the door open. It is left unguarded."

Diakrina laid her hand on the door and gave it a firm push. It swung slowly and silently on its hinges and opened into the dark interior of the Castle.

"One thing more, Diakrina," said Strateia, stepping between her and the door. "Once within, you will not be able to speak directly to me and I will not be able to respond directly to you unless instructed to do so. You will have to make your requests to the Living One—it must go directly through His hands once we are within. This is the law of the Castle and we must obey it as if you had not been brought through the Door of the Rose. I will do and say only what the Living One directly tells me to do or say; or has previously made my charge. So, I will be able to speak to you, but only at His instruction."

"Will the Living One be with us within the Castle?" asked Diakrina.

"He is already. He is always with us. He will be still."

"But I mean . . ."

"I know what you mean," interrupted Strateia. "It does not have as much meaning as you suppose. Simply be assured He is with you in a more profound way than you can now understand. And it is not a less real way than the one you desire, but the most real way presently possible. Out of this will come all the other for which you long."

Diakrina felt as if these words had somehow ripped away a mask from her eyes. She suddenly saw everything differently. The joy, which had occasionally invaded her at the mention of the Living One, now saturated the atmosphere. He was everywhere! He was distinct from everything—nothing could be Him but Him. Yet, simultaneously, He was everywhere. Nothing could avoid His Presence.

Strateia placed his large hand on Diakrina's shoulder. "Translate this insight into secure knowledge and treasure it in your heart. By the very nature of your journey there will be times when this truth will not feel real. You must choose to believe it, even when doing so is not easy."

Strateia stepped aside and waited for Diakrina to enter. She walked through the door into what looked like a spacious reception area. A musty, stale rush of cool air hit her in the face as she took her first step inside.

In a few moments her eyes adjusted to the lack of light and she took note of elegant artistry all around her. The symmetry of the room was delicately balanced, and the works of art were graceful, not ornamental. They appeared to be planned into the design of the room, not added later to fill it or decorate it. In fact, one could almost imagine the room itself was designed around the various statues and forms. Diakrina decided against this, however, because the works of art seemed to contribute to the greater effect of the room and not the other way around.

Three doors led out of this room: a door straight ahead of her, one to her far right and one to her far left. She was about to proceed toward the middle door when she turned to make sure Strateia was behind her. He was not. She looked back through the door and saw him still standing there on the landing.

She then remembered. She had acknowledged what Strateia had taught her concerning the necessity of inviting him in, but she had never actually done so.

"Strateia, I'm sorry! Please come in with me."

He made no motion or acknowledgement of her invitation. She repeated herself, "Strateia, please come with me!"

He still made not even the slightest acknowledgement.

Diakrina walked back through the door and out onto the landing. "Strateia, didn't you hear me?"

"Yes, but I don't think you listened to me."

Diakrina face clouded with questioning.

"Did I not tell you that once you entered the Castle you could not speak directly to me, but must speak to the Living One?"

Diakrina frowned at herself for forgetting so quickly.

"When you are within you must obey the law of the Castle. If you wait until you are within to invite me to accompany you, then you must do it by the house rules."

"I'm sorry, Strateia. I should have paid closer attention."

She was about to repeat her invitation a third time when a sparkle came into her eyes. She looked up and whispered, "Please, Living One, will you allow Strateia to accompany me into the Castle?"

Strateia smiled and his gentle clear eyes danced like a bubbling brook as he acknowledged Diakrina's insight. "Good, Little One. You have learned the Law of the Castle is your privilege everywhere. Speaking to Him is always your privilege."

"Then is it not also a privilege within the Castle?" asked Diakrina, pressing the point.

"Yes, Little One. When this is understood, the necessity of it being a law ceases in one sense. Yet, in a higher sense, it then becomes a law of delight: a natural practice held to for the love of it, a law of reason and order, a law of love."

"And such a law is a delight because it is not a burden?"

Strateia nodded in the affirmative. "I am instructed to accompany you. Shall we go?"

Diakrina retraced her steps (checking twice confirming Strateia was with her) and was soon standing in front of the middle door again. It then occurred to her she had no direction on which door she should open. She wondered if it mattered. She looked back at Strateia, but no communication came from his countenance.

"Living One," she whispered, "does it matter which of these doors I enter?"

She had hardly said the word, "enter" when Strateia stepped around in front of her and turned to face her. He raised his sword and pointed at the door to Diakrina's left. Diakrina smiled and turned toward the door. She was about to reach for it when she spotted a word carved into the door: Κοινωνια. This word she understood to mean Communion or Fellowship. It struck her the other doors might have carvings on them, too, and wondered why she had not noticed until now.

She turned her head and looked straight across the room at the door on the right. She saw no carvings of any kind. It looked smooth and plain. She then glanced around Strateia at the middle door. There in vivid relief was the carved word, Γνωσις, meaning Knowledge or Cognition.

The letters were so deeply and clearly carved she could not imagine how she missed seeing them before. She stared for some moments at the door trying hard to remember if the carved word had been there. She felt certain she had seen only a plain door before— "just like the one on the right," she thought, as she stole a glance at it.

There, before her unbelieving eyes, was a clearly carved word in the third door! Right where she had verified a plain smooth surface only a moment before now was the word, Συνειδησις or Conscience. She stood there with her head tilted to one side with a troubled frown on her face, at a total loss as to how to account for this.

She looked back at the middle door and the lettering was still there and the same. She looked back at the left door, where Strateia now stood to one side, and the word, Κοινωνια, was still there. She read aloud the Greek words on each door and translated them into English, moving around the room from left to right: "Κοινωνια.— Communion; Γνωσις—Cognition; Συνειδησις —Conscience."

"Strateia," she blurred out, pointing at the middle and right-hand doors, "Why could I not see these words before?"

Strateia didn't acknowledge her. She was just beginning to repeat herself as she took a step toward him, "Strateia, why . . ." when she remembered the house rules. She stopped and whispered, "Living One, please help me understand about the doors. I sense there may be something important about all this."

Strateia spoke. "Diakrina, you did not at first see the carvings on the two doors, Cognition and Conscience, because of an interdependent relationship between these three doors. Each door represents a major function or attribute of mankind's immaterial nature—the spirit. There is a definite order in which they must function. The doors testify to this by making it possible to see the function which it represents only after you have seen its prerequisite function—the function on which that function depends."

"So . . ." began Diakrina thoughtfully, "the door on the left, Communion, is what you would call the first door. And once you have seen this door, you can then discern the middle door, Cognition. And only then can you discern the third door, Conscience."

Diakrina stopped and waited for Strateia's approval on her deductions. He said nothing, as if he had not heard her at all.

"I never thought it would be so hard to remember not to talk to you directly," said Diakrina with both hands on her hips. Looking up she asked, "Have I understood correctly?"

Instinctively she looked to Strateia expecting an answer. He said nothing. However, suddenly, the Door of Communion behind him glowed with a warm, golden light. Without visible hand, the door opened gracefully, revealing bright crimson-red steps, ascending into a blinding, yet beckoning light. Diakrina hurried to the steps and began climbing, with Strateia following behind her.

She ascended only one level up, when she came to a wide landing. On her left rose a reddish-brown wall she took to be the inside of the exterior wall of the Castle. To her right stood a crystal wall, as clear as the purest glass one could imagine. Beyond the crystal wall Diakrina could see a hallway about 30 feet wide, lined with book-laden shelves on both sides, reaching all the way to a 20-foot ceiling. The hall curved back to the right in a perfect arc and appeared to circle a voluminous room, though Diakrina could not know for sure because the wall of books limited her view. She looked for any kind of opening in the crystal wall, finding none.

The books were large and thick. They resemble books in which one would expect to find fanciful stories people like to read curled up by a fireplace (unless, like me, you enjoy another kind of book I am about to describe). Some of the book also looked like books of records in which pages and pages of facts and events would be recorded. I am not saying they would be uninteresting facts and events. On the contrary, these books gave the impression they would be intriguing, though unembellished. Diakrina had a strong desire to take one from the shelf and pore over it. The main thing, however, is they did not look to be the kind of books which had been written to be interesting—they would have no hidden design or purpose of appealing to anyone. They would be books written with exhaustive attention to detail and truth, and nothing more.

The golden light, which had first drawn Diakrina, still poured down from a second set of stairs straight ahead on the other side of the landing. Since it seemed certain she could have no access to the hall of books from this landing, she determined to keep following the light. As she said to me later when she was relating her story, "Even if I could have accessed the books, I somehow knew I must follow the light."

Resuming her pursuit of the golden light, she followed the crimson-red floor to the second set of stairs, where, stopping, she looked up. The walls—crystal-clear on her right and reddish-brown on her left—continued up the stairs. A wonderful flood of light poured down the crimson steps like a strong, liquid current against which Diakrina consciously had to brace herself. A deep, stabbing yearning—that pain of joyous longing more pleasing than a thousand pleasures—seemed to lift Diakrina and carry her away in a torrent of desire. She felt so drawn by the light, she had to look down at her stationary feet to confirm she was still standing at the foot of the stairs.

She took her first step onto the staircase and fell suddenly on her face, shaking violently. She had been literally knocked down by . . . , "by . . . Immensity," she later said, searching for words. "I was in a place too big, too great, too vast. I lost all sense of reference. If you had dropped me in the middle of the Pacific Ocean, with nothing but sky and water for thousands of miles in all directions, I would have still felt infinitely larger than I felt at that moment. An ocean can at least be measured!

"An inexplicable dread, a sense of exposure to someone who was unsafe—in the sense you could have no control whatever over him—settled like a huge boulder upon me. I was paralyzed with awe, stricken with panic. And yet, the golden light called to me forcefully.

"Music, which was like a three-dimensional substance, flowed over and through my whole body. Each melodic chord resurrected a sleeping part of my mind and flooded it with enchantment and delight. I was suddenly being thrust into a realm where fear and joy were not opposites, but somehow united in a terrible and yet wonderful marriage.

"This marriage seemed to be the law of this realm—like a law of nature in the physical realm—and I was out of step with it, terribly out of step," she said. "Here, somehow, things which I had only experienced as opposites were revealed not to be opposites when placed back in their proper relation. Yet, in me, they still polarized into a false dichotomy.

"I struggled to reconcile myself to this marriage of terror and peace, Immensity and Intimacy. I was in the presence of awful splendor and beautiful trepidation. I was being called on both to stand at a distance in reverent fear and to leap like a child into a loving Father's lap. These paradoxes were the source of my paralysis. What one act or thought could achieve both—what could marry such seeming opposites?"

Diakrina said at this point she had her first memorable experience of a sense of unworthiness.

"I had always been a rather secular person, even though raised in the Church. I now know this means I was ignorant of much of reality. I had lived with little comprehension of anything or Anyone as exalted. In fact, being a product of western, secular culture, I had a suspicion of anything or anyone who would dare to claim any kind of supremacy. We were always taught 'equality'—even where it didn't, and sometimes couldn't, exist.

"The great offense was to be different. We were told everyone should better themselves, but this 'betterment' was defined in a way to exclude any genuine pursuit of improvements with true significance. To have actually adopted the better and the best would have meant dropping out of step with the masses. This was not only discouraged, it was silently reproved as arrogant and self-serving.

"This all carried over into an unspoken suspicion of anything inexplicable or incomprehensible by human methods of reason and examination. So, of course, the very idea of a transcendent One was suspect.

"We acted like spoiled children who refused to play unless everyone played by our rules—which, of course, were designed to place us in charge of every game. We had blackmailed our way into a position where we could have say as to what rules would be admitted or not admitted according to our liking. That may work for spoiled children, if the adults pay no attention, or do not interfere with their games by bringing in the real rulebooks and settling disputes by authority.

"Yet, here I was at the foot of this staircase with no more room for blackmailing reality. I could no longer demand it to conform to that which made me comfortable. Here was the Unchanging and Unchangeable: The Eternally Decided. I was the one who would have to do the conforming. The very reality of this flowing glory washing over me from the stairs above insisted, in patient silence, I adjust and fall into step. And yet, it was my choice and I understood intuitively that if I made it, it led to freedom and greater individuality, not less. I could not, in my mind, fit all the pieces of this seeming puzzle together, but somehow, I knew they fit.

"One thing I did know was I was not worthy to proceed until I changed my attitude from its present deformity to one which submitted to the healing and adjusting power of the golden Light. I was graciously, even pleadingly invited in, but all on definite terms. There could be no thought of appealing for an exception to the Unchanging and Unchangeable. Anything 'other' would be wrong and one somehow knew He'd never allow it. In fact, you realized only His will was truly real. All else was impossible, a mere deceptive illusion.

"I was being forced to embrace what was once my fear as a joy, and my joy as a grave thing of immense importance. I had to confess to the golden Light I had always lived in a realm of the incomplete and deformed. My 'normal' was subnormal. Here I had met NORMAL for the first time.

"Oh, how strange, yet wonderful, to realize the 'normal' was GLORY, LIFE, JOY; ULTIMATE UNCHANGING, UNCHANGEABLE BEAUTY; not gloom, death and uncertainty. But at the same time, and constantly accompanying it, was the awful realization I was the one deformed; I was of a deformed race. I felt I carried some deadly infection that could not be admitted into the presence of such Perfection.

"Oh, don't misunderstand. This absolute Perfection was in no danger from my infection. I was the one in danger from His Perfection! What held me at bay was kindness! It was mercy which, for the moment, shut the door in my face. One step more and I would have walked into the Presence that would, of necessity, consume me. In love He momentarily excluded me."

Diakrina knew the Living One had already significantly changed her. He had set her free from her internal fears in the cave. She had been given the grace to trust as she entered and passed through Nekus. She had learned to follow His footprints instead of seek her own way, even to the point of leaping into Nekus Falls. And in His healing presence at the Spring of Longings, she had been transformed and renewed.

But now her perception of His infinite Otherness, and seemingly opposite, infinite loving identification with her, were both being corrected, refined and joined into a higher form of perception. These were somehow being revealed as on a higher plane of reality than she had ever been enabled to embrace.

Diakrina heard voices whispering. Yet the whispers echoed like thunder off every surface around her, speaking, and yet, as in song, with voices and melodies indescribably beautiful.

"IS THERE A CURE FOR THIS DAUGHTER OF ADAM?" they sang.

"THERE IS!" echoed the reply.

"WHO PROVIDES THE CURE?" came the next melodic question.

"I, WHO SWALLOWED THEIR FINITE ETERNITY OF DEATH IN MY INFINITE ETERNITY OF LIFE; I, THE LIVING ONE, POURING OUT THE SACRIFICE, WHICH IS THE CURE, IN THE SPILLING OF MY LIFE UPON THEM; IT IS I WHO PROVIDES THE CURE!"

"OFFER IT TO HER. SHE IS ALREADY UNDER THE PROVISIONS OF THE CURE. IF SHE COMES DEEPER, SHE MAY COME HOME, AND COMMUNION WILL BE MORE DEEPLY RENEWED," came the verdict.

Without warning the crystal wall to Diakrina's right erupted into clear liquid fire. The flames did not dance, but flowed in currents of white heat from top to bottom. Diakrina stood up and fell back against the reddish-brown wall to her left trying to raise her shield. But the shield was somehow struck from her arm, clamoring to the landing below her, where Strateia stood.

The heat was overwhelming! She turned her face to the outer wall to escape the flames and to protect her eyes from the intense light. This wall, no longer a dark reddish-brown, was now pierced by the blinding light from the flames, gleaming with translucent, blood-red crimson.

She wanted to scream, but no sound would come. She pressed tightly against the now crimson wall. Her back was being blasted by the heat and light, with the crystal flames engulfing her. Just when she was sure she would be consumed, without warning, the crimson wall suddenly turned fluid: a flowing stream of blood-red liquid. She felt herself falling headfirst into the flowing torrent, as a healing coolness engulfed her.

Instead of falling downward, she was caught and suspended in a crimson current—that was the wall itself—as it flowed upward. She felt, to her own surprise, no fear, as she slowly maneuvered herself upright and turned to face the stairs and the wall of flaming light. The light was still so intense she had to cover her eyes. But she no longer felt the searing heat. How she was able to breathe deeply in this liquid atmosphere engulfing her, she did not know. But breathe she could.

Then, from the blinding flames on the other side of the staircase, she could see a faint, golden silhouette of a beautiful being. She could only look for a few quick seconds without covering her eyes in the direction of the flaming, Golden Light. She could make out little of His actual form. However, what she could see filled her with great awe and joy. Then came a Golden Voice thundering like the troubled sea, and yet caressed Diakrina as a gentle spring shower:

"YOU MUST CLOTHE YOURSELF AT THE DEEPEST LEVEL OF YOUR BEING IN THE CRIMSON CURE WHICH IS PROVIDED. ONLY THEN CAN YOU MORE FULLY EMBRACE THE POURED-OUT LIFE OF THE LIVING ONE AS YOUR THE DEEPEST CURE?"

"Oh, yes!" came Diakrina's eager response still shielding her eyes with her hands. "I have and I do!"

"THEN YOU MUST CHOOSE TO LISTEN CAREFULLY SO YOU WILL UNDERSTAND. HEAR THE TERMS OF THIS COVENANT:

•"THE GATE IS NARROW AND THE WAY COMPRESSED AND FENCED IN BY WISDOM FROM ABOVE. THERE IS BUT ONE CHOICE APPEARING IN MANY FORMS. IT IS ALWAYS THE CHOSING OF ME OVER YOUR SELF—MY TRUTH OVER YOUR OWN PRECEPTION, MY PURPOSE OVER YOUR PASSIONS—SO I MAY THEN CONTINUALLY BESTOW ON YOU YOUR TRUE SELF AND BIRTH PASSIONS IN YOU THAT LEAD TO THE JOY OF YOUR ETERNAL PURPOSE.

•"THE ONLY DOOR IS MY DEATH BECOMING YOUR DEATH.

•"IN EMBRACING ME IN PREFERENCE TO YOUR SELF, YOU MUST CEASE TO BE WHAT YOU ARE, SO YOU MAY BECOME WHAT I WILL MAKE YOU; YOU MUST TURN LOOSE OF ALL ELSE, SO YOU CAN TAKE HOLD OF ME AS I TAKE HOLD OF YOU.

•"YOU MUST LOSE YOUR SELF AND NEVER KNOW YOUR SELF AGAIN OUTSIDE OF ME. MY DEATHLESS LIFE WILL BECOME YOUR LIFE. YOU MUST BECOME ONE WHO HAS SURVIVED DEATH, INSTEAD OF ONE WHO FEARS IT."

A pause followed, making it clear she should speak. It was a question bubbling up from deep within her finding its way to her tongue. "Then . . . I must embrace Your death . . . to embrace You?"

"YOU NEED NOT EMBRACE WHAT IS ALREADY YOURS. YOU MUST EMBRACE MY LIFE AND THEN FACE YOUR DEATH IN ME. FOR IT WAS YOUR DEATH WHICH I EMBRACED—I HAVE NO DEATH OF MY OWN. ONLY WHEN YOU HAVE EMBRACED MY LIFE AND ALLOWED IT TO SWALLOW YOUR DEATH, CAN YOU KNOW THE MYSTERY OF REDEMPTIVE DEATH—DEATH WHICH LEADS BACK TO LIFE. FOR I AM THE RESURRECTION AND THE LIFE!"

"I do! I will!" cried Diakrina.

The whispering, echoing voices sang, "THE OATH OF BLOOD IS TAKEN. THE COVENANT IS CONFIRMED. SO BE IT! GIVE HER THE COVENANT MEAL."

Then the Golden Voice spoke again. "DIAKRINA, OPEN YOUR EYES."

Diakrina slowly opened her eyes and, little by little, lowered her hands. At first, all was fiery clearness, like liquid flaming crystal. Her eyes hurt a little at first but slowly they focused, and then the pain ceased.

There in the blazing glory, a crystal Hand of unspeakable beauty reached out toward her. It entered right into the flowing crimson wall of Sapient Castle touching her lips lightly with the forefinger, like the touch of a burning ember. Although burning deeply into Diakrina's lips, it left only a glowing radiance behind when the glorious finger was removed. Someone placed something in her mouth.

"EAT THE BREAD FROM MY HAND," instructed of the Golden Voice. "IT IS HUMANITY INVADED BY MY DIVINITY."

Diakrina obeyed. An intense bitterness unlike anything she had ever known struck the inside of her mouth and she instinctively recoiled, but only for a brief moment. As she swallowed, the bitterness instantly gave way to a taste wonderfully sweet; like fresh, raw honey.

The crystal Hand now lay open with a cup sitting upon the outstretched palm. The cup itself looked ancient and earthy. It seemed rather out of place in this magnificent palm. Then the Golden Voice spoke:

"DRINK FROM THE CUP OF COVENANT. IT IS FILLED WITH MY LIFE POURED OUT ON YOUR DEATH."

Diakrina reached for the cup. Although it appeared of normal size, she could not lift it. Seemingly it weighed tons and was so dense to the touch she knew, intuitively, she would never elevate it.

"YOU CANNOT DRINK OF THIS CUP ALONE," came the Golden Voice. "PLACE YOUR HAND ON MINE AND WE SHALL DRINK TOGETHER."

Diakrina reached out and touched the glorious Hand, which then closed on her hand and the cup.

"NOW DRINK, DIAKRINA," came the instruction.

She bent her arm to bring the cup near to her lips with the crystal Hand lifting the cup into place. When her eyes cast down over the rim, they widened in disbelief. To look into the cup was to be suddenly suspended above a vast eternal ocean of crimson with no perceived limits. (Diakrina swears her eyesight was by this time so strengthened almost any measurable distance, no matter how great, could be seen in its entirety.) What most astonished her was what she viewed through the crimson ocean. Her sight traveled down, down and farther down, to the bottom of the cup, as if descending into the depths of a vast sea! At the very bottom she gazed through the cup, seeing the surface of the crystal Hand. There beneath the cup, in the palm of the Hand itself, near the wrist, was a cruel wound—the source of the crimson sea. The wound flowed freely up through the bottom filling the cup.

Diakrina drank. She drank deeply of the most intense sorrow full of every conceivable pain. Yet, all this pain was immediately overwhelmed and lost in a glorious, unrelenting joy. And suddenly, the cup was gone.

"REMOVE YOUR TUNIC," came the instruction of the Golden Voice, "BUT SAVE THE BELT WITH THE CHRUSOLITHOS ROSES, AS WELL AS YOUR SWORD, THE GLOWING PAGE, AND THE CRYSTAL CONTAINER WITH THE IMMORTAL FRUIT."

Diakrina complied. While holding all these in one hand, she pulled the tunic, which Strateia had woven of still living grass, over her head. The crystal Hand took from her the tunic and instantly it burst into liquid flames and was gone.

"STEP OUT ONTO THE STAIRS."

Diakrina momentarily hesitated, remembering the blasting waves of liquid heat. Diakrina was afraid to make any move toward the stairs. How could she step out there again? She wanted to ask why she must, but her questions could find no voice.

Immensity waited in incredible, humble, patient kindness. An unearthly silence engulfed everything else—a silence so intense it could not be described as the absence of anything, but rather the presence of absolute attention. An intense consciousness surrounding her. It was as if a thousand beautiful eyes were waiting to see what she would do.

Diakrina was suddenly aware of how her own heart was overflowing with longing for the Living One. The pain of that terrible longing was like a crescendo increasing to an earthquake within her. She felt she must run to Him.

Yet, she couldn't run, not yet anyway. She lacked the spiritual legs for this terrain of terrifying Immensity and this atmosphere of such astonishing Perfection. She was not yet strong enough or dense enough.

But go she would, even if it were the last act of her life! Slowly, almost swimming, she moved to the edge of the wall of crimson. Every part of her being vibrated with intense longing and holy fear. Her mind raced, determined to master these seeming opposites.

"I must marry longing and fear," she heard her mind repeating. "I must know His redemptive death—death bringing resurrection. I must lose what I am to find what I will be. Only in Him—in His Life— can I find my true self."

But when she came to the place where stepping from the crimson wall was possible, she could not make the last move—the step of no return. Something was holding her back. What needed to be set right or was trying to keep her from being set right, she could not identify.

Then she heard a gentle whisper. "YOU MUST NOT SURRENDER YOUR SELF TO GAIN YOUR SELF. YOU MUST SURRENDER YOUR SELF TO BE MORE FULLY HIS! IT IS NOT YOUR SELF YOU WANT. IT IS HIM!"

It was true. Her heart nearly leaped out of her breast as the truth came clear. She cared nothing for having or saving herself if only she might have Him; and that, if only for a moment.

"Forget Diakrina," she heard herself whisper. "I want Him!" Suddenly, she was free. She pushed through the curtain of crimson onto the flaming stairs. She was hardly ready for what happened next.

Although Diakrina had stepped out onto the steps naked (if there is such a state in that place and under such conditions), a swirling crimson light immediately covered her. She looked down and watched herself being clothed in the most exquisite crimson dress of translucent light. The dress and the process producing it were incredibly beautiful.

Then crimson shoes appeared on her feet. She felt something sweep through her hair and, reaching up, found to her astonishment a small crown woven into her long flowing, dark-brown hair.

"YOU MAY ASCEND THE STAIRS, CHILD," came the loving instruction of the Golden Voice.

Then something beautiful happened. Diakrina burst into song. Never one to sing before this, she suddenly was filled with music she could not contain. A glorious voice came flowing freely from her open mouth, as though music were the language of this Place and she had been given the gift of speech.

The song she sang translates something like this:

> *"Covered, I'm covered, dead but alive.*
> > *Lost, but discovered and carried to the skies.*
> *Engulfed in Immensity, insignificant and small.*
> > *Known by Omniscience, thus important to all.*
> *Held by the Power of a great awesome King.*
> > *Sing, yes I sing, of the freedom He brings.*
> *Circle without end, yet repeating never.*
> > *Eternal Friend, who loves me forever!"*

As Diakrina sang, she sensed the impression of noble, immortal children dancing with supernatural delight and skill, up and down the staircase. Yet as soon as she would try to focus on any one child or one aspect of the romp of joy engulfing her, she would again see nothing but the stairs, the crystal wall of flames and the crimson outer wall. Yet the sound of the singing, dancing children never ceased for a moment and she could continually feel herself caught in the current of a welcome celebration.

The mystery of the children dimmed in importance. She was consumed with song. A joy, which previously would have been incomprehensible surged up from within her and flowed without interruption.

How long she sang she was never sure. Time did not seem to move. An audience too large to be seen stood at attention and delighted in her song.

Suddenly, she stopped. It was as if the song within her knew an important moment had come in a grand ceremony. She was instantly silent. Even the incorporeal children stood still in a solemn, yet delighted hush.

From behind her, Diakrina heard steps on the stairs. Before she could turn, the forgotten Strateia was beside her, with her shield in his hand.

"You are to be presented before your King. Place the rose-belt around your waist again and then your sword. Then place your trust, which is in the crystal container, over your shoulder again and the glowing page within your dress above the belt."

Diakrina tied the rope around her waist. The golden-clear roses sparkled with an intense luster against the exquisite crimson dress of light. Then she buckled the golden belt and slid the crimson sword into place. Lifting the strap of the clear crystal container, she placed it over her head and let it come to rest at her left side. Then she took the glowing page from the book, and folding it up, secured it inside her dress. Taking the shield from Strateia, she slid her left arm through the leather strap and grasped the handle.

After securing each of these items, Diakrina, to our mind's eye, might have appeared as a kind of walking paradox. It would be hard for us to understand how all these things would blend: the exquisite crimson dress of light, tied with the belt completed by the golden-clear roses. Then the golden belt and crimson sword, a strap over her right shoulder that held the crystal container to her left hip, which was slightly covered by the shield quietly flaming with blue, white and golden flames. But somehow, it all was perfect.

Strateia then held out his strong bronze left arm and she placed her right hand on top of his. Together they gracefully ascended the stairs surrounded by an invisible, yet certain, romp of serious joy.

Chapter Six

THE BRIDGE OF TRUST

Diakrina walked up the final steps on the arm of Strateia. As she stepped onto the landing, she slowly turned and took in a full panoramic view of the mesmerizing scene above her. A peculiar sensation struck her. She concluded later her normal human sight would likely not have taken notice of this abnormality. However, her newly refined vision was capable of perceiving extreme detail, and she immediately detected something odd. Her view suddenly filled with a far distant horizon that was, at the same time, extraordinarily near. After staring at it perplexed for a few moments, she determined the ceiling above her appeared to be a clear, dome-shaped lens absorbing and reflecting objects that were actually far off, making them look remarkably close.

"Is this part of Heaven?" gasped Diakrina. She was not speaking to Strateia, but to the One who filled the atmosphere.

"It is not," came the emphatic answer from Strateia. "At least, not as you mean. This is a place of communion. But He often lifts it, by His Presence, into Heaven, itself. What you see above you is the Dome of Reality."

Diakrina was entranced by the display of golden light that, having washed over this distant horizon, painted the landscape's smaller twin on the surface of the mysterious Dome. It was indeed a twin, except in one respect: it lacked detail.

When Diakrina tried to note any particulars concerning any mountain, tree or star (she claims brilliant stars dotted the sky even though it was day), a specific examination revealed little more than a splash of general form and color. Specific things could never be made out, though you somehow knew the original behind them must be exceedingly detailed.

"This made the whole display quite maddening," said Diakrina one day when we were discussing the scene. "Everything reflected in the half-sphere of the Dome of Reality was of such a nature as to draw you in, to pull at you and cause you to long to leap within and run deeper and deeper into each unfolding object or scene. Yet, everything was in general outline—somewhat like colorful shadows—with nearly every desired detail obscured."

"Oh, OH!" whimpered Diakrina as she stood on the landing and searched frantically for some single detail which would take her one step deeper into the glorious horizon. "I can't make out anything for certain beyond the general forms. Where is the way in? There must be a way in!"

"You are looking through an obscure glass, darkened by loss of knowledge," came the quiet, yet silvery voice of Strateia. "Only through communion can the knowledge of reality be regained. Come now, your King awaits."

The mention of the King brought Diakrina's eye down from the golden horizon. For the first time she noticed what was immediately around her. The stairs had brought them into a wide aisle running from side to side in this great sanctuary, approximately halfway between the front and back of the room. This aisle was so wide the generous landing of the stairs fit easily into its center and still left ample space. The back of the large sanctuary was to her right and seemed to be on top of the castle, though covered by the great dome. The front, much farther away, was to her left in the direction of the Great Portico.

While surveying the dome ceiling, she had instinctively turned first right, then left and then back to the way she was facing as she came up the stairs on the landing. The aisle continued out in front of her all the way to far side. She could now see she was not centered in the room side to side. She was looking toward the center of the great sanctuary, which lay further along this aisle. At the middle this aisle seemed to intersect another large aisle running back-to-front in this sanctuary—the back on her right, the front on her left. Strateia pointed gently ahead toward the intersection.

Diakrina looked down the wide aisle she was in. It was bordered on the right by the front of pews, like in an immense church, and on the left by the backside of the same kind of pews. To her right it was rather dark, and the pews had little groups of people seated in them here and there throughout the expanse of the sanctuary. But far down to her left and slightly in front of her, a scattering of white light came from a single object sitting in the center of a huge platform, which stretched from side to side in the vast sanctuary.

Strateia led her straight ahead toward the center of the expansive room to where this wide aisle intersected with the other center aisle—as it turned out, a much wider aisle. As they reached the middle of this intersection, he turned to the left and stopped, looking down the Great Aisle (as Diakrina came to call it) toward the large platform.

This cathedral, with its imposing half-sphere Dome for a roof high above, was even more impressive from this vantage point. The floor of the Great Aisle dropped away toward the platform with a gradual slope. There, at the center, far away on this platform—which had seven steps running across its curved front, set a finely carved kneeling bench with crimson cushions at its foot and at its top. And just beyond the top cushion, in arms reach of one who might kneel there, a shining book lay open. From its pages the white light scattered all across the front half of this great cathedral. Behind the shining book, the floor of the platform met with the clear Dome, which rushed up and toward them with golden light and a rainbow of colors stretching high above them and extending into the darkness at the back of the sanctuary.

Something else caught Diakrina's eye. As she looked down the Great Aisle, she spotted only two rows of pews until another gap—like, perhaps, another wide aisle—intersected this Great Aisle running parallel to the aisle they had first entered. But the longer she studied it, the more convinced she was it was not an aisle at all, but some deep break in the floor itself.

This break ran right across the Great Aisle, forming a chasm being impossible to cross, except for the fact a slender, rail-less bridge spanned it at the center of the Great Aisle. This bridge was not much wider than a gymnast's balance beam, with a slight upward arch to its structure.

"I will wait here," said Strateia. "You must cross the Bridge of Trust," and here he pointed to the slender structure crossing the break in the Great Aisle. "You are being called to communion."

Diakrina, already much intrigued as to what it was all about, took a step toward the narrow bridge. As she did so, a nervous cough came from somewhere in the shadows behind her, followed by the whispering of several hushed voices. She stopped short. For the first time she was fully aware of little groups of people huddled together in the shadows. It meant she and Strateia were not alone in this cathedral.

"Who are these people?" She lifted this question to the One she knew was with her. She turned back to her right looking into the shadows at the various groups close enough to see. "Did they, too, come up the Stairs of Communion and Covenant?"

Strateia spoke. "These in the shadows did not come that way. They came another way. Those who have come as you did are now on the other side of the Bridge of Trust."

Diakrina was about to turn around and continue her investigation into the bridge and the strange chasm it crossed, when she heard a concerned voice address her from one of the groups nearest her.

"I'd think again before I crossed that bridge, my dear. It doesn't look safe at all. No supports, you know, and no rails for safety. You'd not catch me out on it."

Grunts of affirmation arose from several within the same group and a few from some of the other nearby groups as well.

"And who might you be?" asked Diakrina, looking in the direction of the speaker.

"My name is Sophidzo Logou. I am an instructor of those who seek knowledge."

"Your name means, 'cunning with words.' What cunning insight can you give me to support your warnings concerning the Bridge of Trust?" asked Diakrina.

"I have told you it appears dangerous. Doesn't reason itself tell us if anything of considerable value is to be gained on the other side of this bridge, someone would have long ago built one which would be more inviting and less of a risk? Then, all could see there is something worth obtaining and would cross in safety to obtain it. I think this line of reasoning is quite clear."

"Hear, hear!" came the response from several in his little group. The members of the group all sounded British with a mixture of educated and less educated accents. The most refined accent belonged to the one addressing her—Sophidzo Logou, he had called himself.

"But I am to be presented before the King. And it has been indicated through Strateia I should cross the bridge. Would you not agree being presented before the King is of considerable value?"

"Why of course it is, my dear. I most emphatically agree. However, I don't know who this Strateia is, but there is one aspect of this you may not have considered." Sophidzo Logou paused for a deep breath before continuing.

"There may be another, even better way to be presented to the King. One need not do something so rash as to endanger oneself on that bridge. We know the King is love. Surely He would not require us to do such a rash thing. Besides, it's not logical. Would he command us to encourage others to come to Him if they must always embrace danger on that unsafe structure to be in His presence?"

With this last statement a much louder round of, "Hear, hear!" and "Good point!" and "Fine reasoning!" filled the air. Obviously, this point had been discussed before. All responded to Sophidzo as if he were using a favored technique in combat. They were cheering him on.

"You see, my dear," continued Sophidzo in a much stronger and more condescending voice (he appeared to gain courage from the support of his little group), "if we get in the habit of doing such rash and ludicrous things, then those we are to encourage to come to the King will write us off as fools. We will lose our influence with them. Then, of course, we could never have the opportunity to encourage them to think about such important considerations."

"But how, then, can we present ourselves to the King?" asked Diakrina.

"Why, by the other ways I mentioned, my dear."

"Hear, hear! There are other ways!" came the unison response from the others.

"All of us here have presented ourselves before the King. Yet we have never been over that bridge," replied Sophidzo Logou smugly.

"Can you tell me how this is done?" asked Diakrina with growing interest.

"Well of course I can tell you," came Sophidzo's belittling, but not cruel laugh. "But it will take more than a little talk. You must be initiated into my school of learning." Then changing to a most intriguing voice of trembling excitement, "There are wonders and mysteries which only those on the inside can know; paths on which one must be led. To see behind the meaning, this is the real source of truth."

Diakrina felt a sense of mystery and intrigue wrap its dark arms around her. She felt drawn in—invited and included into some inner circle. Her mind rehearsed Sophidzo Logou's last statement: "To see behind the meaning, this is the real source of truth." It stirred an excitement in her. She was being offered the opportunity to pull back the curtain, to open the sealed box—become one of the few who knew.

Suddenly, something like an inner alarm began to sound. Something was wrong! Questions came from somewhere: "How can there be anything behind the meaning if it is already the real meaning, the true meaning? Don't we look for the real meaning only when we feel the whole truth has not already been told?"

Diakrina saw how foolish Sophidzo Logou's statement had

been. Before she could voice her thoughts—whether she had betrayed herself by a change of expression, or they too had heard the questions—Sophidzo Logou cleared his throat in such a way as to claim the floor.

"Now my dear, I must not forget to warn you some of the things I have said will sound contradictory at first. That is always the case until you are more enlightened. Take it from one who has stood where you now stand and now sits where I now sit. These apparent contradictions will soon resolve themselves once you are given the secret pieces—the rest of the puzzle—which I can supply. I have been here a long time and I have seen many come and go across the bridge, and I can promise, you will do better with me."

"Did you come up the Stairs of Covenant?" asked Diakrina.

"Well, no, my dear. I should say not! Such an approach does not fit my temperament. Those stairs are not safe. Demands far too much, smacks of some kind of ready-made, Salvationism. If you came that way yourself, it is a wonder you even made it here at all!"

"Hear, hear!" came the resounding agreement.

"There are many ways to get here, my dear. You should not think the way you came should have anything to do with the way anyone else has come. All ways have their own merit."

"Except for the Stairs of Covenant, you mean?" interjected Diakrina with a tone of irony she could not hide.

"Oh, I see. You think I am being inconsistent. Well, I quite agree it seems that way. But if you knew what I know—and you can in time—you would see I am really being quite consistent. However, I confess I do sometimes overreact whenever those stairs are mentioned." (He said, "those stairs" with exaggerated negative tones as if they were an offending and dangerous thing everyone should be warned about.)

"Many have claimed those stairs are the only way one should come here. How arrogant! Why, such closed-minded claims are an insult to the whole history of human inquiry and achievement. It is abundantly clear I am here and I can assure you I didn't come by those stairs!"

Sophidzo Logou's voice was rising ever higher the longer he spoke. Diakrina couldn't see well into the darkness, but it looked like the one speaking had stood up in the middle of the group and was waving his arms in a most passionate way as he continued.

"Think of it! My being here is a clear testimony against such narrow thinking. I have shown there is something more to all this than we have been told outright. Don't I have eyes to see? Don't I interpret the crystal Dome above us and find life's meaning there?"

His voice had reached a stirring climax. "What more could we want from such a place as this, than the inspiration we receive when we apply our knowledge to the display of random patterns above us? Do we not see exhibited there," he gestured dramatically to the Dome overhead, "the truth of how the designs of chance fit the song of our souls? And if so, do we not behold our King as well as any? If chance is our King, and we his improbable children, then do we not see our own selves reflected back to us from overhead into the very depths of our souls? Oh, yes, my dear, there are many different ways to arrive and just as many different reasons for doing so."

Diakrina's head was reeling by the time Sophidzo Logou reached his stirring crescendo. He sounded perfectly sincere and convinced. But she couldn't help wondering if he and the others had arrived at all where they were supposed to be.

She turned slightly toward the bridge, but something other than the bridge suddenly caught her eye. The glorious book shining with white light glowed even more brightly than before. She had almost forgotten about it. Turning back she shot a question in the direction of the shadowy group.

"What about the glowing book with glorious white light? Is it not an important enough reason to cross the Bridge of Trust? Isn't it the true destination to be reached?"

After a long silence came the now smooth, noticeably controlled, and now slowing speaking voice of Sophidzo Logou. "What … book, my dear? We see no glowing book."

"The one on the platform, at the front," replied Diakrina, pointing in the direction of the obvious light.

"I knew it!" declared Sophidzo Logou to those around him in a stern and troubled voice. "Those stairs have done the same thing to her as to the others. She is seeing things, too. It always has this unfortunate effect."

He then turned from the others and addressed Diakrina. "Look, my dear. You can take it on good authority there is no glowing book up there. A book, yes. And I will grant you, quite a good book; and interesting, I'm sure. But it is not a book glowing with any light or is of any unusual quality. Books are books.

"That platform is nothing but darkness. The book does contain some good and interesting material, maybe even valuable," and then he almost whispered under his breath, "if one has wisdom to understand. But in that darkness up there you will get little benefit from it."

"But it isn't dark at all!" cried Diakrina in utter amazement. "The whole platform is blazing with the light coming from its open pages. How can you not see the light?"

"Because, it only exist for you, my dear. It is merely a subjective perception affecting those who come here as you have—by those stairs." Then he added to the others just loud enough for Diakrina to hear, "I think it does something to their eyes, somehow; maybe even their minds." Solemn grunts of pity sounded from all in the group.

Diakrina was bewildered and becoming angry. "You said you have never been across the Bridge of Trust, Sophidzo Logou. How is it that you know so much about the book there?"

"Why, I have accurate knowledge from reliable sources, my dear. You see … there are some in the other groups who have sent representatives to investigate the reports of the shining book. We have conferred with them on what they found. All agree it is hopelessly dark up there and the only way to read the book is to take your own torch along. What we have discovered in our research is only those who come up those stairs see this supposed light coming from the pages of the book.

"Now … don't interrupt, my dear … you might wonder if we should not then conclude there is some relationship between the book and those stairs."

"I would think so," interjected Diakrina.

"Well, this we have considered, I assure you. But it seems logical to us if this shining book story held any true reality, at least some of us who have come here by so many other ways would be able to see this light. For you must remember, Miss, we have all come here by different paths and surely one of those paths would equip at least one of us to see the light if it really did exist. But none of us have ever seen it. Only those who come up those stairs say they see it. Now it must . . ."

"I am puzzled," interrupted Diakrina in a firm and determined voice, "how any of you were able to cross over to the platform if you did not use the bridge, which you have made quite clear you would never use."

"Well, my dear," sniffed Sophidzo Logou in a confident and rather arrogant fashion, "I am glad you asked. For our studious efforts in this matter only prove how committed we actually are to discovering and understanding truth.

"You see, Miss, in conference with these other groups, we planned an expedition and helped them draw up a design for a kind of human catapult. It took some time in building—and it was an imperfect tool, I will admit—but given our limited resources, it was rather a triumph."

"Do you mean what I think?" gasped Diakrina. "While you would not trust the bridge, you yet were willing to hurl someone across the chasm from a catapult?" Diakrina was dumbfounded.

"Great undertakings call for heroic actions, my dear. If you look on the back of one of the pews over there near the chasm," he motioned toward the area of the bridge, "you will find a plaque in memory of those who were lost in the great expeditions. Until we got the trajectory perfected, we were ill fated in losing two into the abyss and one, landing unfortunately on the bridge, went mad. He was able to make it back to us but was in a most unfavorable state of mind. He soon left us to go down those stairs, returning a few weeks later. His madness was such he rushed out onto the bridge. We have never seen him since. Poor fellow.

"But when we did succeed, and the projectiles we sent with them came flying back with their accounts attached to them, they spoke only of darkness, confusion and obscurity. They even reported some unsafe presence was evident beyond the chasm, which made them all deeply unnerved indeed. We wish they could have gotten back to us. Their verbal reports would have been useful, I'm sure.

"It can now be concluded the evidence of our investigation points to the non-existence of the light. And since this insight was gained by much sacrifice from the groups supplying the men, we are duty bound to honor their work.

"It is only reasonable to conclude, Miss, those who claim to see this light are experiencing some perceptual damage. And since all who make this claim have come up those stairs, ergo, those stairs somehow are responsible for causing this distortion of mind or eyes."

"Could we not rather conclude, just as reasonably, instead of damage, it is some enhancement of perception which the Stairs cause?" countered Diakrina.

"See, what did I tell you?" shouted Sophidzo Logou abruptly to those around him. "The journey up those stairs always causes this delusion of superiority."

Then addressing Diakrina, "Surely you do not believe yourself so above us? We, who have been here much longer, sacrificed greatly, who have seen so much more and, therefore, have greater wisdom than you, will not be so easily taken in by such arrogant accusations."

"Hear! Hear!" came the resounding approval from the group. "How dare she teach us?"

"Now, now," Sophidzo's commanding voice quieted the group. "We must be patient with her. She has been through quite a damaging experience. Remember, we have cured others, and we may hope—if she will trust herself to us—we can cure her. Why, some who lead other groups are the very ones we cured. So we will not be so quick to judge her, as she does us."

"Judge?" retorted Diakrina. "How have I judged you?"

"Why, your very assertions are judgmental to our position and our beliefs. If they were true—which they are not," he added under his breath—"then we would be wrong and you alone right. It is not good for the few, or in this case, the one," he added with stern force, "to look down on the many."

"I do not look down on you. But I do see your accusations as fulfilling in you, the exact thing of which you accuse me. But it is reason which drives me to my conclusions, not any desire on my part."

"Well, now. You are suddenly reasonable," taunted Sophidzo in an arrogant voice. "I may then hope we are making some headway?"

Diakrina was growing furious. She decided to have it out with this accuser at close range. She turned fully toward him with a swift jerk, and taking two steps toward the shadows, suddenly lost her footing and fell backwards into a sitting position.

She was startled to find herself on the floor in the middle of this intersection. She rose quickly to see what behind her could have caused the fall. As she did so, her eyes met those of Strateia standing down the Great Aisle by the Bridge of Trust. His eyes were fixed on her, his sword lifted, pointing at the shining book laying across the Bridge. She knew he was warning her to continue her journey immediately. How he had caused her to fall, she did not know, but she was sure it was Strateia.

For a moment her eyes pled with Strateia. How she wanted to set Sophidzo Logou right. She was boiling over at his arrogant spin, his irrational conclusions, and unfair accusations. But she found nothing in Strateia's gaze repenting in the least of the command to obey immediately.

She cast one last glance in the direction of the little group before turning fully toward Strateia and the Bridge of Trust. She then began making her way down the Great Aisle.

She could hear a commotion of whispers behind her in the shadows as she took her first steps in the direction of the bridge. "I knew it. She's one of those what can't be told anything." "Sad, isn't it," responded another voice. Then a third, "Once that fanaticism gets a hold of them, they are hard to cure. Just best leave her alone."

For a moment, Diakrina felt herself wanting to reengage the battle. But the commanding gaze of Strateia broke through and she took her next steps toward the great abyss.

∞———————————————————————————————∞

When at last she joined Strateia at the foot of the narrow bridge—so narrow in fact only one pair of feet could fit on its width—she was immediately entranced with what she saw looking over the edge into the abyss and forgot Sophidzo Logou and his group, altogether. "Strateia, it's . . . it's the Porticos!" she blurted in amazement.

Strateia gave no notice of her comment.

Diakrina stared wide-eyed into the chasm, appearing to be the gap between the edge of the Castle and the roof of the Great Portico—as though she were peering over the south wall of the Castle. Yet, the longer she looked she realized she was seeing more than the Porticos.

The scene puzzled and disoriented Diakrina. She was seeing between the Castle wall and the roof of the Great Portico down to the top of the Lesser Portico, connecting to the Castle wall. Yet, at the same time, she was seeing another view with very different content. At first she could not make it out, for it would not come into focus with the Porticos.

Then, at the edges of her vision, she saw something which looked familiar—though it seemed so out of place. She was looking, not at the Porticos (though they had not disappeared, but had merely gone out of focus), but at the great gorge that had ripped itself into the landscape of the Garden, creating the Severed Lands. She was seeing the Chasm as she had seen it from the arms of Strateia thousands of feet above the Garden.

Somehow, here, straight below, lay the Tree Bridge, which Strateia had cut clean except for the crossbeam of limbs resting on the inside bank of the circle in the Severed Lands. She could also see the features of the Chasm descending into infinite depth; its jagged, scarred sides dropping into impenetrable darkness.

This perception of enormous height rapidly made Diakrina

dizzy. At the very moment she felt she could take it no more; the Chasm went go out of focus—but not out of sight—while the Porticos came back into focus. She could never clearly see both at one and the same time. To fix on one, was to lose focus on the other.

This alternation happened several times. Each time it did, Diakrina became increasingly aware of a correlation between the three things she was seeing: the Tree Bridge, crossing the great Chasm with its cross-beam resting on the Severed Lands; the Small Portico, connecting to the Castle and extending across the gap between the Castle and the Great Portico and then out under the Great Portico; and then the Bridge of Trust, crossing this same gap here in the sanctuary where Diakrina stood. These three things appeared to be in some kind of synchronization, or alignment, if you could call it that.

She found herself absorbed in their amazing relationship. To confirm this apparent alignment was real, it seemed she needed to be out on the Bridge of Trust, at its very center.

What is more, if Diakrina were perceiving correctly, the two crimson-red columns of the Great Portico were exactly in the place one would expect nails to have been driven into the crossbeam of the Tree Bridge if it were used as a cross to nail the base of someone's palms.

Slowly, but steadily—her dizziness and concern forgotten—yet never taking her eyes off the three objects as they alternated in her perception, Diakrina began walking, step by step, out onto the narrow bridge, looking much like a tight-rope walker staring at her own feet. This side of the bridge was crimson and nearly translucent. Step by careful step she proceeded toward the center of the bridge. When she reached it, exactly ten and one-half steps out, she stopped, for there at her feet—precisely halfway across the Chasm—the two ends of the bridge appeared to join. The crimson, translucent material on which she had been walking ended, and the rest of the bridge was the color of the Great Column far below—that clearness that was somehow, also, a color.

Diakrina—who would have looked to anyone watching from the outside as if she were in a trance taking instructions—was keenly aware of everything she was doing. Somehow, she just knew what she must do. An inner voice, which was not her own, yet belonged, was gently taking hold of her and directed her in each movement.

Very deliberately she placed her right foot on the clear portion of the bridge while leaving her left on the crimson. Then, turning sideways, she looked straight down through the place where the two translucent substances joined between her feet.

Diakrina discovered by looking through the Bridge of Trust, at its center, she could see all three realities at the same time. But as she did, all three became so much one she could not tell where one ended and the others began; and yet if you can imagine it, they were ever and continuously distinct.

You might say a new fourth reality emerged which was only a fourth in that it was a new perception of all three together. The fourth reality was a perceived union of the three. They were one, yet three. The one they composed was the deeper reality out of which the three emerged, rather than the other way around.

Even when she tried to consider each of them distinctly, still a deep interrelationship existed between them. If she looked at the Small Portico, she was not only aware of it as the Small Portico, but also as the deeper reality of the Bridge of Trust. At the same time she knew—and could somehow see—the Tree Bridge in the Garden was the deeper reality of the Small Portico and so, also, of the Bridge of Trust. Or to say it the other way around, something in the Tree Bridge merged into the Small Portico and then something—which was somehow the same something—in the Small Portico blended into the Bridge of Trust. And they were all within the context of the Great Portico.

But here comes the hard part. The Bridge of Trust did not just exist as a small, narrow walkway across this Chasm which fell away into the Great Abyss. It was made of the Chasm and of the Abyss!

Somehow, that which she was crossing became the crossing; that which needed to be healed was the means of healing—was healing itself. Through the Tree Bridge, the abyss became part of the Bridge of Trust. Also through the Small Portico, the Chasm was transformed and became part of the Bridge of Trust. And when all this was understood, or we should say, seen, one could no longer worry about falling off the Bridge of Trust. It could not be fallen off of, because to fall was to fall into the Bridge itself and so into safety!

Suddenly, Diakrina was no more concerned about falling off this narrow bridge than a bird is of falling off a branch. Even less. Still, the Abyss and Chasm remained real. In themselves alone, sad or even evil, and yet, at the same time, conquered and swallowed up by the Tree Bridge and the Small Portico which were, and were not, each other and both of which were, and were not, the Bridge of Trust.

While all this was happening as an almost instant revelation, another insight flooded Diakrina's mind. (Here the reader will need to be patient with me and be willing to stretch his or her own perceptions a bit farther.) She suddenly knew the Great Portico— the roof onto which she was about to step—was the heart, the centerpiece, the key to it all. (Don't ask me how she knew this. But I assure you she did know this with complete certainty.) The Small Portico swallowed the great abyss and crossed the Chasm because of its connection to the Great Portico. The Small Portico was one with the Great Portico, and the Great Portico was deeper than the abyss and, therefore, was the deepest reality of all. The Tree Bridge, then, was sustained by the deeper reality of the Great Portico.

Being one with the Great Portico, the Small Portico was also the deeper reality of the Tree Bridge, which was itself the deeper reality of the Small Portico. So we might say, the Small Portico both preceded and followed the Tree Bridge. (If you are by this time feeling a little confused, I am sorry. Trust me, I also have known that feeling many times in trying to understand Diakrina's descriptions.)

Suddenly, Diakrina was drawn back to her immediate surroundings. Without instruction she knew she must now turn and run the other ten and a half steps across the bridge. When the final step landed her on the roof of the Great Portico—which was the floor of the sanctuary on the platform side of the Chasm—she was immediately engulfed in a warm swarm of singing, praising children dancing in the noblest romp she had ever seen.

She splashed into a living sea of glorious beings and was caught in their current. She was flowing with them like a small boat pulled by a powerful swell. This swell was headed ashore toward a platform filled with the blinding light of a glorious book.

On the other side in the shadows, Sophidzo Logou and his group saw Diakrina disappear from the bridge. "She fell!" was the cry of shock. "Poor creature. Just wouldn't listen."

Chapter Seven

THE SHINING BOOK
AND THE DOME OF REALITY

When finally the glorious romp came ashore at the base of the seven steps mounting the platform, Diakrina was all but deposited on the first step. She turned and took a long look into the eyes of the rejoicing children all around her.

She had never seen such children. They were beautiful. They were so unrestrained and yet in perfect harmony with each other. Their movements were spontaneous and free while being well-choreographed as a group. Their joy was individually and corporately expressive, each willingly contributing synergistically their singing and dancing. They all appeared to possess an ability to collaborate immediately and continually on every movement. They clearly found joy individually and corporately in the patterns emerging. Their dance literally trembled with meaningful expression as each willingly submitted to a visual articulation of what was within them.

As she looked into their clear eyes, she saw a noble mirth, a serious joy, which was so deep it astonished, if not actually frightened, Diakrina (if one could experience fright in such a place). This was no foolish riot of pleasure, but the serious business of proper and beautiful rejoicing.

Light dripped from everyone and everything. Entranced by it all, Diakrina tried to rejoin their celebration; however, every time she stepped onto the crystal-clear floor, she was lifted in a delightful swell of little hands, as if a child herself, and firmly placed back on the first step.

The dance came to an elegant conclusion. One child stepped forward and taking Diakrina by the hand, turned her around with an endearing smile and guiding her up the seven steps. Reaching the top, Diakrina was amazed by the platform's vast size, spreading left and right like a raised plateau. And its depth was also astonishing.

However, the impressive platform was erased from her thoughts as her attention was captured by the wonderous shining Book. It was not merely light coming from its pages. Colorful moving images projected from the pages in the atmosphere between her and the Book. The Book had come alive, luminous with living images in rainbows of magnificent color.

Entranced, she was led forward by the same glorious child to the small altar with its crimson cushions. When she stood directly in front of the Book, the child gently released her hand and graciously bowed and glided nimbly away to join the others now assembled along the seven steps.

The images from the Book were somehow familiar, though slightly out of focus, as Diakrina stood in front of the Book. Then, placing her hand on top of the little altar on which the Book lay, she lowered herself kneeling on the crimson cushions. As her knees touched the cushions, her vision cleared, as if someone suddenly focused the images.

As her eyes focused it was like another whole world, which had always surrounded her, came into clear view. She discovered a new reality encircling her. It did not replace the platform, but filled it with living, moving images.

In front of her appeared two men, one old with a full grey beard, but he was not feeble. The other was a young man, in his late twenties or early thirties. The young man stood facing the older man in front of a stone altar, little more than waist high. It was made of uncut, yet carefully positioned stones. Diakrina seemed to sense the two of them had only finished constructing it a few moments before.

The expression of the older man showed determination and grief, his eyes rimmed with tears. He began a long explanation—a story—which Diakrina could not hear. She could only observe the changing expressions on both men's faces as the story was obviously unfolding with serious weight. Then, suddenly, she could hear their conversation.

"Son, I only know it is He who has demanded this of us. I cannot disobey Him, even though I cannot understand. I would just as soon tear my heart from my chest and lay it on this altar, but He will not let me make a lesser sacrifice."

Diakrina detected the old man's shoulders trembling with restrained grief.

The younger man spoke, slowly at first, but with the same resolve, "I will do exactly as the Almighty has told you. I trust you, my father, that if another way existed, you would embrace it. I do not understand this, but He has not told us we always will understand His ways.

"As we made the climb to this mountaintop, I asked about the absence of a sacrifice, and you answered He would provide. If I am His provision, so be it. For indeed, He caused me to be when I could not have been but by His miraculous intervention. And by that miracle I became the child of you and mother's old age. If He provides another sacrifice in my place, we will have cause to rejoice. But whatever, we must precede. We must continue, for to disobey Him would be worse than death."

Father and son fell into each other's arms, weeping.

Diakrina soon had tears streaming down her face along with them.

After some time, in a slow but deliberate manner, the son reached down and lifted the last firewood onto the top of the altar. After arranging it in the traditional fashion, he climbed upon the altar presenting himself to his father to be bound in the sacrificial manner with leather cords.

After tearfully binding his son, all was finally ready. The father then removing his sacrificial knife from a leather bag, approached the altar, and stood motionless. No one moved for a very long, tortured moment. The only sound was from the wind playing with the flames from the burning torch. His delay was not one of uncertainty, but of sad dread of what he knew he was determined to do next.

Then, slowly, he lifted his son's chin, exposing the length of his neck. He raised the knife little by little, until his arm was fully extended. The knife hung over the son's throat. Still weeping noticeable, and lifting his voice to a commanding shout, he looked toward the sky, "Receive, my Lord, the sacrifice You demanded!" The father's body tensed; his arm thrust downward.

Diakrina heard herself cry, "No! NO!!"

The knife was only inches from the son's throat when another—more commanding—voice cried, "ABRAHAM! ABRAHAM!"

Diakrina stared wide-eyed as a being more glorious than she had ever imagined appeared on the other side of the altar. His right hand lay open, palm up, over the throat of the son, above where the knife was to strike. Abraham pulled back hard on his downward thrust but not before Diakrina saw the knife cut deep into the glorious hand, at the base of the palm, just below the wrist. Blood spilled out and covered the throat and head of the son, but the knife had not touched him.

Abraham did not appear to see the glorious man, but he immediately answered the voice in a startled whisper, "I am here."

"DO NOT LAY A HAND ON THE BOY," came the instructions. "DO NOT DO ANYTHING TO HIM. NOW I KNOW THAT YOU FEAR GOD, BECAUSE YOU HAVE NOT WITHHELD FROM ME YOUR SON, YOUR ONLY SON."

Then raising his hand from the throat of the son, the glorious man placed it on Abraham's head and the blood flowed from his hand down over Abraham's head like a crimson anointing. Then, He disappeared.

A bleating cry was heard. Not far away, a white ram had its horns caught in a thicket. The father burst into tears of joy and cut the cords binding his son. Both men fell into each other's arms sobbing and laughing.

Together they went to the ram and, binding it with cords, untangled it from the thicket and placed it on the altar. They joined hands rejoicing as the father raised the knife and cut the ram's throat. The blood covered the altar. He then prepared its various parts for sacrifice, took the torch, and set the wood of the altar on fire. Then, together, father and son bowed to the ground and worshipped.

Diakrina saw, high above them, the glorious being once again. He called to Abraham a second time.

"I SWEAR BY MYSELF, DECLARES YAHWEH, THAT BECAUSE YOU HAVE DONE THIS AND HAVE NOT WITHHELD YOUR SON, YOUR ONLY SON, I WILL SURELY BLESS YOU AND MAKE YOUR DESCENDANTS AS NUMEROUS AS THE STARS IN THE SKY AND AS THE SAND ON THE SEASHORE. YOUR DESCENDANTS WILL TAKE POSSESSION OF THE CITIES OF THEIR ENEMIES, AND THROUGH YOUR OFFSPRING ALL NATIONS ON EARTH WILL BE BLESSED, BECAUSE YOU HAVE OBEYED ME."

∞———————————————————————————————————∞

The living story faded. The light from the Book changed, glowing bright with a whirling, rainbow-colored spotlight shooting a beam toward the crystal Dome. Diakrina's eyes widened as she followed the multicolored ray.

Like a door opening, the patterns of obscure design, which she could not make out before—those which called you into themselves, yet gave you nothing but nonspecific, unintelligible generality—were changed. Obscurity vanished. Specific details, which literally tugged at Diakrina and carried her aloft, manifested.

She could see beyond the Dome into the splendid reality it reflected. Other tales unfolded. She could see a thousand cascading stories emerging from the story she had just experienced. The intricate themes of these stories wove a masterful reflection.

The deeper she investigated this illuminated spot on the Dome the more new and increasingly wonderful facets revealed themselves in the light of the Book. Stories unfolded. In only a moment of time she saw a thousand stories, which somehow all connected to what she had just seen on the mountaintop; they seemed to emerge from it. The intricate themes and design of these stories were woven into a masterpiece of reflection: truth highlighting truth and life illuminating life.

Diakrina traveled deeper and deeper into the illuminated place. Ages unfolded, each telling its story. Story ran beside story and birthed hundreds of new stories, which all ran side-by-side while also interlacing with each other. Nations were birthed and nations died. Dreams shaped lives and Diakrina lived as a million different people and loved and hated in more ways than she knew possible. And yet, deeper and deeper she was drawn.

Soon, all the intertwined stories, which now danced as living multitudes, converged on a single place, and there before her was a wide reddish expanse. This reddish expanse was a circular spot with definite boundaries in the middle of an immense expanse of blue—the same vast expanse, she was sure, on which she had seen the Great Dance.

In the middle of this reddish circle danced all the living multitudes she had seen interlacing with each other in the countless stories she had watched unfold. But now, the dance was confused and chaotic—astonishingly so.

The multitude danced as if each defied all the others. Sometimes a kind of harmony would appear briefly among small groups of dancers, but only as an organized attempt to trample some other group that formed.

Each group danced riotously into one another. Thousands were trampled as screams of pain and shouts of rage echoed across the reddish, and now clearly bloody, expanse. And as they danced this dance of trampling death, the expanse under them became even bloodier than before.

The music could hardly be called music at all, except it was a roaring confusion of millions of different melodies all playing at the same time. Diakrina held her throbbing ears as the discordant din ripped and tore at the air around her. She could not remember seeing, hearing and feeling such ugliness and horror all in one place and at one time. She became weak, sickened and pale as she watched. Even at its best it was a dance of frenzied, ugly pride. The motions, though sometimes intricate, were always grotesque and hateful.

The dance thrust itself at her. It laughed a hellish laughter and dared her to join in and make her mark—to prove herself able to dance this dance; more than that, to out-dance the others and prove herself superior.

At this point a bad memory flashed like unexpected lightning across Diakrina's mind. She had seen this dance before! But where? The thought had hardly formed the question when she suddenly saw the answer.

She now recognized one pattern to the mayhem: one source of origination for almost everything happening. Right in the center of this screaming, trampling mob danced a leader. All this chaos moved out from him in a ring—like a constantly reoccurring tidal wave of horror and confusion.

He danced a spellbinding and intricate choreography; filled with awful pride and hatred. So overpoweringly hideous was his dance Diakrina wanted to scream. Yet, at the same time, she could not take her eyes away or close them, so cruelly did this horror fasten itself on her. She felt like the fabled bird, hypnotized by the eyes of an awful serpent and spiraling downward against its will into the waiting jaws of its devourer.

"Oh, Living One, help me! Please, help me!" cried Diakrina.

A crystal hand reached from somewhere and covered her eyes. Instantly, the spell was broken. The hand remained for a moment as if bestowing something; then it was gone. The ghastly dance reappeared but Diakrina was no longer being drawn in like a helpless fish on a hook. She had been cut free.

As she opened her eyes she heard herself whisper in recognition, "Anomos!" He was the leader at the center.

She watched an inner circle of those who danced closest to Anomos. They tried to mimic his moves, yet always poorly and with their own silly embellishments. Anomos appeared to be trying to organize patterns he hoped would spread throughout the reddish, bloody expanse. But arrogance does not lend itself to submission. Those surrounding him mimicked his defiance more than his actual dance steps, and any sense of order disintegrated as the circle widened into a screaming, writhing mob.

The patterns at times took hold and would spread by trampling and murder from the center to the edge into a temporary obedience of the majority. But like a rebounding wave, the defiance and murder would backwash over the whole. It would all fuse again into a blood-soaked mass. The spirit of hatred and violence seemed to be better mimicked than the patterns of organization Anomos tried to infuse into it all.

Diakrina watched as Anomos tried method after method— some more successful than others, but all in the end failing—to bring this mob more fully under his direction. His methods were unmistakably self-defeating.

He resorted more and more to certain former patterns of the Speaking Music, which Diakrina still remembered. These were somewhat more effective, yet those in the reddish expanse would quickly destroy any patterns emerging by their more faithful imitation of Anomos' arrogance.

Diakrina watched this hopeless enterprise for some time. Then out of the corner of her eye she noticed something happening on the blue expanse outside the bloody circle. As she lifted her eyes to the vast horizon, shock waves of glorious contrast suddenly flooded over her. She had never known beauty could be so wonderfully militant.

"The Great Dance! Oh, Living One, it's the Great Dance!" She was instantly on her feet in unbridled delight. (Yet, she had to kneel again to keep the scene in focus.) There on the horizon, with noble steps of splendid grace and harmony, moving ever closer with sublime and majestic patterns, danced the magnificent participants of the Great Dance.

Over the thunderous din of the hellish romp and discordant music before her, Diakrina could hear the ever new and glorious strains of the Speaking Music. Its empyreal fire caused a dancing song of pure light to spring up within her whole being. She was filled with serious joy which made her want to dance in swirls like a child at a circus.

The Great Dance came to the edge of the reddish expanse

and then, without anyone placing even one foot within the circle, they danced gracefully out around the whole circumference of the scene of confusion and death. Diakrina could hardly endure the contrast. Glorious beauty, noble splendor and holy joy surrounded unspeakable ugliness: screams, horrors and murder, and arrogant defiance.

Within the circle, nothing changed. They seemed unaware of anything not within their reddish domain. In fact, if you looked closely at anyone of them, most were unaware of anything outside of their own self, until someone got in the way of their "dance." Then they would turn in hateful awareness on one another.

Suddenly, the whole company of the Great Dance came to a stop. The Speaking Music became unfathomably beautiful—full of love and gentleness. Far on the horizon (for the company of the Great Dance stretched beyond what the eye could see in all directions) Diakrina could see an aisle forming among the noble company. The flowing aisle opened elegantly toward the reddish expanse like the parting of a sea. Then, she saw One so bright she could not look directly at Him, dancing gloriously down the aisle.

I could never get much more out of Diakrina as to a full description of this Person of Light. She would always, upon the very mention of Him and this moment, begin to sing strange, yet incredibly beautiful songs to Him in an ancient language I could not understand. This was not some "unknown tongue," for Diakrina understood the language perfectly and used it with full knowledge of its meaning, as though she had learned it by visiting another place, like one might learn Italian by living in Italy. Yet it did not come to her through study or effort, but was given to her as a gift as you remember by Strateia at the Spring of Longings. In our world such a gift would seem miraculous—indeed Diakrina's entire journey was miraculous. However, she insisted on the other side of reality, as she called it, this manner of acquiring language was not uncommon.

As she sang, a wonderful unearthly glow would radiate from her face. Her eyes would turn so clear and so filled with golden light you would have to see it for yourself in order to appreciate the transformation in her as she recalled this Person of Light. I often sat, after having brought up the subject of this moment, for half an hour or so, lost in the beauty of her song. Eventually, she would become quiet and say in a whisper, which echoed from the walls, "It was Him, the Living One Who brings the Dance of Life." After some time, if I said nothing else (indeed it felt unholy even to speak), she would relate the rest of the events.

The blazing glory of the Living One was such that those closest to Him hid their faces joyously to protect themselves, as He danced with resplendent beauty and grace to the very edge of the reddish, bloody expanse. There He paused and gathered Himself. Then, with a swift motion, like lightning, and a thunderous crescendo from the Speaking Music, He danced out onto the bloody expanse.

He danced up to several different men. Through Him the Speaking Music could now be heard within the bloody domain. He and His Music surrounded them. While they continued their dance of confusion, He danced steps of beauty, meaning and life. At first none paid much attention. But then, one man began to respond to the sound of the Speaking Music. The Living One danced closer to him and around him, inviting the man into each pattern.

The man hesitated. Then he tried his first move in step with the Living One. At the precise moment he did so, the Living One reached out and touched him. Instantly, he became able to follow the patterns the Living One had shown him.

The Living One's humility was wonderful to behold as He danced simple yet meaningful patterns for his new follower. Only after this man had mastered the simple was something more complex added.

Finally, after much time, the man was dancing with some elementary grace. At this, the Living One led him aside from the screaming confusion all around. When they reached the edge of the reddish expanse, the man faced Him and bowed low to the floor.

Then Diakrina heard the Living One speak: "I AM A SHIELD TO YOU AND YOUR EXCEEDING GREAT REWARD. I MAKE A COVENANT WITH YOU TO BLESS YOU AND MAKE YOU A BLESSING TO ALL THE WORLD. THROUGH YOU I WILL BRING THE ONE WHO WILL TEACH THE DANCE OF LIFE."

With that said, this glorious One was suddenly like Two. He stood behind the man as well as in front of him. Behind, He was sheer Majesty—Eternal Fire. In front, His form was like that of a Man, though radiating glorious light. He raised both His right hands, from behind and in front, and brought them together at the base of the palms over the head of the kneeling man. From where His hands met, blood flowed, pouring down over the man's head in a crimson anointing.

This done, He was as One again—but now like the One who looked like a Man. He and the man now danced together and the man learned, little by little, to dance even more beautiful patterns.

Soon, they were joined by a third. It was the man's son. He grew up learning the patterns of the Living One's dance instead of the confusion of the reddish expanse. Soon he had a son, also, and his son had twelve sons. At this point the Living One led them back close to the dance of confusion and death, but not into it.

There they prospered and many sons and daughters were born who learned to dance the patterns of the Great Dance in this simplest of forms. Time past and they grew into a great multitude dancing in simple beauty next to the continuing blood bath of Anomos' followers.

Anomos soon grew furious and danced with hateful vengeance toward this multitude who defied his patterns and danced the simplified patterns of the Great Dance. He led his followers in a dance surrounding this beautiful multitude in a closing circle of ugly confusion. Then they struck.

Like a pack of screaming wolves, they attacked. They tied heavy burdens of harsh cruelty on their backs to weigh them down so they would stumble and could hardly dance the simplest patterns of the Great Dance.

But most continued to follow the patterns taught them by their fathers. They danced much slower, for the burdens they bore were painful and made the dancing of the patterns decidedly difficult. Yet, they preferred to suffer and dance the beautiful patterns rather than join the bloody confusion all around them. That is, most of them.

Some altered the patterns. Their goal was to fall in step with the mob whenever it looked like a confrontation was coming. Once Anomos saw this, he made sure of many such threatening confrontations to pressure them to conform. Soon, these few who compromised polluted the patterns of the Great Dance within their circle with the arrogant moves of Anomos.

But because the majority still danced the patterns of the Great Dance, Anomos instigated the binding of larger and larger burdens onto their backs. Slower and slower they danced, until it seemed they would drop.

Soon they cried out to the One who had given the patterns of the Dance to their great father. They reminded themselves He had promised to be their Shield and Reward.

In response, the Living One, who was still among them, laid His hand on one of them and gave him power and knowledge to lead the dance. To him He spoke inspired words of promise and instruction and then taught him a dance of deliverance. Together, he and the Living One danced a glorious battle against Anomos and his followers.

Diakrina watched as this man chosen as their leader received more instructions from the Living One. Then dancing into the center of Anomos' circles he warned them of what the Living One was about to do if they did not remove their burdens. But Anomos' followers refused.

Then the Living One danced in among them, and lay upon Anomos' followers burdens so heavy they could not stand up. This continued until the followers of Anomos finally agreed to remove their burdens. But in the end, the Living One had to take many of them away with deserved judgment.

With immense joy the liberated children danced the beautiful patterns of the simplified Great Dance with all their strength. Together they danced to another part of the reddish expanse.

There the Living One gave them wonderful instructions and promises. He appeared to them all for a short time and thereafter, spoke to them through their leaders. They renewed and expanded their covenant with Him and vowed to be faithful to the patterns of the Great Dance. And this they did, agreeing (as one must do in such a covenant) they and their children should be punished should they corrupt their patterns with the patterns from the bloody mob.

It may seem strange, but they had hardly finished making these vows before some began to change the patterns by unlawful interaction with the mob. The Living One would punish them and, through the leaders He gave them, would warn the others not to do the same. This He did while gently reminding them of their vows and how exceedingly important were the keeping of those vows, so the One who would teach all mankind the Dance of Life might come.

Diakrina watched in amazement as times of profound beauty and times of dark confusion passed like changing seasons among them. At times the patterns were danced in marvelous splendor, so much so some of those who had grown up in the dance of death and confusion repented and joined them in the patterns. When this happened, they became a part of the children through whom the promised One—the One who would teach the Dance of Life—was to come.

At other times, too numerous, they polluted the patterns and danced with little difference from the murderous mob around them. Over and over this happened. When it did, the Living One would pull certain of their number aside and instruct them to warn the children to rejoin the proper patterns. Many times these ones whom the Living One sent to warn them were trampled underfoot by the arrogant patterns already being danced. Sad indeed was the sight of these children of the life-giving dance adding blood to the reddish expanse by joining in the dance of death.

Through these men who gave warning and instruction, the Living One taught them about some new and wonderful patterns; patterns announcing the coming of the ultimate Dance of Life. They were instructed to pay close attention so they might recognize this greatest moment in the Dance when these new patterns would appear. For indeed, they were taught, this was the central purpose of their Dance of covenant with the Living One. One Great Moment was to come which would give meaning to all going before, and, also, all that would ever after follow.

In the end, however, only a few danced the patterns with any courage and love for them. The rest altered them to accommodate various forms of interaction with the mob—and this while often refusing to dance with the mob. (They claimed purity from the mob, but still mimicked its patterns within their exclusive circles.)

On the edge of the reddish circle, the members of the true Great Dance stood at elegant attention and watched all happening. Then, the Living One danced to the edge of the reddish circle and stepped out onto the vast blue expanse. The Great Moment had come.

The children of the covenant within the reddish circle continued to dance their patterns. Though often interrupted by those who broke step, and slower than they had been taught, yet surely, they danced the patterns bringing them close to the edge where the Living One stood.

As they reached the edge, all but a handful seemed unaware they were beginning to dance the patterns they had been foretold would bring the Great Moment. But though most danced blindly, and only a few with understanding and excitement, they moved together into the final steps which announced the momentous event. These children of the covenant danced to the very edge of the reddish expanse where the Living One stood quietly. Diakrina held her breath and wondered what wonderful thing would now happen.

The Speaking Music gave a musical pause, and for a moment not a sound could be heard, save the din of the mob (and even it sounded small and drowned out by a huge glorious hush). For a moment, everything stood still.

Then a baby cried.

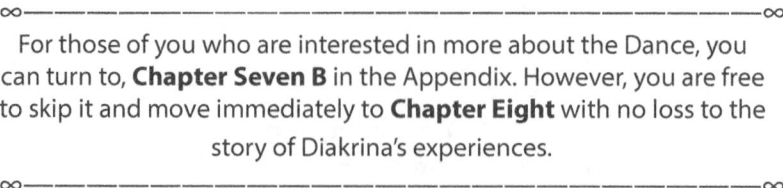

∞———————————————————————————————∞

For those of you who are interested in more about the Dance, you can turn to, **Chapter Seven B** in the Appendix. However, you are free to skip it and move immediately to **Chapter Eight** with no loss to the story of Diakrina's experiences.

∞———————————————————————————————∞

Chapter Eight

THE TRUTH WITHIN

As Diakrina's vision continued she could hardly believe her eyes. There in the arms of a simple peasant woman, who danced with greater joy and understanding than any, was a child with immensity shining from his face.

"How can anything so small and helpless be, at the same moment, so grand and transcendent?" she asked me rhetorically one day. And without giving even symbolic pause for the unexpected answer, she turned it around as the answer: "Only Someone so grand and transcendent could become small and helpless to that extent."

"What do you mean, Diakrina?" I asked, puzzled.

"Can't you see one must be eminently great to endure such immeasurable humiliation? We miss this, much like we miss the interdependence between the transcendent and the intimate attributes in God. We forget it is His transcendent attributes of omnipresence and omniscience making it possible for Him to be super-personal and deeply intimate with every conscious being in the universe at the same moment.

"Unlike so many conclude, His greatness is the source of His nearness. A lesser god would be obscure and unknowable. The transcendent, unlimited God is limitlessly knowable, as far as we have capacity to know Him and as far as He chooses to reveal Himself. He is able to bridge the great Chasm between Himself and us."

I must confess she was forever challenging my former ways of thinking.

Many more glorious scenes followed. Diakrina and I have spent long and precious days, and late into many nights, discussing the wonderful stories playing out before her there on the platform of the sanctuary, illuminated by the Shining Book. Some of them were even too wonderful for her to relate. All she could say was, "You'd have to see for yourself!"

Something supernatural characterized those moments, which I never got over even though I never understood what Diakrina actually experienced. An unseen door between where we were and where she had been, opened just a crack, and a sweet fragrance from another and better world filled the whole room. One breathes deeply in those moments, not with one's lungs alone, but with your whole being.

One scene which Diakrina did describe for me followed immediately after the cry of the baby. The Living One, Himself, took on the form of a mortal dancer and brought the Music of Life to all those on the bloody expanse, leading many away from the chaotic dissonance of Anomos and into the glorious Great Dance of Life. I hope you will want to read it for yourself, and so I'm including it, at least in part, at the end of the book as an appendix to chapter Twenty-Nine. For now, however, I feel compelled to push on with our story.

The Light from the Book of Truth—she now knew it should be capitalized as it was the Light that was the source of all other light—suddenly returned to its former state. It was glistening from the pages, but not shining on any one place on the Dome of Reality. Yet for Diakrina, this one particular place on the Dome overhead remained illuminated—speaking and forever meaningful. She said, "Somehow you just knew deeper stories were yet to be revealed even from this same place." But for now, what had come forth was exactly what should.

Diakrina said ever after, this particular place on the Dome always was clear and beautiful to her, even though other parts of the Dome yet remained obscure. However, when she looked at this one particular place and then looked at other places, they became less obscure and often a story, which related to the former, would come dancing at her with majestic choreography. This happened with so many places that after several hours (she was never sure of the time measurement) there seemed to be hundreds of places on the Dome related to this original spot.

What is more, they somehow interacted with each other. When she had understood how this one story, here, fit with this other story over there, and then the two of them with this third one over there and so on, their combined meaning would begin to "peel back" the obscurity from another part of the Dome. No part of the Dome became as clear, or presented as much insight, as the first part which the Book of Truth had illuminated. Yet each was no longer as obscure as before.

Diakrina knelt looking at the shining pages of the wondrous book. She longed to turn every page and learn its wisdom and truth until the whole Dome of Reality above her head turned crystal clear with meaning. But just then, she felt something inexpressively wonderful approaching from above her head. She turned her face quickly upward in time to see the crystal Hand coming to rest upon her.

As Diakrina related this moment to me, she sang with that unearthly beautiful voice which she always possessed after she had returned. I cannot express what her singing did to me or to anyone else who heard her. A mass choir of the world's most beautiful voices cannot compare. It seemed to me she did not sing with her physical voice only, but some part of her, deeper and more substantial, had been brought to life and would rise in song out and through her mere physical voice—playing it like an accompanying instrument.

When Diakrina's singing ended the day she was relating this part of the story, she fixed her crystal-clear eyes on me. "Communion with the King is such severe joy. It goes beyond both the extremes of our mortal terror and our mortal delight. And somehow, they are one."

Later she related, as best I can understand, when the crystal Hand came to rest on her head she found herself mysteriously gathered up into the lap of what she called, "absolute Love and terrifying Immensity." And she added, "My joy was indeed, in ways no one can imagine, complete."

When Diakrina rose from the crimson altar, Strateia, standing beside her, reached past her to the pages of the shining Book. His hand, reaching into its pages, lifted out a swirling rainbow of wondrous Light—a sphere not quite big enough to fill the palm of his giant hand. But when he handed it to Diakrina, it filled both her hands as full as they could possibly be.

"You must take this knowledge with you gained from your communion with the King," he said. "This Light is the Lantern of Logos which we came here to obtain. With this Light you must bring to life the great Stone of Perception and later enact a necessary resurrection."

Diakrina wanted to aske Strateia about this last comment concerning a necessary resurrection. But asking him questions while in the Castle was not allowed and Strateia's manner made it clear she should table it for now. Instead, he quickly turned around, and said, "Now we must go."

Diakrina began to be fascinated again with the sphere of Light in her hand. "So, this is the Lantern of Logos. It is so wonderful," said Diakrina to the One she knew to be listening as she gazed deep into its colorful swirling illumination. "But where and how shall I carry it with me? I mustn't lose it."

Strateia, who had turned away and walked a few steps, turned back again toward her, and walking up to her, took her by the shoulders and looked down into her questioning face. "Hold it close to your heart, Little One, and embrace all you have been given. The Lantern of Logos is His gift to you to illuminate your inner being."

Diakrina took the swirling rainbow of light and pressed it lovingly to her heart. Slowly the swirling glory sank into her breast and out of sight deep within her.

"Now, Little One, there is a Sword of deliverance in your mouth," said Strateia. "Obey the knowledge the light has given you and it will pour out of you as a mighty power to push back the darkness of Anomos. And when you speak its truth and apply its principles in battle, it will be a Sword in your mouth. It will cause him to tremble and fall before you in the Great Mist Forest.

"But for now, we must find the Stone of Perception here within the Castle. This light of the Lantern of Logos must rekindle this Stone and set it burning with the flame of truth or we will have no hope of overcoming the forces of Anomos, which are already seeking us out. What is more," he added, "we must hurry. I sense time is limited."

Strateia looked up, and then down at her. "I am instructed we need to change your attire slightly to be better fitted for what lies ahead." With that, Strateia took his sword and lifted it up and out to his right so that the tip was just above Diakrina's head. He looked up for only a moment, and then touched the tip lightly to the top of her head. Light poured down over Diakrina's head and shoulders as though she were standing in a waterfall of light. It poured down over her until it reached the hem of her dress, which was about mid-shin in length. The dress began to change. The long sleeves disappeared and the dress became sleeveless. The hem shortened until it was now slightly above Diakrina's knees. The whole dress remained like crimson light as before, but now it was much less formal and less restrictive to her movement.

When the light reached her shoes, they also changed. They transformed from the formal crystal shoes to red leather sandals with straps that crisscrossed around her ankles and lower shins several times.

Strateia stood back and gave her a once over. "That's better."

He then turned and walked a few steps away making it clear Diakrina was to follow him. She took one more longing look at the shining Book and then fell in step with him. The glorious little children, who had been at solemn attention all the while Diakrina had been kneeling at the shining Book, began to dance a majestic yet light-hearted dance.

Diakrina looked to her right out over them as she followed Strateia across the vast platform and watched with delight their effortless and perfect artistry. Beyond them she could see the Bridge of Trust over the expanse and beyond it the shadows of the back half of the great sanctuary.

A slight movement in the shadows beyond caught her eye and caused her to remember Sophidzo Logou with his little groups huddled all around. "Living One," she whispered as she came to a stop, "could Strateia and I return to instruct and convince those in the shadows of the sanctuary to cross the Bridge of Trust? They are so close, and yet so very far."

Strateia stopped and turned back, closing the few steps between them. "Your request cannot be granted in full. The King has other work for you that must not wait. He has sent others before with little results; and He will send others again if there is even a chance one might come. But so you will learn it is not evidence which they lack, nor will mere evidence convince them, your request will be granted in part."

Strateia then turned to their right toward the front of the platform and led Diakrina down the seven steps into the throng of dancing children. As they made their way toward the Bridge of Trust a living, moving aisle formed ahead of them like a parting wave among the dancing ones.

When they reached the place where the Bridge of Trust joined the crystal clear floor, Strateia turned and spoke. "Little One, you may go as far as the center of the Bridge of Trust and no farther. From there you may call to Sophidzo Logou and those with him. You will learn, I suspect, that when confronted with your evidence they will only shift the ground of their arguments and reveal an even deeper unbelief. You are given a short time to do what you can. When I call, you must return here at once and dispute no longer with them. I sense the approach of Anomos' forces outside the Castle. You will not be given long."

Diakrina understood. She walked out onto the bridge and made her way to its center. Though she knew she could not fall, the effect of the Chasm was still considerable on her, but she was determined to give herself to her purpose.

She stood there for a moment allowing her eyes to adjust as she peered into the shadows. Just as she made out the little groups here and there, she heard a commotion of voices in a group which she soon understood to be the one led by Sophidzo Logou.

"Look on the bridge!" she heard someone exclaim in a whispered shout. "It's the girl! She didn't fall after all."

Before Diakrina could speak she heard the familiar voice of Sophidzo Logou: "Well, well," he said, "there may still be hope. Perhaps she can be coaxed off before she does."

"You need not trouble yourselves about my safety," said Diakrina in a firm voice. "I am most certainly secure—more so than ever I have been. Rather it is I who finds myself concerned for your safety. You are here in this sanctuary, which is made for but one purpose: to commune with the King. Yet you lurk there in the shadows more concerned for yourselves than for knowing and loving Him, though there is no need to be afraid of this bridge. Your fear is born of illusions and lies.

"I have crossed over this bridge, the Bridge of Trust, and I have danced among the glorious ones on its other side. I have knelt before the shining Book—which indeed does shine—and I have seen its light make the Dome above clear with meaning where before was only obscurity. It must now certainly be clear to you all your warnings to me were unnecessary. For though I am surely of little significance compared to you in many things, yet I have faced your fears and conquered them. I have possessed the truth of the shining Book and now the true knowledge of the Dome above. Will you not do the same?"

A considerable commotion arose among the group as Diakrina asked her question. Finally, after several minutes of confusion, Sophidzo Logou stood and called for order. All fell quiet.

"Now I must confess this is an exciting turn of events," said Sophidzo Logou in his most scholarly voice. "And it certainly merits our full consideration." Some half-hearted grunts of approval were heard. "However, we must be guided by what we know to be true already in judging this matter. We are people of wisdom and we must not allow such facts . . . (he corrected himself) . . . I mean, eh, events, to turn us too quickly.

"I have no doubt about the girl's sincerity. She believes she has indeed crossed the bridge and returned and has seen a shining book and been given new insight as to the meaning of the Dome.

But to keep ourselves from running headlong into disaster, we should remember we have found what is true for one of us is not necessarily true for all."

"Hear, hear!" came a resounding response. Sophidzo continued.

"Apisteo, do you see the same thing as Antilego when you both look at the same spot on the grand Dome?"

"I believe not," responded Apisteo.

"Most certainly not!" joined in Antilego

"And haven't I been able to show you how each of you has a right to what you see there? That what you see is certainly valid for you, but not for the other, and vice versa? (He didn't wait for an answer.) Well, I think we should consider this event in view of this principle."

By this time Diakrina felt she was practically forgotten. They had replaced her with a discussion about her. She, as a living fact, was no longer in consideration. This did not set well with Diakrina and she determined to turn this foolish conversation back to reality.

"Sophidzo Logou," interrupted Diakrina, "will you not concede there are some things most certainly true apart from our awareness, observation or interpretation? That these things have a definite existence and nature which does not change regardless of our correct or incorrect observation of them?"

"Now that is indeed an interesting question," responded Sophidzo Logou. "But I am not sure it can be answered. I would certainly allow for such a possibility, but then, I am not sure it would be of any importance."

"Is it not true each of you can see me standing here, unharmed and safe, on the Bridge of Trust? In other words, you all see the same reality?"

"Well, as far as we are capable of knowing each other's perception, I would say that is true," squirmed Sophidzo Logou. "But then there are surely important differences, which should be correlated and contrasted, and then the essential common facts could, of course, be agreed on. But we would have to do the same with those facts in correlating and contrasting it with other things we hold to be true. For example, gentlemen," (he turned away from Diakrina) "we have information—not of a less reliable source in my humble estimation—which says this bridge is dangerous, near impossible to cross without harm, and there is no shining book on the other side giving new understanding, but rather . . ."

"Why do you shun the garden of simple truth and make hard-to-follow paths through the junkyard?!" shouted Diakrina in amazed frustration. "You waste reason and logic on the meaningless. You weave mazes through piles of nonsense and pride yourself on their complexity. But you forget you remain only in this scrapheap of foolishness and vain reasoning—you make not even one step on a journey of truth. What is it you are afraid of?"

Sophidzo Logou turned around toward her again. "Afraid?" he parroted in mock tones of fear. "We are not afraid, my dear. We are simply cautious. With life filled with so many illusions—in fact, life itself may be an illusion for all we know—we are determined not to be taken in. We will define reality for ourselves, in our own way, as it best suits itself to our comfort."

"Comfort is your highest principle then?" asked Diakrina. "What if there is One who can and will clear all illusions? What if there is One who will give you truth without lies; One who Himself has complete knowledge of reality and does not have impaired perception as we have? Would you risk anything to come to Him? Wouldn't a little discomfort be a small price for such insight?"

Sophidzo Logou was clearly upset by Diakrina's continual interruptions; he wished to keep the floor and go on with his rhetoric. "Madam, please keep to the subject! That is another matter, altogether. Who can know if such a One exists, and if He did, that He would take the slightest interest in us? In fact, to my thinking, such a One as could be as you describe would necessarily be so great we could not be a matter for His concern. We would hardly exist in His mind at all."

"This last point is not well taken," challenged Diakrina. "One who is truly great, without limitations, would be not only infinitely 'large' but infinitely 'small'; He would be great in all 'directions.' He would be great in the vastness of His knowledge and equally great in His knowledge of unlimited particulars concerning every microscopic detail. You do not speak of a truly great One but of one limited by your own mind and your own concepts of what such a One could be. You are reasoning from a connotation of the word 'great,' not from its definition. Your mind is moved by the emotion which such a thought creates in you instead of true reason, which might lead you to realize your own emotions are limited and highly subjective."

"Well, now," smirked Sophidzo Logou in uncomfortable resentment to her last point, "you have your definition of 'great' and I have mine. And if you think I am going to be taken in by a schoolgirl, you can think again! I trust no one! I trust nothing but my own understanding. And since I cannot understand such a One as you attempt to describe, I will not trust He exists. And I certainly am not going to take some foolish risk."

"But can you not see you have reasoned in a meaningless circle?" countered Diakrina. "To be such a One, He would of necessity have to be beyond your understanding. For, if He were not, He would not be great. All you have said says nothing about His possible existence and possible attitude toward us. You have spoken only of your attitude toward Him. And that attitude is such as seals you, without doors or windows, from the knowledge of Him.

"If He exists, you could never know it under such bigoted demands—which means you are no seeker after truth or reality. Rather you seem to be one who is determined to lock himself in with his illusions by stubbornly locking out any and all facts which cannot be dismembered or blackmailed to serve your private, subjective illusion of reality."

"Gentlemen," said Sophidzo Logou, turning his back on Diakrina, "I find this line of discussion most unfruitful for me. I do not think there is anything to be gained by it. For you there may be. But as for me, I would rather consider this when she is not here to interrupt my thoughts. I think this is a matter challenging a longstanding position . . ." then he added, ". . . which we have all held. I am comfortable with myself and my position. I see no need to call it into question. Now if you wish . . ."

"Diakrina! Come!" came the silver voice of Strateia.

Diakrina was about to object when she remembered Strateia's instruction she was to obey immediately. She took one last glance into the shadows and observed Sophidzo Logou was putting something like cotton in his ears while he continued to drone on.

She turned and walked sadly and thoughtfully down the bridge to the crystal roof and floor. But her sadness could not survive the glorious romp of the children. She was soon skipping in and out of their accommodating patterns as she followed in the wake of Strateia.

When they were back on the platform, Strateia turned again to the right and resumed their former journey with Diakrina following close behind. As they reached the far side of the platform, Diakrina saw steps turning again to the right and disappearing into the platform floor in the direction of the sanctuary. Diakrina followed as Strateia turned and descended the steps.

She soon discovered these steps were carved into the very crystal of the floor, which was also the roof of the Great Portico. The stairs descended about 50-feet and then emptied into a crystal tunnel leading back toward the Chasm beneath the Bridge of Trust: the same Chasm separating the roof of the Great Portico and the south wall of the Castle.

After just a few moments of walking, Diakrina, catching quick glimpses around the broad form of Strateia in front of her, could see the glow of moonlight up ahead. She concluded they must be coming to the end of the tunnel. Soon the roof of the tunnel gave way to the open sky and the walls tapered down until they reached the floor about 10-feet further along the path. There the path suddenly ended at the edge of the great Chasm. Stars shone in the night sky above them and a full moon beamed down from their right.

Diakrina looked up and saw, high above them, the Bridge of Trust. Far below was the roof of the Small Portico crossing the Chasm and attaching itself to the outside of the Castle wall. Diakrina knew beneath and behind her—out of sight from her current vantage point—would be the massive columns of the Great Portico holding up the roof through which she and Strateia had just tunneled. "The spatial dimensions of this place defy physics," she thought to herself, almost aloud.

Strateia suddenly stepped off the edge of the landing into the Chasm. Diakrina gasped from old habit, but immediately reminding herself Strateia was a master of the air as well as the ground. Yet, as she watched him, having moved to the edge herself, he appeared to be walking down steps, not flying. She rubbed her eyes and looked hard at the places where his feet fell, but she could see nothing but empty space. He was descending in a matter-of-fact way across the Chasm toward an arched opening far below in the outer wall of the Castle. This opening created a landing some seven or eight feet deep into the Castle wall where she could just make out what appeared to be the bottom of a door. But the moonlight was not quite enough to determine any of this with certainty.

"Are you coming?" asked Strateia, stopping and turning around in mid-air and looking back up toward her.

"Yes . . . of . . . course I am," said Diakrina hesitantly. "I was trying to find . . . the steps."

"Follow my footsteps and you will," smiled Strateia. "There is more than one way to find something sought."

Diakrina looked into Strateia's dancing clear eyes as he stood looking into hers. She smiled back and stepped forward into what appeared to be the emptiness of the chasm. As she did, the step under her foot materialized. She took another stride and the second step appeared. Now with two steps visible, she could predict where the next, yet invisible, step would be.

"It seems," said Diakrina, standing on the second step looking down at Strateia, "that some things can only be seen by trusting first."

"True, Little One," smiled Strateia. "But you saw them first in my eyes because you trusted me. A trustworthy companion is often an aid to faith."

Strateia turned and continued down the steps toward the arched opening in the Castle wall. Diakrina took her next stride, and then another, each step materializing the moment she committed to walking onto it.

As they made their way down the rest of the stairs, which had no rails and were extremely narrow, Diakrina's thoughts were much about Strateia's last statement. She was about halfway between the Portico and the Castle when the thought hit her that out here, suspended between the Great Portico and the Castle, Strateia had answered her directly. But before she had time to organize her thoughts about any of this, a sudden intense flash of greenish light came from behind and above her. She turned quickly around, only to be startled by another greenish burst of light, this time from below her on the stairs.

Diakrina could see nothing for a few seconds, but every instinct shouted whatever was happening was not good. "Strateia! Strateia!" she yelled. Then, through squinting eyelids, she discovered she was between two winged creatures—one in front and one behind. They were much like those she had encountered in the dark swamp outside the Castle, but these were three times larger. Instead of standing on the stairs, they hovered with enormous wings beating the air. With one look at their red, glowing eyes Diakrina realized what they were.

She swung the shield on her left arm up and toward the creature behind her, while with her right hand she grasped the handle of her sword, which was strapped on her left side. The shield blazed up with blue, gold and white light and caused the creature to retreat several feet. Her sword came out of its sheath pulsing with crimson light as she swung out at the creature just in front of her. She missed it, but earned enough respect from her singing blade the creature flew backwards a few feet to keep well clear of it.

"Strateia! I need help!" Diakrina shouted again as she thrust her shield in and out in the direction of the creature above and behind her to keep it at bay, while fending off the darting creature in front of her with her sword tip. Then she heard the unmistakable sound of Strateia's singing sword. She glanced down toward the bottom of the steps hoping to see Strateia coming to her rescue, but that was not the scene which greeted her.

Whether Strateia was standing or flying, she could not tell, because the steps below her were still invisible, but she could see he was fully engaged in an intense battle. Eight or nine of the same terrifying creatures surrounded him and were attacking him. Diakrina heard a hideous scream as Strateia's blade sliced one of the creatures literally in half from the side of his neck down through his winged body. The two halves of the creature, each with a fluttering wing attached to it, fell away to either side of the stairs and disappeared into the shadows below.

Diakrina had to keep looking back and forth—in front and behind—to maintain the shield and sword in the right places to keep the creatures off her. Fortunately for her, they feared both the sword and the shield. But even so she found it difficult to keep them away and to maintain her balance on the narrow steps so high above the Small Portico. The creatures' beating wings threw long and fluttering shadows across the steps by means of the moonlight. This disoriented Diakrina and made her somewhat dizzy.

All the while, constant screams and shrieks accompanied the song of Strateia's blade and testified to the battle still going on below her. When she again found a split-second to glance toward him she saw parts of creatures and dislodged greenish swords spinning down and away from him in all directions. But though by now he had certainly dismembered at least as many as she had originally seen around him, the number of hovering, attacking creatures increased, not diminished.

Many more of the creatures hovered above and around them in the air—maybe hundreds. And as Strateia would dispatch any one creature, another would take its place. Certainly the creatures understood they could not get to Diakrina without keeping Strateia completely engaged. So, while the main force kept attacking him, the two creatures around Diakrina constantly tried to find a way around her sword and shield. They were not using their swords but were reaching in at her with their legs, which had long talons on their feet, trying to get their claws into her.

She then realized what they were after. They were trying to get the crystal container which held the Atheos. She pulled the container tight to her left side, and though constantly thrusting with her shield at the creature above her, she always brought the shield back close to her side and over the container to protect it.

Then the creatures started circling around Diakrina in a

clockwise direction, always with their feet and legs lifted toward her and thrusting in at her. This made it necessary for her to turn around and round, or constantly turn back and forth on the stairs, to keep her shield and sword between her and the creatures. When one of them, which was now to her right, darted in at her, she gave it a hard thrust with her sword. The creature retreated quickly enough only one of its talons was cut off. But at the same moment Diakrina felt a sharp pain in her left shoulder as one of the clawed feet of the other creature gripped down hard on her. She threw her shield up and out against the leg of the creature and a blaze of blue, gold and white light flashed. The creature screamed as the smell of singed flesh filled the air. At the same time, she spun hard to her left while swinging the crimson blade of her sword fiercely over her left shoulder.

The blade hit its mark. Part of the creature's right wing and its left leg were sliced from its body. But more importantly, though she had not realized it, the creature had embedded its right talon into the strap of the crystal container behind her. Her sword swing continued around and also severed the right leg of the creature. The clawed appendage of the left leg fell away from Diakrina's shoulder into the darkness. The right appendage fell at her left heel as Diakrina reached behind her to ensure the crystal container was still safe. It was! The creature screamed and fluttered down and away from her. But it no sooner fell away when another one took its place.

Evidently deciding, however, not to risk her shield and sword again, which they clearly feared, both creatures took out their swords and moved above and below Diakrina on the stairs, just out of her reach. They then proceeded to swing their sword blades from over their heads down onto the stairs with a terrible shattering force making the stairs shudder beneath Diakrina's feet. She looked up at the still-visible steps above her and saw an ominous gash where the sword had struck. Cracks radiated out from the gash in all directions through the structure of the stairs. While she could not see the steps below, the shuddering report of the creature's sword told the story all too well: they intended to collapse the stairs and send her plummeting to her death onto the roof of the Small Portico or, worse, into the darkness of the chasm on either side. When the creatures struck the stairs a second time, the whole structure convulsed, and

Diakrina saw chunks of crystal fall away from the steps above her.

Diakrina panicked. She needed to do something fast. But what? The stairs clearly could not take many more blows without collapsing. The creature below her raised its sword over its head preparing to strike for the third time. The creature above her did the same.

"Up the stairs to the Portico roof, Diakrina!" shouted the silver voice of Strateia. It came from below her and off to her left. Strateia had tried to fly toward Diakrina, but as he did a horde of 30 or more of the creatures descended on him. They surrounded him and, encasing him like a sickening green globe, began driving him down and away from the stairs. Diakrina could hear the rising pitch of his singing sword. Crimson lightning blazed around him as creature after creature met its doom.

But Diakrina's own crisis snapped her back to attention. The instructions Strateia had shouted appeared to be her only hope. It would mean charging the creature above her in a desperate effort to fight her way through it and back up the steps to the tunnel.

As frightening as that idea was, the alternative of falling from the stairs and hurling helplessly into the darkness below terrified and emboldened her. A surge of determination swept over her and she turned in the direction of the upward steps. Pulling her shield tight in front of her and raising her sword out in front, she ran up the stairs toward the creature. The creature was focused on striking the stairs and did not see her coming.

When she was almost upon it, the creature's blade struck the steps with such powerful force the vibrations nearly bounced Diakrina off the stairs to the right. At the same moment, by providence, her left foot landed on a crumbling portion of the stairs, throwing her weight back in that direction. The combined effect caused her to stagger, but kept her from falling over the edge.

Without stopping to assess her footing, Diakrina lunged forward with all her might, stretching her whole body and right arm out with the sword toward the soft underbelly of the creature, which was hovering above her, its sword still stuck in the crystal stairs. At the last moment, before her sword found its mark, the creature saw her and attempted to extricate its weapon from the structure, while desperately striking out at Diakrina with the horrible talons of its left leg. But it was too late. The claws of its foot only parted her flowing hair as she thrust forward and drove the blade deep into the creature's heart, if indeed it had a heart where most creatures do.

The blade sank deeply and Diakrina pulled the sword hard to the left and down, tearing the whole torso open, greenish liquid bursting everywhere. She pulled her sword loose and the creature fell with a thud onto the stairway before bouncing into the darkness of the Chasm.

Diakrina could hear and feel the stairs collapsing beneath her, as a crack—two steps above her—suddenly opened from left to right. She had only moments to reach the remaining stairs above the crumbling fissure.

With all the strength she could summons, and with a cry for the Living One to help her, Diakrina threw herself toward the upper part of the stairway, though she knew its smooth surface offered no place to secure a firm grip. As she did so, a memory flashed through her mind of driving her sword into the stone like an anchor when she was about to fall off the platform leading to the Immortal Fruit in the realms of Thanatos. Lunging upward, inspired by the memory, she turned the point of her sword down, grasped its handle with both hands, and plunged it into the steps above her as high up as she could reach and with as much force as she could muster.

The sword penetrated the stairs three steps above the crumbling break, and Diakrina's upper body landed on the two steps still intact below the sword. The weight of her body instantly shattered the lower of the two steps, and it fell away in several pieces into the chasm below.

She clung to the sword handle with desperate strength and managed to pull herself up far enough to rest her waist on the edge of the remaining lower step. Her arms were now drawn tightly to her body, and she could not pull herself up any further. She tried turning loose of the sword handle with her left hand and grabbing hold on the left edge of the stairway above her, but the step was too smooth and she could get no grip on it allowing her any leverage to lift herself. She seemed to have no choice but to cling to the sword handle with both hands, with the lower half of her body dangling over the edge of the broken step.

Then she saw it. High and to her left, one of the creatures was descending on her. Its talons were extended and she could see it was clearly aiming at the crystal container with the Immortal Fruit, which was now hanging unprotected behind her on her left. Diakrina gripped the sword as hard as she could with her right hand and forearm and, reaching back with her left hand, pulled the container up onto the bottom step and covered it with her shield. Though the container was safe for the moment, Diakrina hung helplessly exposed. The creature had her where it wanted her.

The creature, seeing the container was under the shield, pulled up short. Flying up and around, it landed on the stairs above Diakrina, folded its wings and stared at her with red, hellish eyes. It appeared to be studying her predicament and determining the best way to achieve its purpose. Its gaze roamed slowly from the shield and up Diakrina's arm to her shoulder, and a look of diabolical glee settled in it eyes as it raised its sword. Diakrina read its look and instantly knew it intended to cut off her left arm at the shoulder so the shield would drop away and leave the container exposed. It raised its sword walking down toward her. She stared with horror at the greenish glowing sword as it was fully extended above the creature's head, ready to strike.

Swoosh! The creature's head and arm flew from its body. Swoosh! The sword of Strateia, who was now in the air behind Diakrina, sliced the headless body in two with such force the pieces propelled outward into the night to fall like shrinking, fleeing shadows in the dim moonlight.

Before she could say a word, Strateia lifted her and placed her on her feet and took a defensive position in the air behind her. "Quick!" he said. "Retrieve your sword and get up those stairs!"

When she had her sword in hand, he rushed her ahead of himself up the stairs. Reaching the landing, he held her back for a moment while he lit up the mouth of the tunnel with his crimson sword to make sure no creatures lurked inside. Then he hurried Diakrina into the tunnel ahead of him and, walking backwards, followed her until they were about 20-feet inside.

"Things have changed, Little One," said Strateia in a firm whisper as he starred back into the night beyond the mouth of the tunnel. Diakrina followed his gaze and saw shadows hovering back and forth in the moonlight. Beating wings could be heard echoing along the tunnel walls. "I will have to get you to the second story of the Castle by a different route."

Chapter Nine

THE BATTLE FOR KNOWLEDGE

Diakrina slowly regained her calm. The reality of what she had just experienced settled on her and she admitted to herself how frightened she had been.

Her left shoulder began to sting where the horrible talons had gripped her. She gingerly inspected the wounds with her fingers. Her dress of crimson light was in no way damaged, but the flesh under the dress was pierced in at least three places on the front side and one place on the back. Diakrina concluded she was not severely injured. The wounds would likely heal in due time, but the pain, though mild, brought back the terror of the moment the creature had fastened onto her.

"What are they, Strateia?"

"They are called the Nekros. They were sentient creatures living in Heylel's domain. They were corrupted by his fall when he plunged into the delusion of self-idolatry and evil. They were intelligent, with self-consciousness on a par with that of a three or four-year-old human child. They originally had rudimentary speech capabilities but have since lost the power to speak. Now, under the full control and training of Anomos, they have become his vicious servants. He uses them to make war continually against all light and truth. These are what we call Medialnekros. They are small compared to the Meganekros, which are the size of large dinosaurs … perhaps dragon would be the better comparison as they can fly," added Strateia.

"Anomos has made sure they understand you carry with you not only the Āthēos, but also the knowledge of the truth gained from the Book—the Lantern of Logos. If this knowledge reaches the Altar in Sapient Castle, it will change the balance of power in the final level, the level below the one we are headed toward. In this lower level is where good and evil are weighed.

"The Nekros know enough to understand if the fire begins to burn on the Altar, it will endanger their hold on the Castle. If the Castle is set right by the truth coming forth from the Light burning on the Stone of Perception—which is the flame of knowledge you carry inside you coming from the Book—Anomos knows the Āthēos will likely escape him. So, the Nekros are under orders to steal the Immortal Fruit or keep you from reaching the next level."

"Are these Nekros the same as the smaller ones we encountered earlier?"

"Yes and no," answered Strateia. "The smaller ones are of the same species, as you would say, but are a smaller sub-species than the Medialnekros. We refer to them as Minor Nekros. However, the smaller Nekros are just as deadly. Their bite can be like a viper. You must always keep your sword between yourself and one of them."

Diakrina shuddered as she remembered how close she had come to these lesser Nekros without knowing their danger. She had no desire ever to meet one again, nor these larger versions, either. Both were hideous. Diakrina wanted to change the subject.

"What is this next level down there where you say the Altar is?"

"It is Γνωσις—Cognition (Knowledge). And the one below it is Συνειδησις—Conscience."

"Oh," interjected Diakrina, "the same as the doors below the Stairs. I remember they which could only be discerned in a certain order. Is that why I had to come to the place of Communion first?"

"Yes, Diakrina. In the spirit, communion is the foundation, our reason for existence. He created us for relationship. He had no need to create for He is without any need—He is perfect, complete in Himself. He chose to create us out of the motive of pure Love: pure giving; the overflow of His infinite fullness.

"Through communion with Him we gain insights into reality and experiential knowledge, which activates and fills our cognition. This understanding is needed for conscience to function correctly. It needs Light revealing truth. In the darkness of lies and ignorance, the conscience cannot give proper guidance."

"Strateia, you speak about this Castle as if it were a person. How can a structure like this have functions like communion or cognition or conscience?"

"Diakrina, Sapient Castle is a psychomorphic entity. It projects, in living metaphor and sentient forms, the nature of any human who enters it. When you entered this Castle, it began to externalize to you aspects of your inner self. In a sense, you are traveling through a materialized reflection of yourself, Diakrina—a psychomorphic representation."

Diakrina's mouth fell open in stunned amazement. "You mean all these creatures and people I am encountering, all these things that are happening are not real?"

"Oh, you would be quite mistaken to draw that conclusion," responded Strateia. "It is all real. The Castle reflects and translates into living images what is true about you, but not you only. This journey through Sapient Castle is no mere dream or fantasy for anyone here. I assure you the creatures we have fought have their own objective reality, which you have just encountered. They are not part of the Castle but try to invade it, and you, in order to achieve their purpose within you and the others here.

"This Castle is like a visual language by which your inner reality is materialized and actualized to you. It enables you to interact objectively—in conscious ways—with aspects of yourself otherwise hidden within you. Yet it does not keep you from perceiving, encountering, and interacting with other realities which are not elements of your own soul.

"However, it is also doing this for others who are here as well. Your interaction with them plays a role in their inner revelations. Real persons and beings enact these revelatory roles in each other's lives without the slightest knowledge they are doing so. Each possesses their own real story. This is no mere drama-performance or virtual reality for anyone here."

"But how can that be if the thing I encounter represent something true about me?" asked Diakrina clearly puzzled.

"Because your interaction with the others is revealing something true about them as well. This is a somewhat symbiotic interrelationship. Sapient Castle is like an intersection where many lives converge; where many individual stories and journeys intertwine. By means of this designed intertwining, a mutual transformational energy is brought to bear on each one by all the others through the work of the Living One. Yet, each must, and will, determine how they interact with this favor given them. Each person possesses a sovereignly decreed freedom. They are predestined to choose, yet free to determine what those choices will be within limits. All individuals here will be changed: some for the better, others for the worse. They have limited freedom to help determine which change they will embrace, but none have absolute freedom. They must choose between the alternatives offered them, each with its predetermined consequences."

Diakrina whispered an interjection, "Kind of like real life in many ways." Strateia raised an approving eyebrow. Then continued.

"For you, Diakrina, Sapient Castle is a crash course in transformation: like an intense boot camp helping you gain strength, faith and wisdom quickly so you can continue your quest. But many here experience a lifelong confrontation before any good is realized. Others merely confirm their rejection of reality and their insistence on following Anomos into the illusions spun by self-idolatry."

Diakrina was silent for a moment. "I don't understand much of this, Strateia. And surely what we have encountered outside the Castle is not a mere pyschomorphic representation!"

"No, Little One, this out here is all real, independent of the pyschomorphic realities inside. As I said, it all has its own objective claim on reality. But neither is anything within Sapient Castle merely a pyschomorphic representation. The revelation communicated to you is pyschomorphic. The components, so to speak, of this revelation are all real with their own claim on actuality. Each person reveals and also receives revelation and insight."

"So . . . what aspect of myself am I encountering here, now, at this end of the Castle?"

"You are walking through your spiritual nature, Diakrina, with its primary functions of communion, cognition and conscience. Your spirit needs to be set right in all these respects if you are to succeed in your quest."

Strateia placed his hand on Diakrina's shoulder like a comforting older brother. "Your success is more important than I can express. The road of history for your race divides at the point of your success or failure. If you succeed, that road will put you and your race forever beyond Anomos' nightmarish schemes in regard to the Ātheos. But if you fail, I see the road dropping into the depths of the great Chasm. If there is a way back from its depths, no creature could comprehend it. I have looked deep into that dreadful possibility, but it remains dark to my understanding."

As Strateia spoke these last words, his countenance shadowed for a few moments with the first, and only, expression of deep bewilderment she ever observed on his face.

"Remember, Little One, this is all real and the changes you will undergo are all profoundly important. Nothing is merely blueprinted, so to speak. Freedom is real and necessary with all its blessings and possible curses. The curses need not actualize, but they will unless the blessings of loving trust are embraced."

Strateia walked closer to the opening of the tunnel. The Nekros still flew back and forth waiting to see if their prey would venture into the open again. He watched them thoughtfully for several moments.

"I will have to carry you across the Chasm, Little One," he finally said. "But it will be quite hard on you. You may pass out from the speed with which I will have to accelerate to keep the Nekros from attacking us before we can get you through the door. What is more, you must be the one leading the way through the door once we are on the landing outside the Castle. And for that, you need to be conscious. You must invite me to join you inside the Castle again. For I can only enter at your invitation."

"Why don't we just ask the Living One to vaporize these

creatures like the ones in the swamp outside?" interrupted Diakrina.

"In time He will. Indeed, He will deal with all these creatures. But some of them still have roles to play in His sovereign purposes for now. Though He is always able to annihilate His enemies, He often chooses short-term restraint for the sake of a greater victory. No, we will have to risk the crossing."

Resisting the urge to question Strateia further, Diakrina forced herself to stay focused on the immediate crisis, and asked, "But Strateia, I can't invite you in or lead the way through the door if I am unconscious."

"True, Little One, this is our dilemma. Our best hope is for me to find a speed just quick enough for safety and yet not beyond your ability to maintain awareness. And if—just out here on the landing, before we cross over—you invite me to accompany you into the Castle, that will fulfill the law of the Castle. You can then put your sword in both hands and hold it out in front of you, prepared to pierce the door and pass us through. I will have my sword ready in my other hand to deal with any Nekros who might attack."

"What do you mean about passing through the door? Are we going to destroy the door?"

"No, Little One. The door below in the Castle wall is somewhat similar to the Door of the Rose by which you passed into this side of reality—though it certainly is not as impressive, nor does it lead to as profound of an exchange of reality. Unlike the Door of the Rose, however, this door is always open to those who have a right to enter and who bear the Sword of Truth."

"So, I have that right?"

"Yes, Diakrina. The inscription on the door below says this: (He then spoke in a very strange and ancient sounding language. The translation is, 'For Fellowship-partakers with the Altar bringing knowledge of Him,' or as you would say, 'For those bringing knowledge of Him by means of communion with the Altar.' That is you, Diakrina."

Diakrina's face appeared thoughtful for a moment and then looking up at Strateia, "Ok, let's do this."

Diakrina pulled her sword, and Strateia with his left hand reached behind her putting his hand through the belt holding her sword's sheath.

"The belt is strong and will hold you without fail," said Strateia. "Keep both hands on your sword and keep the blade pointed straight ahead. When we step out from under the roof of the tunnel, you will need to give me the invitation quickly. Do you understand?"

"Yes, Strateia. I am ready." Diakrina straightened her arms out in front of her with the sword in place.

"Be prepared. The attack will be quick—of that, I am sure. But, whatever happens, do not forget the invitation."

Strateia and Diakrina moved to within a few feet of the tunnel's mouth. "Take two steps and give the invitation, and we will be off, Diakrina."

Together they stepped quickly out onto the landing. Diakrina said, "Strateia, come with me into Sapient Castle."

Just as she uttered the word "Castle," two Nekros fell out of the sky with their talons flared open with cruel intent. Strateia lifted Diakrina from her feet and flew straight up into the Nekros with his sword singing. Fiendish body parts and greenish blood-like ooze showered in all directions. But before a drop of the greenish liquid could touch them or a single body part fell, Strateia suddenly gave a burst of speed taking Diakrina's breath away. She struggled to keep her sword in position, or even to hold on to it.

During their blink-of-an-eye descent, Strateia turned slightly sideways and led with his right sword hand as he held Diakrina slightly behind him with his left hand. The speed was such, Diakrina has little recollection of it. She recalls the sound of Strateia's sword, and the crimson propeller-like pattern it formed in front of them as bursts of greenish goo and body parts exploded in all directions like tiny bombs.

Just before they came to the arched opening in the wall, Strateia maneuvered Diakrina around toward the door while his crimson wall of protection from his sword covered them from behind and above. Diakrina, fighting to stay conscious, struggled with all her might to get the sword fully raised in front of her as they entered the arch. Just as they approached the door, she managed to point the blade so it hit the door remarkably close to its center.

Before she knew what had happened, they passed through the three-foot thick substance of the door. Then they came to an abrupt and complete stop. Diakrina would have tumbled out of control without Strateia's firm grip on her belt. She felt like her insides would spill out. For several moments she rubbed her forehead and concentrated on regaining her sense of orientation and equilibrium.

"I trust you are okay, Little One."

"Yes, I think I am," responded Diakrina. She looked around trying to peer into the dim light as Strateia gently released his grip on her belt. "Where are we?"

Strateia did not answer.

But then turning to her, he said in an earnest voice, "What we are here to do we must do quickly. Anomos' forces are outside. The doors of the Castle have been temporarily sealed so none can exit or enter. But his forces will likely be working to batter down one of the small physical doors on the north end of the castle. From there they will make their way through the material domain and then the center—soulical—aspects of the castle to try and reach us here. Don't fear. But be diligent."

"I will," answered Diakrina.

She then turned to engage her surroundings. As best she could determine, they were standing in a wing off of what at first appeared to be a huge, circular, elegant ballroom. It had a 70-foot-high ceiling and a massive open marble floor, surrounded by black marble columns with gold bases at the floor and gold capitals far above.

In the center of the marble floor loomed an immense, beautiful, rose-red polished Stone of square marble, about 20-feet high. From where Diakrina stood, she first saw the Stone from the side, but she described it to me—and I will describe it to you—from the front.

Seven steps of black marble surrounded the base of the Stone leading up to an elongated oval platform about six feet above the floor and stretching left and right. The Stone stood embedded, and perfectly centered, in the black marble platform. On both sides of the Stone, another 14 steps continued up from the platform to the top of the Stone. These steps were also of black marble and appeared to be an unbroken continuation of the lower seven steps, except they did not encircle the Stone but only rose up its right and left sides. Diakrina was, at first, looking at the structure from its right side.

"This must be the Stone of Perception, the Altar of Sapient Castle, Strateia mentioned," thought Diakrina to herself. "It is indeed impressive."

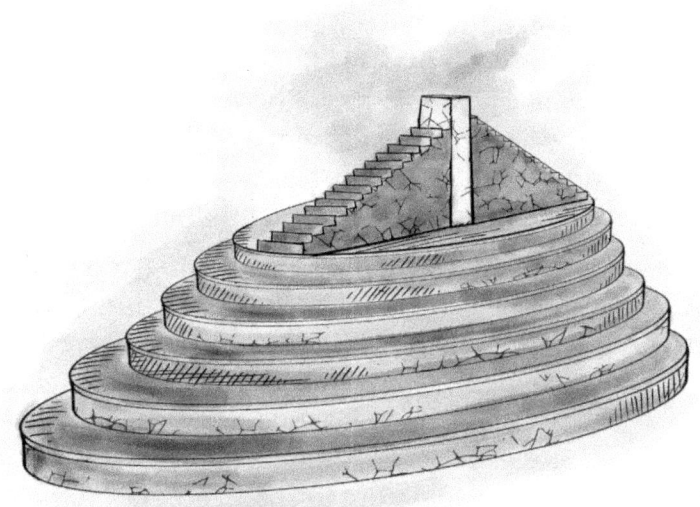

Diakrina's first notion of being in a ballroom faded quickly, for the atmosphere felt much more severe than a ballroom. The wing in which they were standing was dimly lit, illuminated only by what light spilled in from the great room beyond the row of columns.

Diakrina and Strateia stood in an aisle between tall, square objects, set in rows on either side. Diakrina opened her eyes wide and stared, trying to make out what they were, as her vision slowly adjusted to the dim light.

"Books!" whispered Diakrina to herself. Then quite out loud, "Why it's books. The kind of books I saw through the glass at the first landing on the Stairs of Communion. This is a library!"

With this new insight, Diakrina suddenly understood her surroundings realizing they had entered the level of Cognition— Knowledge. What she at first thought might be a wing off a great ballroom was a small break—to accommodate the doorway through which they had passed—in massive rows of bookshelves skirting the outside of the giant black columns and completely encircling the enormous oval-shaped room. The shelves were laden with books; large, thick, leather-bound books, venerable and important looking volumes.

Diakrina stepped out from the bookshelves and stood between two of the enormous black columns. The scale of the room made her dizzy as she looked up at the ceiling. She felt like an ant in a great cathedral. The Porticos were the only things she had seen surpassing it, although they were outside. Here, in this enclosed space, she felt overwhelmed by the sheer largeness of it all. To steady herself she rested her hand on one of the square golden bases of the nearest column and noted the base itself was taller than herself.

The ceiling was flat—without arch or vault—and rested on top the great columns. In the center, right over the rose-red marble Stone, was a large, round, stained-glass window, surrounded by a complete circle of six smaller stained-glass windows. From the center of the large window a heavy black chain reached down to within a few feet above the marble Stone. On its end hung a giant crystal chandelier, with six arms of crystal reaching out from its center. A somewhat smaller black chain attached to the end of each of these arms. Each chain rose in an outward sweep all the way up to the imposing ceiling and attached to the center of one of the six stained-glass windows surrounding the larger window.

The effect was astonishing. The six black chains all descending in a diminishing circle, with the greater black chain descending straight down the center. They all attached to an amazingly contrasting work of art: a completely clear crystal chandelier. Diakrina stood for several minutes taking in the grand impression of it all.

Movement suddenly caught her eye from across the great central room. From the shadows of the bookshelves came a hooded figure, passing between two of the black columns on the opposite side of the room. He was dressed in a black robe covering him from head to foot with long, full sleeves, giving him a look of dignity. He walked with what could only be described as educated grace. In his arms, he carried one of the heavy books.

The book was highly ornate, with a leather cover so thick, the deeply carved symbols did not go all the way through the leather. She could see the front of the book, for the monk-like figure carried it in an upright position, with a hand gripping each side, the front cover facing away from him. His arms were outstretched—almost as if the book were leading him. The cover, inlaid with gold on its top half and silver on its bottom half, flashed beautifully as it came from the shadows and reflected the light from the great room.

A long oak table stood about 20 feet in front of the Stone of Perception stretching across the great room, from the side near where Diakrina stood to where the hooded figure had emerged. High-backed chairs lined the table all along the side opposite the red-rose Stone. Anyone sitting in them would be facing the Stone.

A chair also sat on each end of the table, with one lone chair in the center on the side near the Stone. This chair was different from the others: it was two-sided. It had two seats. There was one facing the table and one facing the Stone, both sharing a common back between them.

The hooded figure walked along the side of the table closest to the Stone until he reached the two-sided chair. After placing the book on the table, he turned and walked up the seven steps to the Stone, where he bent over and picked up something leaning against it. As he raised it, Diakrina could see it was a hefty mallet, like one might use to play a big bass drum, or to strike a metal gong.

The hooded figure raised the mallet in the air with his right hand and firmly struck the rose-red Stone. A low rumbling seemed to begin in the floor. At first it was more felt than heard. But the pitch rose (not the volume) resulting in it becoming an audible sound. Diakrina heard a low, full voice speaking in a gentle tone seeming to come from everywhere. The words she heard were in the language she had been gifted by Strateia. They would translate to English as:

"BRING LIGHT FROM THE ALTAR TO ILLUMINATE THE STONE, TO ADD UNDERSTANDING BY MEANS OF SIGHT."

Immediately, Diakrina knew this invitation was for her. As the voice died away, she was about to step forward from the shadows of the columns when a quiet commotion caused her to pull up short. The sound of many footsteps echoed from everywhere.

Emerging from the columns all around the great room came hooded figures of various sizes and shapes. Each carried a large book in his arms (it always took both hands to carry these large books). They held the books close to their chests as they walked. Walking to the chairs on the opposite side of the table from the Great Stone, they took their places facing the Stone and the hooded figure who first appeared.

When all were standing in front of the various chairs, the one who had struck the Stone positioned himself to be seated on the side of the double chair facing the others. He gave a solemn look up and down the length of the table in both directions, and then gave a nod. They sat down in unison as they each placed the books they were carrying on the table. All the chairs were occupied except the two at the two far ends of the table.

No one moved for several moments. A cold and empty silence spoke of severity and rigid discipline. But then, just when Diakrina thought she could take the silence no longer, the one seated in the double chair removed his hood. The others then, in unison, did the same. Immediately, the tension lifted and they were all at once a warm, friendly, even playful bunch, discussing, joking and laughing in various little groups forming along the table.

Diakrina was stunned by the sudden change. They went from a medieval-style university sternness to something akin to backslapping chaps gathered at the end of the day in their favorite pub. Indeed, a kind of relief filled the air for which Diakrina was thankful. The cold quiet had been insufferable. But this good-natured frolic had not gone on long until Diakrina noticed how out of character it all was with the noble surroundings and the call coming from the Stone on moments before.

Now, it was not the light-heartedness or joy that was out of place—not at all. But the roaring laughter—the course jesting which soon came from almost every little huddle. It all felt defiant to the very purpose of this great room.

The invitation had been to, "Bring Light from the Altar to illuminate the Stone, To add understanding by means of sight." Nothing they were doing appeared to have such a lofty prospect in mind.

Diakrina walked out from among the columns. Though she was slightly behind and to the left of the single hooded figure in the double chair, she was certainly within sight of those sitting facing the Stone. One would think they would have spotted her immediately as she made her way across the open floor toward the table, but they seemed oblivious to her approach.

Diakrina intended to walk to the near end of the long oak table where one of the two empty chairs was placed. As she walked toward it, she passed near the seven black oval steps leading up to the Stone's platform. Suddenly, the deep resonant voice from the Stone spoke again with the same command Diakrina had heard when the hooded one had struck the Stone with the mallet.

**"BRING LIGHT FROM THE ALTAR TO ILLUMINATE THE STONE,
TO ADD UNDERSTANDING BY MEANS OF SIGHT."**

Diakrina stopped short in front of the steps, and the cachinnatory laughter around the table dissipated into a stunned silence. A quick, but amazingly quiet, scramble for seats ensued, and hoods went up over every head.

"This is most unorthodox," came the nervous thin voice of the hooded figure in the double chair. He spoke without turning to look at Diakrina. "Whoever you are, we must ask you to present yourself to us."

"Please accept my apology if I have somehow offended in matters of which I am ignorant," said Diakrina. "I fully intended to present myself to you. But it now seems I am being summoned."

"Summoned by whom?" inquired the hooded figure softly.

"Why, by the Stone, of course," answered Diakrina.

"This is most unorthodox," snapped the hooded figure.

"May I ask what is unorthodox and why?" inquired Diakrina.

"What can you possibly mean by such a question? It couldn't be the fact of merely hearing the sounds from the Stone?" the hooded figure shot back.

"If you mean the rose-red Stone, yes, I certainly did hear it. And I thought what I heard most wonderful and appropriate." Then she added, "But I am still at a loss as to what is unorthodox. I am afraid you must teach me."

"Oh, my, my . . . teach you? . . . I guess I could. But you must come to the end of the table and present yourself."

"I will most gladly do so, if that is what I should do," responded Diakrina. "But may I ask a question before I do?"

"I guess so, if you must."

Diakrina was somewhat bewildered at the nervous manner of this stranger, but placing it aside she proceeded with her question.

"Shouldn't I obey the invitation of the Stone of Perception first?"

A long low sigh came from the hooded one.

"Ohhhhh, I knew it might come to this," Diakrina heard him say in a half whisper. Then in an anxious but audible voice, "I believe there is something which speaks to that in one of the ancient books. But you have to be careful about taking anything found in them too literally."

"Can you recall what exactly the ancient book says on this

matter?" asked Diakrina.

"Oh, my, my . . . this is most unorthodox. You have not been presented, yet, and already we are entangled in such matters. ... Well, let's see ... there is a passage in which one of our forefathers, who first came here, was taught that one who is qualified (he emphasized this word strongly), upon receiving an invitation from the Stone of Perception, should present themselves immediately to the Stone."

"Does the passage indicate what would determine if one is qualified?" asked Diakrina.

"Well, it says, and I quote:

'When trust has crossed the Chasm and faith the invisible revealed, When Light has opened patterns and obscurity has been healed, Then the Light must be reflected, so perception may be known, So obey the invitation to be presented at the Stone.'"

As he quoted these ancient words, a stately warmth surrounded Diakrina. The massive marble surroundings were no longer cold. For the few moments the words were on his tongue—which Diakrina noted he quoted eloquently—it felt as though warm sunshine and a flower-scented breeze invaded from somewhere. Diakrina was instantly at home.

"Then I must obey without delay," responded Diakrina joyously and she turned to mount the first of the oval steps.

"Now, now, NOW! We mustn't become impetuous. An incautious approach to these ancient writings is not wise. Not wise at all!"

The hooded figure's voice was firmer than Diakrina had yet heard it, but she could tell it was on edge with fear, not conviction.

"But sir, I meet the qualifications," she retorted kindly. "I have crossed the Chasm on the Bridge of Trust. I came back across to this place by faith revealing invisible stairs, though I needed Strateia's help to complete the crossing. And I came from a most wonderful place where a glorious, shining Book of Light unlocked the patterns on a beautiful Dome and took away the obscurity. I have communed at the Altar and have been welcomed by the King. There I was given the Lantern of Logos and I bear it within me even now."

"These are grand qualifications indeed, if they truly be yours. But there are things of which we must be certain."

Diakrina had paused in front of the first step and now turned toward the hooded figure, though she could hardly see him at all, for he still sat with his back to her, mostly hidden by the high back of the double chair.

"I will submit to any proper investigation, but the investigation must not be such it would cause me to disobey the clear instructions of the Altar. And besides, the time is short."

"Altar! Did you call the Stone an Altar?"

"Yes, I did, for I have been informed it is the Great Altar of Sapient Castle and it needs to be kindled by the Lantern of Logos which I bear. That Lantern shines Light from the Great Book, the one from which I was illuminated resulting in the Dome of Reality losing its obscurity."

"This is most unorthodox. Unorthodox indeed!"

"Are you saying this is not the Great Altar of Sapient Castle?" ask Diakrina pointedly.

"Oh, no, I'm not denying that. Nor, mind you, am I confirming it. It is a matter to be studied and discussed."

"Are you asking me to disobey the command of the Stone by submitting to you?"

"Oh, not disobey, madam, but be willing to submit to orthodox timing and understanding."

"And what is the authority for this timing and understanding which you call orthodox?" asked Diakrina.

The hooded figure was quiet for several moments. When he finally spoke, he again spoke nervously.

"I am not sure I know the answer to this question. I can only say it has always been so since I came here. And I think those who went before me found it the same."

"And why do you think so?" asked Diakrina, trying to keep her tone of voice respectful and inquisitive. "Is it written somewhere in ancient books of truth?"

"No. It is written no place I am aware. I think it is simply something reasonable which has become settled tradition."

"If indeed it is a proper and reasonable tradition, would it not be deduced from an understanding of evidence or logic?" responded Diakrina.

"Well . . . yes," came the reply.

"Then, do you know of such evidence, facts or logical arguments to make it reasonable to conclude things have always been as they are and should be as they are?" Again, Diakrina tried to pull any sharp edges off the tone of her words.

"Well, no, but it is what we are used to believing and that should count for something," retorted the hooded figure.

"Then," offered Diakrina, "I think you mean not reasonable but comfortable. And I am sure the two do not always go together."

The hooded figure stood up, turned, and walking from behind the large chair, took several steps toward Diakrina. Diakrina could now see he was a slight man with a drawn but friendly face. The other hooded ones, on the other side of the table, sat motionless—completely motionless. In fact, she suddenly realized they had sat this way—with their large unopened books in front of them and their hands folded on top the books—since the moment they had replaced their hoods.

"My name is Meletao . I am the servant of the Stone of Perception."

"It is good to meet you, Meletao," said Diakrina as she bowed her head in reverent greeting. "My name is Diakrina."

"You just now suggested," began Meletao, picking up the previous discussion, "that I was substituting comfort for reason. Please explain more fully your meaning."

"I simply mean," answered Diakrina, "you seem to base your

decisions more on what you are accustomed to, or comfortable with, than on any understanding of facts or information which has been presented to you. You seem to impose a predetermined course of action on each decision as if, for example, the answer to every math question is, for you, four."

Meletao looked troubled. He folded his hands together and looked nervously at them while alternately stealing quick glances at Diakrina's face.

Diakrina watched this nervous twitching for some moments, then asked, "Can you tell me what your purpose is here, Meletao?"

"Well, I am here to learn and understand truth and to increase knowledge. This is my stated purpose. By serving the Stone of Perception I hope to gain knowledge and understanding."

"And you do this by obeying the commands of the Stone of Perception and the directives of the ancient books?" asked Diakrina.

"Well ... yes ... in a way," answered Meletao.

"I do not understand your answer," responded Diakrina.

"Well, you see ... it is much more complicated than that," continued Meletao. "One cannot just start acting on the basis of what seems obvious. Things are not always as they seem. You have to see beyond, and understand the objectives before you do anything. Otherwise, you quickly lose control and knowledge and understanding decrease not increase."

The look emerging on Diakrina's face must have been clearly one of perplexity, for Meletao immediately discerned the failure of his explanation. He raised his hands slightly in a gesture of helplessness and countered her expression by saying, "I'm sorry you can't understand, but it is complicated. There are things of which you are not aware—things which must be taken into consideration." His response seemed to Diakrina to be both fearful and defensive.

"Of my ignorance, I am certain, and I am gladly reminded by you concerning it," said Diakrina in a firm but kind tone. "But is there some reason why you cannot inform me? I have been sent here to bring Light to the Stone of Perception. If you are the servant of the Stone, then shouldn't you enable me to obey its command and the directives of the ancient writings?"

"Oh, this is most unorthodox," groaned Meletao once again. "We are sure to lose control and knowledge is going to be lost."

Diakrina was becoming a little impatient with Meletao's complaints of unorthodoxy. As for his other statement, the one about knowledge being lost, she could make no sense of it, one way or the other.

"Meletao," she challenged, "why do you respond with complaints about orthodoxy to every reasonable and obvious conclusion I present? Your response itself concedes my conclusion to be right and unanswerable. If it is right, and unanswerable, why would it be unorthodox? Is your orthodoxy based on truth or is your orthodoxy itself unorthodox?"

The look on Meletao's face could not have been more pitiful if you had told him he was scheduled to be hanged at dawn. Wringing his hands, he muttered frantically to himself. Meanwhile, Diakrina stood with question marks in her eyes, unable to understand why this strange little man was so obviously shaken.

After a few minutes of handwringing and muttering, none of which made any sense to Diakrina, he looked once again at her with troubled and focused eyes.

"This is most unortho ... I mean ... I've never dealt with this situation before. I had been warned it would come, but I had hoped it wouldn't."

"Is it possible you can explain to me why you see obedience to the Stone's directive as something so dangerous and undesirable?" asked Diakrina in a more compassionate tone, for she could not help but be moved by the little man's obvious intense pain.

With strained effort clearly etched into his face as he fought with fear, Meletao tried to speak. At first nothing came. Then, in an explosive whisper, "It's the Stone! Once it happens like this, we will lose control. The Stone will respond to the Light and not to us. Who knows what might happen?"

Diakrina was more confused than ever. She could not understand the basis of his fear. Yet, he was clearly worked up over the whole situation. What did he know which could cause such fear? What would the Stone do in response to the Light from the Lantern of Logos? And how could anything evil or dangerous come from the glorious Light from the shinning Book of Truth? And what could he have meant by the words, "Once it happens like this, we will lose control"?

"Meletao, what control will you lose?" Diakrina heard herself asking almost before she knew she was speaking her thoughts. "Isn't it right the Stone of Perception should respond to the Light from the Great Book of Truth?"

"That's what the ancient books say," said Meletao quietly. "And that is why you have to be careful about what you read in those ancient books. Sometimes, they simply are not practical." And then looking anxiously, first at the Stone and then at Diakrina, "I was afraid it would come to this."

"Meletao, you are not making any sense to me. You must explain more fully what you fear about the Stone not being under your control."

Diakrina notice a sudden change in Meletao's countenance. The fear previously dominating his face gave way to an expression of puzzlement. Then, after a moment, it became a look of amazement which washed away the anxious lines in his face.

Still, he stood motionless looking at Diakrina like we might at someone who had two heads. He wrinkled his brow as if in deep concentration and then, with a questioning face, asked, "Do you mean to say, Madam, you have no fear of the Stone acting without being under our control?"

Diakrina at first wondered if he were mocking her. But she could see in his eyes he was sincere.

"No, I have no such fear," responded Diakrina softly. "I have never been given any reason to form such a fear."

The same amazed look replaced the questioning expression on Meletao's face for several moments. Then, as if amusingly bewildered, he shook his head and slightly pursed his lips and said, "Madam, you are either very ignorant or very brave. I am not sure which."

"As to how brave I am, I am not sure I know. I have not been sufficiently tried. As to being ignorant," added Diakrina, "you may well be right." Then pausing for only a moment, Diakrina asked, "Can you inform me why you believe one or the other must be true of me in this matter?"

"Madam," said Meletao, with less nervousness than she had yet seen—he appeared to take on a teacher's attitude—"if you were in a chariot with four powerful spirited horses pulling it, wouldn't you want to have hold of the reigns?"

"I'm sure I would if I had no one better with me to hold them. But if someone more skilled and stronger than I were with me, then I would want the reigns in their hands."

"You didn't answer my question," snapped Meletao in a decidedly teacher-to-pupil fashion. "I said nothing of another. Certainly nothing of one more skilled and wise."

"And may I ask why?" retorted Diakrina. "This may be our very point of difference—it shows in the markedly different ways we picture the issue: the very assumptions from which we are reasoning."

"Do you mean to say you believe there is someone who will guide and direct the Stone of Perception other than us?" asked Meletao with an even more wrinkled forehead than before.

"Of course."

Meletao's mouth dropped, "And who, pray tell?"

"Why the One who made the Stone and put it here to serve us in regard to the Light He has provided from His Great Book of Truth," answered Diakrina firmly.

Meletao's face turned pale, then flushed slightly red with a sudden anxious anger.

"You have been reading the ancient books of truth. You are only saying what they say. And I already told you those books do not always make sense."

"If the shining Book of Truth under the Dome of Reality is one of the ancient books—or, in fact, the most important ancient book—then, yes. I have read from it."

"However, you need to know the Great Book of Truth told me nothing about this place one way or the other. Indeed, I did not know then this place exists as it does. And as to other ancient books, I have read none. What I believe is a matter of mere deduction from what I see here in this place and from what was revealed to me from where I came—the place of Communion before the Great Book of Truth."

This last statement by Diakrina took the wind out of Meletao, as if she had punched him in the stomach. His face went pale again, and it stayed that way as he wrung his hands together and started muttering to himself all over again.

Nonetheless, Diakrina pressed her point.

"If my conclusions are reasonable and match the directives of the ancient books, could it be the ancient books are more trustworthy and practical—even, might we say, reasonable—than you have suspected?"

Meletao clearly heard her. He doubled over more than before, as if again hit in the stomach, and began groaning in addition to his muttering.

Then without warning he straightened up and shouted angrily at Diakrina.

"Confound your reasonings, Madam! You have upset everything!" Then as if regaining some control, he looked at her with focused and somewhat apologetic eyes, and said, "But I see it must be. But mark my words: I don't like it."

It was quiet for several long seconds. Two intimate strangers stood face to face, both confused by the other in an embarrassing silence.

Meletao eventually broke the aging hush. "Madam, I must confess there is something about you which both troubles and excites me. In one way, it all sounds so right when I think of what the ancient books say. But when I try to fit it with my present level of understanding, it troubles me indeed.

"I am comfortable being in control. I have always felt—and been taught, I might add—this was the only hope for order and understanding. Yet you claim to bring news and insight of One who may be greater and more capable of bringing order and understanding than any of us. But how can I know this to be true?"

Diakrina looked thoughtfully at Meletao. "Before I attempt to answer your question, I wish to ask a few questions of my own," she said. "In what manner do you control the Stone of Perception? And how does this control protect knowledge from decreasing, as you have previously asserted?"

Meletao was thoughtful for a moment. He started to answer, then stopped. He made another attempt, but thought better of it, also. Then for the first time, Diakrina saw an innocent bewilderment come over his face; a childlike admission of ignorance without fear. This bewilderment was not self-conscious but wholly absorbed in the pursuit of an answer—lost in the desire to know. When he finally spoke his whole demeanor had changed.

"Madam, it now occurs to me we never have controlled the Stone of Perception unless you call refusing to use it a form of control. We have sat for hours and discussed its beauty, wondered and argued over its true purpose, exchanged theories and papers without end concerning its origins, but never once have we attempted to follow the commands it gives. In fact, without the Light from the Lantern of Logos which comes from the Great Book of Truth, we could not fulfill its commands. And we have become accustomed over the years to seeking to interpret its meaning and purpose without any attempt to discover how we should obey its commands concerning the Light. For some reason, we never considered going up to the place of Communion to seek understanding from the Great Book of Truth."

Diakrina's mouth was now the one hanging open. But she caught herself. She determined not to interrupt or distract Meletao. He appeared to be really thinking and honestly facing his own irrationality, and she did not want to stop his moment of insight.

She composed her expression as he continued. However, it was not necessary as Meletao was not looking at her but was now gazing at the great Stone, as if seeing it for the first time. As he continued to speak he walked slowly toward it.

"We were afraid for it to come to life," she heard him saying more to himself than to her. "Afraid ... it would have a life of its own or

... a purpose which we could not foresee. Could it be our fear of the Stone of Perception was more a fear of who had made it and for what purpose?"

This question he was clearly asking of himself. Diakrina was all but forgotten for the moment. Yet, all this was somehow right, and she knew it. She was watching a sunrise, as it were, piercing the dark of a long and deep night, of which Meletao had never seen the beginning. She saw a man entranced by the golden rays of light and the warmth of truth which had rudely broken in on him.

At first, he had responded in anger, like a person might do when the light is unexpectedly turned on in their dark bedroom, hurting their eyes. But now the light was doing its work. He was not seeing just light, but the Light—and beginning to engage those things which Light illuminates and reveals.

His inner eyes were focusing. A new nature, another dimension of reality, was unfolding before him and in him. Diakrina watched reverently as Meletao continued.

"And so, we turned from illumination to the darkness of our fears and the seeming control of our independence. In so doing, we made the Stone useless. We have never seen . . . never known . . . its true purpose or power. For its purpose and power will not surrender to our fears, nor honor the impoverished expectations of our attempted self-sufficiency."

Suddenly, his eyes opened wide and he raised his head to view the pinnacle of the Stone. "Indeed!" he shouted in an intense whisper, "the Stone is not tame or safe, that is true. But it never could be! Not and be the Stone of Perception. For no one is ever safe from the truth nor should they be! That I now perceive.

"So ... that is what the ancients meant by untamed. They meant it as a cause for joy . . . not fear. Ohhh ... how foolish we have been," he confessed, most apologetically, to the Stone.

"Madam!" Meletao almost shouted. He turned toward her as a man she had not yet met—changed before her eyes into someone new, as if some noble purpose for which he had been created was being activated by this new understanding—as when a key turns on a motor or opens a formerly locked door. "You are right, and I am caught suddenly ashamed," he continued. "You must obey—we must all obey—the command of the Stone and the directives of the ancient writings. It is now so clear! Oh! What fools we have been!"

"Meletao," interrupted Diakrina, "has your fear left you so quickly?"

He stopped short, searching his spirit, and then burst into the first smile Diakrina had seen on his face. "Why, yes, Madam. I believe it is gone. Amazingly ... gone!"

"Then we must not delay," answered Diakrina. "I will precede at once." Then pausing, she asked, "Meletao, what about them?" as she glanced past him to the ones still seated motionless at the table.

Meletao followed her gaze and turned around to face the row of solemnly hooded men. "I am not sure," he responded as his face became rather solemn, too. "I guess we will have to wake them and see if they will cooperate."

"You mean they are asleep?" questioned Diakrina in astonishment.

"No, not exactly asleep. But something like it."

"They were certainly awake a few minutes ago before the Stone spoke for the second time," reminded Diakrina.

"True, true," agreed Meletao. "But when the Stone speaks, I and the members of the faculty must cover our heads. When that happens, we come to the table and are seated—they as you see, and I, in the Chair of Focus. All of them, but myself, go into a deep focus on the Stone. This makes them attentive to any instructions from it, but unresponsive to the outer world. If I remove my hood while seated in the Chair of Focus, they then awaken and can remove theirs and become interactive with their environment again."

"Most interesting," observed Diakrina out loud. Then remembering Meletao's mention of the chair, asked, "This, Chair of Focus, the one you sit in, Meletao, must you be sitting in it for them to awaken? If you removed your hood without sitting in the chair would they awaken?"

Meletao turned around to face Diakrina. His face once more looked serious and Diakrina noted some of the former fear in his eyes as he spoke. "Madam, we mustn't speak of doing such a thing. The ancient books forbid it. Some who have held my place have tried it and it resulted in dire chaos."

"Can you explain what you mean by 'chaos'?" asked Diakrina, intrigued by this last bit of information.

"They say a kind of madness comes over each member of the faculty. They lose the ability to concentrate on their work and they are not able to communicate properly with each other. Some run in circles howling disgracefully or laughing or crying while others babble for hours to themselves. My job is to see this doesn't happen, for it is most unseemly. Regaining sanity again is hard, close to impossible."

"So ..." questioned Diakrina thoughtfully, "would you say your job is to focus the faculty, Meletao?"

"Yes, I guess that would be an appropriate statement. My chair is called the Chair of Focus."

Diakrina looked thoughtfully at the strange chair. It was remarkably beautiful: carved of a dark and heavy-looking wood. The seat and arms facing the Stone were inlaid with gold. But from what she could see of the arms and the seat facing the table, they appeared to be inlaid with silver, as were the chairs of the faculty.

Diakrina considered how beautiful and yet strange was this chair. She had never seen a chair like it. She was about to ask about the unusual doubleness of the chair, when suddenly the answer burst upon her mind.

"Of course!" she gasped out loud before she knew what she was doing.

"Of course, what, Madam?" asked Meletao, seeing her sudden change of countenance.

"Why of course, the Chair of Focus!" Diakrina nearly shouted. "It must be a double chair facing in opposite directions. It is all a matter of focus!" Then remembering herself, "Is that right Meletao?"

Instead of an immediate answer, which Diakrina expected,

Meletao looked intently for several moments at the chair. Then looking back at her with questioning, but excited eyes—eyes which said, "I think I see something, but help me!"—he leaned forward and whispered, as if in the presence of something sacred, "The ancient books say I must sit facing the Stone whenever one who is qualified brings the Light from the Great Book of Truth. I have never sat in the chair in that manner because it has not happened until now."

"Do the books say what will happen if you do?" asked Diakrina excitedly.

"Well, yes, there is a passage . . . if I can recall it. Let's see . . . oh, yes," and he quoted:

> "'When seated on gold, real knowledge unfolds,
> While the silver must be abandoned.
> The glory of the old, which has never been told,
> Comes forth from that which commanded.
> But to face the Stone, you must sit as alone,
> Both bearings you cannot embrace.
> For what will be known, of self is not sown;
> You must focus on the smile of His Face.'"

"Don't you see, Meletao," squealed Diakrina with the delight of certain discovery. "The Chair of Focus determines the focus for you and the faculty. When you sit on the silver, you are all focused on each other—or you might say, focused inward. But when you are 'seated on gold' you are abandoning the silver—the inward focus—the focus on self. You cannot look in and look up at the same time; 'both bearings (both directions) you cannot embrace' simultaneously.

"And when you are seated on the gold, you, and they (here she motioned to the faculty) will be focused on the Light, which is 'the smile of His face' coming from the Stone. And what will come from the Stone, 'that which commanded,'" and here she turned and looked upon the Stone's pinnacle, "will be 'real knowledge' of 'the glory of the old'—that which was before the great loss. And that, Meletao, does not come from self—'of self is not sown'— it comes from Him: the Living One. He is the One who controls the Stone of Perception by His

Light!" she almost shouted.

When Diakrina said, "the Living One," she suddenly felt the deep rumbling coming through the floor from the direction of the Stone. Then the rumble became a voice and she and Meletao heard the ancient language again. What it said translates to:

"AMEN! PRAISE AND GLORY AND WISDOM AND THANKS AND HONOR AND POWER AND STRENGTH BE TO OUR CREATOR FOREVER AND EVER. AMEN!"

Meletao, trembling in fear, fell to his face on the marble floor. Diakrina raised her face to the Stone as joy flooded over her and she was pierced by a painful longing for the City—as if it were her long, lost Home and the voice of the Stone was a breeze carrying a glorious fragrance which invited her there.

Again, the Stone rumbled and spoke in the ancient tongue:

"THE SPIRIT OF TRUTH AND THE LIGHT SAY, 'COME!'"

Clearly, the discussion was finished. Meletao, still trembling, rose to his feet.

"I will take my place on gold in the Chair of Focus," he said with a nervous, yet decidedly excited voice.

He was not sure Diakrina even heard him. It didn't matter. He could see by the look on her face, and the silver tears on her cheeks, she was being called and was thinking of only one thing.

Meletao made his way to the Chair of Focus. He stopped in front of it, and while still facing it, reached out one hand and rested it lightly on one of the golden inlaid arms. He had never stood here before. And suddenly it seemed strange he had not. The exquisite beauty of the finely carved dark wood with the shining gold inlay was astonishing. He turned around in front of the chair and faced the imposing rose-red Stone.

By this time Diakrina had walked to the front and center and stood at the base of the black marble steps between Meletao and the Stone. She had her back to Meletao, but was keenly aware of everything he was doing. (Don't ask me how, but Meletao somehow knew this, too.)

Meletao knew the moment had come for him to sit in the Chair of Focus. He reached back with both of his hands for the golden arms. As he started to shift his weight onto his hands and lean back into the seat, a sudden wave of mixed panic and alien strangeness struck him from within. Something in him fought to keep him out of the Chair. Doubts, all unreasonable, yet nonetheless convincing, screamed in his mind: "No! You can't! Unorthodox! Unorthodox! Stop before it's too late!"

Something inside him was both demanding and begging. And it seemed to be more than one voice. They pled like a pitiful child one moment, then without warning rose up in dark cruel shouts and demands. Meletao's face drained pale as he froze in the act of sitting. Then the voices started a fearful, threatening chant: "Control will be lost! Control will be lost! Control will be lost! Control will be lost!"

Over and over they chanted in ever-increasing volume in Meletao's mind. And all the time the alternate pleading and threatening continued as before. An insane mob seemed to divide into three shoving, screaming groups trying to out-shout each other. Meletao felt as if his head would burst.

He tried to break the grip of panic and confusion in a renewed attempt to lower himself into the Chair. A deep, sickening feeling hit the pit of his stomach like the powerful blow of a fist. Waves of pain and weakness spread over his body and through his limbs. He closed his eyes and clenched his teeth to keep from screaming.

Suddenly, above the screaming of the insane mob, he heard a piercing whisper in his heart: "Open your eyes, Meletao, and believe."

Meletao opened his eyes. Diakrina had turned around where she stood about 20 feet away. When their eyes met, Meletao could see bitter tears of sorrow flowing down Diakrina's beautiful face. They were tears of compassion. Somehow, she knew what he was suffering and it was her voice he had heard in his mind.

She took both of her hands and held them to her breast near her heart for a moment. Then slowly she extended them together, holding something bright. There in Diakrina's hands swirled a rainbow of Light more glorious than Meletao had ever dreamed of seeing. Diakrina raised the swirling glory until Meletao could only see her face by looking through the Light. Then she spoke softly.

"Peace, servant of perception. The Light is stronger than the darkness of lies and ignorance. Look deeply into the Lantern of Logos. In His Light is Life."

Strength surged through Meletao. The mocking voices were stunned into astonished silence. The pain vaporized from his body, and all became a living quiet—a silence pregnant with expectation.

Meletao lowered himself slowly, but determinedly, into the Chair of Focus. As he did, something like a dark mist (this is the best Diakrina could explain it) fled from within Meletao and then out of the room as if in a panic.

At the same moment, the Stone of Perception began to glow with a warm crimson light, which became increasingly brighter. Diakrina, still holding the swirling rainbow in her hands, turned again toward the Stone and started her ascent up the seven steps of the base. As she reached the top of the base and stood in front of the Stone, the deep rumbling, which always signaled the coming of the voice of the Stone began again. This time the Stone spoke in Greek:

"Ουδειζ δε λυχνον υψαζ καλυπτει αυτον σκευει, η υποκατω κλινηζ τιθησιν αλλ επι λυχνιαζ επιτιθησιν, ινα οι εισπορευομενοι βλεπωσιν το φωζ. ου γαρ εστιν κρυπτον ο ου φανερον γενησε ται ουδε αποκρυφον ο ου γνωσθησεται και ειζ φανερον ελθη."

The translation is: *"NO ONE LIGHTS A LAMP AND HIDES IT IN A JAR OR PUTS IT UNDER A BED. INSTEAD, HE PUTS IT ON A STAND, SO THAT THOSE WHO COME IN CAN SEE THE LIGHT. FOR THERE IS NOTHING HIDDEN THAT WILL NOT BE DISCLOSED, AND NOTHING CONCEALED THAT WILL NOT BE KNOWN OR BROUGHT OUT INTO THE LIGHT."*

When the voice had finished speaking, the swirling rainbow in Diakrina's hands went aloft from her and ascended upward toward the top of the glowing rose-red Stone. It continued rising to about a foot above the Stone, and then moved over its top at the very center.

A flash of intense Light with every color of the rainbow (plus some which Diakrina claims we can't see here with our normal eyes) filled the whole expanse of the great room. The flaming rainbow ascended all the way up to the enormous crystal chandelier. The six arms of the chandelier filled with the most magnificent display of dancing colors of the Light, which, in turn, reflected throughout the great room.

As Meletao watched the stunning display from the golden Chair, he thought of how literally the last words quoted by the Stone had been demonstrated. Indeed the crimson glowing Stone with the glorious flame on its top now looked like some awesome divine candle. Its rays of shimmering beauty filled the great room and danced from the chandelier to every corner, leaving no dark spot anywhere. Then something even more wonderful happened.

"'Ελθε!, (COME!),'" said the voice of the Stone. Everywhere the dancing Light from the chandelier touched an ancient book of the library surrounding the immense columns, the book began to glow and an angel (at least, this is what Diakrina perceived them to be) of brilliant beauty appeared. Each angel took from the shelf the particular glowing book that had occasioned his appearance and walked out just beyond the columns. There, facing the center of the great room, he stood at relaxed attention as others did the same. Soon, a circle of angels three rows deep lined the perimeter of the great room just inside the enormous columns.

When all were in place, the Stone spoke again. "Ανοιξον! (OPEN!)"

Each angel then opened his book to the first page. Each book, when opened, radiated a small, yet definite wave of the Light, casting a color unique from any of the other books. All around the great room, the waves of Light emanating from the books organized themselves into six distinct shafts of Light. Each shaft then focused itself on one of the six stain glassed windows overhead.

Each window in turn took on a particular reflectiveness, which made it appear like a colored mirror. Each "mirror" reflected a different color. Diakrina instantly recognized the colors as those she had seen in the columns of the Porticos. Two windows, which were opposite each other on the ceiling, glowed a glorious crimson red. The other four windows blazed respectively in brilliant crystal green, shocking purple, deep blue and dazzling yellow.

Diakrina and Meletao watched all this in stunned wonder. Then, the swirling Light from the chandelier began to climb the six black chains, which stretched from the six arms of the great chandelier to the six glowing windows above. As the Light covered, and appeared to soak into, each link, one at a time, the links would slowly lose their black color and take on the color of the window-mirror to which its chain was attached.

When a link was fully changed and glowing its respective color, then the Light would climb to the next link and begin the same process over again. This continued in an upward and outward choreographed sweep until, simultaneously, at the top of all six chains, the last link changed to match the window to which it attached.

At the moment the outer chains completed their transformation, the center, heavier chain began to glow from the chandelier upward toward the large center window. Only now the chain morphed—one link at a time—from black into that same clear color of the Great Column of the Great Portico.

Link by link the heavy chain glistened. Higher and higher the Light climbed until finally the last link, connected to the center of the large stained-glass window in the center of the circle of six windows, turned clear. As it did, the great window burst forth with the same clear color.

At that moment, Diakrina and Meletao gasped as every feature of the ceiling disappeared, except for the window-mirrors, and was replaced with a golden expanse of patterns and colors. The giant black columns with their golden capitals still rose visibly into the expanse, but they looked as if nothing rested on them. The columns stood naked against an immense sky.

Suddenly, Diakrina gasped out of recognition, "The Dome! Meletao, it is the Dome of Reality from the Sanctuary!"

Chapter Ten

THE AWAKENING

There—above Diakrina, Meletao, the faculty and the angels—appeared to be the Dome of Reality. (Diakrina later learned it was not the Dome itself, but a knowledge of the Dome made visible above them.)

A swirling rainbow of Lights blazed from atop the rose-red Stone of Perception, which danced in the clear liquid of the chandelier, as the smaller chains glowed crimson, green, purple, blue and yellow, and the larger chain radiated that unearthly beautiful clear. All the while, each window-mirror pulsed the same color as its chain and reflected the shafts of Light gleaming from thousands of glowing books. The effect was hypnotic. Glorious shining angels held these books, encircled by massive black marble columns with golden bases and capitals, which blazed naked against the shining Dome of Reality. For us in this world, the great room would have been an unimaginable sight of grandeur.

The whole atmosphere appeared living and organized into animated beauty with transcendent complexity. This was no static beauty. It seemed literally to breathe.

Diakrina turned around on the raised platform where she stood so she could take it all in. Everything for a moment was suspended. But not suspended in such a way as to mean still. It is true no one—Diakrina, Meletao, the faculty, nor the angels—were moving. Yet, the Light—which all now knew should be understood to be Light, with a capital L—made everything vibrate with life and flow together in inexplicable ways. And yet, one felt a certain kind of suspension, a solemn hush.

Where before, so many new and wonderful things were happening one after the other, this activity had now reached a climax—the end of a visual crescendo—where everything suddenly synchronized. The effect on the observer was as if a living, moving, perfectly balanced calm had been born.

In explaining this to me Diakrina said, "You know, it was a bit like when you hear one of those high-powered industrial electric motors, which drives heavy machinery, starting up. At first it is loud as it is spinning up to speed. But when it finally reaches its top running speed, it is only a revolving whisper, a steady quiet whine or hum, which says, 'Everything is working right.' It is even a pleasant relaxing sound to those who understand it. Well, I can assure you, this was most pleasant!"

This synchronized suspension lasted, uninterrupted, for several minutes. Then a sudden shaft of crimson Light shot from the top of the Stone over the back of Diakrina's head and, like a laser beam, focused on the hood-framed face of Meletao, drenching him in dancing Light. As it had soaked into the chains of the chandelier, the Light now appeared to soak into Meletao, transforming him before Diakrina's eyes. The Light was so bright she could only faintly make out his appearance was altering; but to what, and to what extent, the brilliance of the Light kept her from discerning.

As Diakrina watched—spellbound at the transformation going on before her—the angels standing at relaxed attention around the room began to sing. The melody was so incredibly beautiful, so beyond a mortal's ability to learn, Diakrina felt a twinge of grief such beauty could not be captured—learned and remembered. Yet this grief could not diminish her transported joy, as blessed and quiet tears of wonder and elation traced down her cheeks.

She could never remember the words the angels sang, until one day when we were reading a Psalm together out of the Bible. It was Psalm 36. When we got to verse nine, "For with You (Lord) is the fountain of Life; in Your Light we see light," Diakrina jumped to her feet clapping her hands.

"That's it!" she declared with delight. "Now I remember what they sang over and over in different and creatively beautiful ways. It was this verse!" And then, almost without taking a breath, "Do you see it? In Light we see light. In His Truth we see reality: the true character of things. He illuminates—reveals—and only then do we correctly discern and are invited to understand accurately. Then we see the true character of things we have thought we already knew.

"We only have partial knowledge. We don't have enough to really know how this should relate to that, until His Light illuminates our understanding and brings together everything into synchronous wholeness. Then, and only then, do we really begin to know! He is the source and the context of wholeness—true knowledge.

"The Light comes from the Great Book of Truth, and it removes the obscurity from the Dome of Reality. It is in the Light of His revelation our understanding of reality is healed, and we are again introduced the Edenic knowledge—redeemed Edenic knowledge," she added.

As the angels sang of a Light that brought understanding, the great room, now full of this Light, was transforming Meletao. When finally the crimson beam completed its metamorphic work, there before Diakrina's startled eyes sat a noble and glorious prince. Clearly Meletao was larger, stronger and amazingly filled out as to his frame. He was no longer a slight, little man.

One look also told you he was no vain or silly prince. You could tell, somehow, by just looking at him, he was a prince full of kindness, yet fierce in understanding; gentle, yet alarmingly powerful; playful, but noble and purposeful in manners. He was dressed in the most stunning clothes, woven out of what appeared to the eye to be strands of gold and silver. (The golden threads ran top to bottom, while the silver threads ran side to side.)

While Diakrina was still trying to take everything in, this prince raised his right hand and spoke. As he spoke Diakrina could hear both his voice—which was strong and silver now, almost like Strateia's—and the voice of the Stone speak in unison: "Εγειραι! (Awake!)"

For the first time since they had replaced their hoods, the members of the faculty showed signs of life. Diakrina could not see the two or three in the middle of the table because Meletao and the Chair blocked her view (as I'm sure they also could not see her). The others—spread out to each side—she could see quite well.

They raised their heads slightly and their eyes opened. Expressions of astonishment and even fear peered out from under their hooded brows. No wonder. They had gone to sleep in one atmosphere—familiar to them—and awakened in another, which was beyond anything anyone could have ever dreamed on their most imaginative day.

With bewildered faces, they looked in unison at the empty silver side of the Chair of Focus. Then, simultaneously, they raised their eyes to the Stone of Perception and the flaming rainbow of Light dancing on its top and in the chandelier. Stunned amazement covered each face: their mouths were wide open, and their eyes dilated.

The angels were still singing the same glorious melody as they wove it intricately around the words of the Psalm: "For with You (Lord) is the fountain of Life; in Your Light we see light,"

Then the Prince spoke: "The Living One has sent us Light. Now the ancient books of knowledge can be judged, corrected, explored and understood; for there is now a standard of Truth shining from the Book of Truth. It is living and certain. All knowledge can now be appreciated without fear. For the Light from the Living One will stand as a guard over all. In His Light we see light and discern it from darkness even when it tries to masquerade as light. Yes, it is in His Light that we see light!"

When he spoke the last sentence, it somehow fell in unison with the song of the angels. With his back still to the faculty, and his face toward the Stone, he continued, "The faculty will open their books."

Each of the hooded members of the faculty obediently took hold of the great book in front of him opening to its first page.

"Now," continued the Prince, "you must write all you can of the knowledge available from the books which have been illuminated. First, however, you must give your attention to the Light itself."

Then the rumble of the Stone began and the Stone and the Prince said together, "Ἰδού! (Behold!)" A blinding flash of white Light filled the great room. When they could all see again, the replica of the Dome of Reality high above appeared to be rushing at them with extraordinary speed, until one of the spots, which earlier had been opened to Diakrina, was so wide it covered the entire ceiling. It appeared as if someone had drawn this spot up close through a high-powered telescope and then displayed it on the ceiling.

All eyes, even those of the angels, turned upward. Then, an Emerald Hand reached from somewhere and rested on the head of Diakrina.

"LOOK AND SPEAK, DIAKRINA," came a Golden Voice. "YOU ARE ENABLED TO EXPLAIN WHAT YOU HAVE BEEN SHOWN."

Diakrina looked up into the Dome and there she saw again the unfolding truths, the stories she had seen in the sanctuary. Suddenly she spoke—though she claims her speaking was more like song and harmonized perfectly with the song of the angels still continuing—describing what she had seen and was seeing anew. As she narrated each scene it appeared in three-dimensional form on the pinnacle of the Stone—where the flaming rainbow blazed between the Stone's top and the chandelier.

She spoke (or sang) and the faculty, never taking their eyes off the unfolding drama in the flame of the Stone above her head, wrote with exacting precision onto the blank pages of their books. When all Diakrina had seen in one spot of the Dome of Reality was recounted, another place would come into focus, and she would begin a new lesson (or song) that concerned this area of the Dome. All the while, the forms, which looked as real as the persons, places and things they represented, continued in breathtaking dramas above her head and held the absolute attention of the faculty.

Everything else—the Light from the books to the windows, from the Stone to the chandelier, and so forth—continued uninterrupted in a visual and auditory symphony of stories, insights and glorious music. Diakrina does not know how long this continued, but the Emerald Hand rested on her head until she finished narrating all she had seen. When it finally lifted, she fell silent.

Then the Prince spoke again. "This is the Light of Truth. Now judge, correct, explore and understand the knowledge of the world by this Light. Do not attempt to change the Light. You cannot. You will only deceive yourself. Bring all else into harmony with the Light of the Stone. In so doing, the knowledge around you will yield its deepest fruit to you—fruit that otherwise would have been hidden from your eyes. Bring all truth home to Truth/Reality."

The Prince then stood—indeed stunning to behold—and walked around to the other side of the Chair of Focus where, for the first time since his transformation, he was visible to the faculty. They all gasped at his appearance.

He then reached for the arms of the silver side of the Chair to seat himself facing the faculty. As he touched the arms of silver, he went, for only a moment, out of focus like one reflected in a pool of water in which a pebble has been dropped. The next moment he was again in focus, but was no longer the Prince, but once again the hooded Meletao in scholarly robes.

When Meletao sat down and removed his hood, he was still stunningly changed from what he had been before. He was a strong prince in the robes of a scholar. As he removed his hood, so did the others, and an amazing process began.

He and the faculty conferred together. They studied and shared. When more information was needed, they would summon an angel, carrying the appropriate book, to one of the ends of the table where the empty chairs held sentinel.

While this got underway, Diakrina descended the seven steps of the Stone's front and walked out to the side of the Chair of Focus so she could see all that took place. She arrived just in time to hear Meletao say to the faculty, "You will notice the Light from each book is different not only in color but in intensity. They have different colors because they touch on different subjects. The different intensities of their light, all the way from dimly faint to brilliantly bright—though none ever come close to the bright intensity of the shining Book—is due to the amount of useable truth contained in them.

All books must use some portion of reality, or they cannot even be written. But if the reality—the truth in them—is mixed with error, it becomes dim and unusable. Thus, we must judge, correct, explore and understand each book through the Light of the Stone of Perception, which has come from the shining Book of Truth on the Altar of Communion."

Diakrina then watched as they conferred together and wrote in their books the truths they confirmed. Whenever they consulted a book and lacked a clear understanding and agreement on whether a certain idea put forth was in harmony with Reality, Meletao would rise from the silver side of the Chair of Focus and walk to the other side. When his hands touched the golden arms of the Chair on the other side facing the blazing Light on top of the Stone, he would once again, in the observer's eyes, go out of focus and refocus as the noble Prince.

The Prince would lift the book in question up to the Light or ask the question being debated. When he did this, a particular spot on the Dome would come into view and the story contained within it would be displayed in the swirling Light above the Stone. Often the Prince would watch the story many times before fully understanding the principle which related to the question he had brought.

Once he understood, he would state its application out loud to the faculty while still seated on the gold of the Chair of Focus. If he had understood correctly, the Stone would respond, "Αμην! (Amen!)" By this means the faculty understood the ruling was not merely the understanding or wishes of the Prince but of the Light itself. For the Prince was under the authority of the Light as was everyone else.

Diakrina watched this process for some time. She was intrigued by the various discussions and could have been quite happy if allowed to continue listening in while the angels sang their glorious song.

But soon she felt the hand of Strateia on her shoulder. "Come, Little One. Your job is well done. We must go. This Light with all the knowledge it is unlocking must invade one more domain of your spirit."

Strateia then led Diakrina back to a place between the Chair of

Focus and the Stone of Perception. He walked about equal distance between the two and stopped, waiting for Diakrina to catch up to him.

"Remove your sword, Diakrina," instructed Strateia. This she did obediently. "We must reopen an ancient passage which should never have been shut. It lies just before us here in the floor."

Diakrina looked hard at the marble floor but could make out nothing looking unusual or like a place where an opening should be. The spot Strateia indicated did have an ornate circular work of art painted on the marble floor. It was strikingly intricate and, in its own way, beautiful. Other than that, the closer she looked, the more impressed she became with the sturdy, unbroken appearance of the solid floor.

"Things are not always as they appear to the eyes," answered Strateia to the unspoken question giving itself away in her countenance. "Sometimes we must see with more than mere eyes. Besides, this work of art—a religious work of art—which many would say should not be destroyed, was placed here to dissuade anyone inclined to look here for the opening that should never have been closed. They revere this painted symbol, and it is embedded deep into their traditions of Light avoidance, but it must be destroyed. It is religion hiding truth rather than submitting to it and proclaiming it."

Then placing himself opposite of Diakrina, Strateia took two steps back and motioned for her to move back the same distance (which was more like four steps for her).

"Here, equal distance from the Stone and the Chair, where this symbol is painted, is where the passage should be," informed Strateia. "Raise your sword and when I give the command, strike the floor with all your might at the same moment I do."

Then, turning toward the Chair, he said, "Prince, we are ready."

Meletao walked around from the other side of the Chair of Focus. When the ripples cleared after he touched the Chair's arm, there stood the Prince, who then seated himself on the golden chair.

"We, too, are ready," said the Prince and the Stone together. "May knowledge now bear its proper fruit."

Strateia, turning to the Stone, raised his sword toward the flame and shouted in a voice shaking the whole room, "In honor of His Light we restore knowledge! We invade immoral deception with the Light bringing moral understanding to the conscience!" Then turning again toward Diakrina, he caught her eye and together they raised their swords.

For a moment, the crimson swords hung suspended in the song of the angels and the Light of the Stone. Then Strateia slowly closed his eyes and gathered himself to a fierce attention as he placed his other hand also on the sword's handle. Diakrina gathered herself into the best imitation she could manage with every muscle of her body trembling as she awaited the signal.

"NOW!" came the rending command from Strateia. Swords of crimson flashed in a downward arc and struck the floor with an ear shattering report. Instantly, where the swords struck, the floor cracked and crumbled, like a spider's web, from the center outward to the edge of the painted symbol.

(Far below, participants in a strange ritual were stunned into motionlessness with their eyes fixed high above them into the darkness from where a terrible thunderous, rending sound came blasting down over them.)

When the cracking and crumbling stopped, a perfect circle— just larger than the size of the painted symbol—could be seen. It was about 10 feet in diameter, just within the barrier of Strateia and Diakrina's feet. The floor had not given way within this circle, but was visibly demolished until it appeared even the slightest pressure would collapse it. The floor within the circle even sagged somewhat toward its center. Outside the circle, the floor was as before—solid and beautiful.

Strateia replaced his sword and motioned for Diakrina to do the same. "Follow me," he said, and walked to one side of the Stone, where he turned and began ascending the 21 steps leading to the top. Diakrina followed him up each step until they reached the pinnacle where the swirling rainbow blazed.

When they had reached the top, Strateia stopped and turned toward Diakrina. "Reach into the Light and take your portion, Little

One."

Diakrina walked up to the blazing wall of dancing Light and reached into the flame with both hands held together. A small sphere of Light, the same size as the former one, formed and filled her hands. As she withdrew her hands, now enveloped in Light, the blazing flame of Light on the top of the Stone continued, not in the least diminished by the portion in her hands.

Diakrina looked deep into the swirling radiance in her hands. The effect was like falling upward into inexplicable beauties inviting her into an unending story. Strateia reached out his hand under hers and slowly lifted them toward her heart. As the Light touched her body it sank into her as before. A sense of utter peace—a peace filled with meaning, purpose and health, and the knowledge being revealed by the books—washed over Diakrina, flushing her with extraterrestrial joy.

"Come, Little One," said Strateia laying his giant bronze hand on her shoulder. "We must finish what we have started."

He led her to the edge of the Stone where he and Diakrina could see the circular pattern in the floor below them. "You must trust me, Little One," said Strateia, lifting her into his arms like a child in a sleeping prone position. Diakrina looked into his clear eyes and relaxed.

Without warning Strateia stepped off the pinnacle of the Stone. As if walking on some invisible surface, he took several steps until they were directly over the crumbled pattern in the floor.

The Prince stood and raised his hand in a salute. The faculty did the same from the other side of the table. The Prince then walked within about three feet of the circle and raised both hands together like he was holding an invisible sword. The Stone began to rumble and then the voice of the Stone and the Prince together shouted, "Εγειραι! (Awake!)," as the Prince brought his arms down as if striking the center of the circle with an unseen sword.

Light burst into the air in all directions from the center of the circle. At the same moment Strateia and Diakrina began an explosive acceleration downward. With an ear-shattering crack, the floor and its crumbled surface rushed at Diakrina. Strateia's feet hit the center of the circle and with a thunderous explosion he and Diakrina plunged into an opening of collapsing stones.

Chapter Eleven

THE INVASION

You have no doubt heard of someone "making a grand entrance." Well, most of the time you would use this phrase when someone has gone to great pains to be impressive in their entrance into a room or theater or stadium or such. Diakrina had made no such plans. In fact, she did not even know she was making an entrance. But an entrance—a grand entrance—she did make.

When she and Strateia had fallen into the circular opening in the floor of the great library, she had no idea where they were going. One moment they were crashing through a floor in an explosion of crumbling stones, the next they were freefalling along with chunks of marble and debris.

Instinctively she looked down. Through the falling rubble she could see a room far below with people standing in a large circle around an open space and looking upward with stunned faces. As she, Strateia and the escorting avalanche of stones fell further, for a moment the sound of the crumbling floor had ceased and no sound from below had yet reached them. She felt caught in a fast charging vacuum of silence. Then suddenly the sounds from below broke in on them like a tidal wave.

She heard screaming voices. Most of them were unintelligible, but the few she could make out were shouting things like, "Run, the cupola is falling!" "Stand still, its falling in the center!" "It's the end, it's the end!"

Not until later did Diakrina understand why she also had the sensation of falling into a narrowing space—like a large hole became increasingly narrower as it descended; like a funnel. Yet, at the same time, this was offset by things below appearing increasingly larger at the breath-taking rate of her fall.

In the arms of Strateia, Diakrina had not given any thought to how they would land safely among all the falling debris. But as the floor below rushed at them and the ant-sized people quickly grew to normal size, for a brief moment, just before the avalanche hit the floor, Diakrina felt uneasy and began to wonder if Strateia was going to do anything. Then she felt herself go heavy in his arms as falling stones rushed past them. The next instant a thunderous roar announced hefty chunks of stones ending their journey just below.

Diakrina hung suspended in midair in the arms of Strateia. At first she could see nothing, as dust filled the air around them. Strateia, who had been holding her cradled like a child, now repositioned her so she was in a standing position—still in midair—with her back to him while his strong hands held her by her waist.

Diakrina felt a little "on display" as the settling dust not only made it possible for her to see the room and the people around her, but for them to discover her. Little by little, coughing and squinting into the dust, one person after another spotted the intruder and, with looks of amazement, nudged the person next to them and pointed upward. This went on until Strateia and Diakrina, and the pile of stones below them, were encircled with stunned and curious faces.

As the air cleared, Diakrina began distinguishing the circle of faces, about three persons deep in most places. The room itself then became discernable.

Her first impression of the room was it was rather drab. Everything seemed to be in earth tones. The walls were paneled in rich, dark-brown wood, which had a twisted, swirling grain, giving the impression the trees from which the wood had been cut were enormous and old. The room itself was square in shape. It would have been particularly dull except for its one impressive feature: the height and design of the ceiling and the ascending walls.

The walls appeared to go up endlessly, but not with flat,

unbroken surfaces as one would expect. Instead, in upward intervals about every 60 feet, the walls were interrupted with what appeared to be something like a ledge. Each ledge held a balcony encircling the entire room and extending back several feet before hitting a further wall which ascended to the next ledge.

Every level created a larger space than the level below it. Six such ledges—the ceiling sitting on the seventh—gave the effect of an enormous funnel with something more like the sky above than a ceiling. It felt larger than a ceiling should; as if it stretched beyond sight. As Diakrina took this all in, she began to understand why she had had the sensation of falling into an ever-narrowing space.

The clearer the room became the more Diakrina could see, in fact, it was much more unique and impressive than she had first perceived. Elaborate banisters completely enclosed the center of the room where the rubble had fallen. Diakrina could now see the people were all on the outside of these banisters peering over them in her direction.

Suddenly someone spoke.

"Your Honor," sneered a condescending voice making Diakrina start, as the voice sounded somewhat familiar, "I don't know who this is, but this is most irregular. I don't see how we can come to vital conclusions with this kind of turmoil and destruction crashing in on us." And then almost as an afterthought, "To say nothing of the fact that evidence is totally ruined and buried beneath this rubble. I think you should do something about this kind of . . ."

"Order! Order!" interrupted a gruff but not unpleasant voice. "I'll determine what should be done. And right now, I want those of you blocking my view to remove yourselves."

Looking in the direction of the voice, Diakrina saw—from the expressions appearing on the faces of those between her and the speaker—the audience around her suddenly remembered where they were and how they ought to be conducting themselves. A moment later the crowd began to part to the right and left revealing an imposing structure on which sat a generously-proportioned silver-headed man in an impressive black robe. It occurred to Diakrina as she studied this structure it was a judge's bench, and she was in a courtroom.

"Now," continued the Judge in a controlled and confident voice, "would the young lady who just made such a grand entrance into my Courtroom like to inform us who she is and why she is here?" As he spoke, he rose to his feet, spread his arms wide and downward onto the top of his bench as he looked up at Diakrina.

Every eye turned again to the suspended Diakrina. An uncomfortable silence followed for about 15 seconds or so, because she was not completely sure why she was here. It then occurred to her Strateia must be invisible to the Judge and occupants of the Courtroom, for the Judge—as well as the collective gaze of the others—had acknowledged only her.

"Your Honor," she began in a soft but steady voice, "my name is Diakrina. As to why I am here, I must confess, I do not yet know the full answer. But I know enough to be certain I am supposed to be here. As to how I have come to enter your Courtroom in this manner, that is a long story.

The Judge eyed her for several moments. He looked up into the expanding expanse over their heads and then back to Diakrina. Then lifting one eyebrow with a quick glance toward the ceiling he asked, "You came from up there?"

"Yes, your Honor." (Diakrina was pulled into the decorum of a judicial atmosphere by the aura of dignity that surrounding the Judge.)

"Did you come from beyond the ceiling?"

"Yes, your Honor."

The Judge eyed her as if trying to size up if she were the kind of person who would tell the truth about such things. He then glanced up again at the expanse above.

"How did you pass through the ceiling, young lady? I have climbed to the top of these ascending balconies several times, and there is no opening up there."

"You might say we made one . . . or rather, reopened one that, for some reason, had been sealed."

This last statement had a visible impact on the Judge's countenance. Diakrina could not be sure, but she thought she detected a slight expression of hopeful excitement in his face.

The Judge lowered his eyebrows into a thoughtful gaze at Diakrina. He gripped his chin with his right hand and looked up again. Evidently realizing his bench was far enough under the lowest balcony he could not see the center of the ceiling high above, he turned and walked out of his place and came down onto the floor where all the others were standing.

The crowd of people parted as the Judge made his way to the banister below Diakrina. He looked again at her and then lifted his head and peered long and hard at the center of the ceiling above them. After a moment his eyes widened with recognition as he evidently found what he was searching for.

He then looked straight at Diakrina and said, "Madam, this heap of rubble beneath you, and the opening I can see far above, tells me you speak the truth. I think the sooner you share with me your story, the better." The Judge turning, and walking back around and up the stairs to his bench, took his place again.

"Now, Miss Diakrina, I am most earnest to hear your story." With that he leaned back in his chair.

All the proper sternness in the Judge's manner softened and was replaced by a serious attentiveness. Diakrina was not sure if she should share everything with the Judge or not. Should she tell him about her quest and the Immortal Fruit which she still carried hidden under her shield?

Something about the Judge made Diakrina instinctively want to trust him, but she had to be sure. She closed her eyes momentarily and whispered, "Living One, I need wisdom."

Strateia leaned forward and whispered in her ear. "You can tell the Judge all. Hide nothing from him," he said.

So, Diakrina began at the very beginning of her story about how she had first met Strateia in voice only, on the other side of the Door of the Rose. The Judge listened with rapt attention.

As Diakrina talked she couldn't help but notice some of the

Judge's mannerisms. He had a certain peculiarity in the way he folded his hands together and rested his chin on them—Diakrina was to observe this trait many times in her further dealings with the Judge. He would fold all but his index fingers and thumbs together. His index fingers and thumbs he held tip-to-tip unfolded. This made a kind of hook out of his thumbs on which he rested his chin while the index fingers were placed together over his mouth and mustache, like a steeple pointing to just under his nose. Above his hands, she was always drawn to his animated and thoughtful eyes, which searched her face as he listened.

One could not help but notice at these times how stately and wise the Judge appeared. He was a fine looking older gentleman with a full head of very thick, loosely combed white hair which had an appropriate freedom in how it lay on his head. His face was handsome and strong with just a splash of kindness across it. But though this hint of kindness never left his face, it did not hide the resolute authority with which he ruled his domain. One instinctively knew it would be unwise to tell him anything other than the truth.

Diakrina took her time in sharing each detail of what she had seen and experienced since passing through the Door of the Rose. The Judge never took his eyes off her for a moment. All the while, Strateia held her aloft just above the rubble. No one else dared to speak, for the Judge had given her his full and determined attention.

When at last she finished her account, the man who had previously protested cleared his throat as if to speak again. But the Judge's eyes darted quickly toward him and shouted a silent but unmistakable, "Hold your peace!" The gentleman, who had stepped slightly forward in his anticipation of taking the floor, melted quickly back into those standing around him.

Then the Judge spoke. "Madam, if what you have shared is indeed true, this is a most important moment. It is a moment when I find all my former knowledge and resources arraigned and placed on trial. If the information you present is fact, then nothing short of a complete reversal of many of my former decisions would be required."

He paused for a moment, but no one dared to speak. Then continuing in a soft but unwavering voice in which he seemed to be addressing himself rather than anyone else: "Both a reluctance and an anticipation stir in me. I am taken by surprise at the strength of my longings."

Then coming to himself and focusing his eyes on Diakrina, "Madam, you last spoke of the Light, Light with a capital 'L'; Light in which truth can be seen. This Light, giving meaning and purpose to the otherwise seemingly disconnected stories of history, would be no small issue if it can be proved true." Then in a kind of personal digression the Judge said, almost in a whisper, "In fact, this Light seems to shine from your face."

Then recovering himself, he inquired in a more formal voice, "The existence of such Light has been, until this moment, little more than a hopeful myth among us. Could its existence be real?"

"I will give you my word, under the sternest oath, that it is so," replied Diakrina.

The Judge looked long and hard at her. "Already the radiance from your face disturbs and begins to dispel a darkness I did not know held me prisoner. It invites me . . ." here the Judge paused as he searched for just the right word ". . . Home!" he finally said in a forceful whisper as a look of pleased astonishment spread over his face. "Yes . . . Home . . . Home to where I have never been."

As he continued, he spoke more to himself again than to Diakrina. "I don't know how, but this hint of radiance from your face haunts me by whispering truth and beauty have their own Face—a Face I long to see more than life itself. Yet . . . it makes me tremble with fear. Has myth become reality? Is the radiance from your face caused by this fabled Light?"

For a moment the Judge appeared to be completely lost in his own thoughts. "Has this myth always been reality? Could it be even in our ignorance we created the myth of such Light because of a need in us—a void—giving shape to what we hoped could fill it?"

His voice trailed off and the Judge fell silent for a moment. Yet, still no one dared to speak. His eyes narrowed in thought as he placed his chin in his hands. Then sitting back in his chair and looking wide-eyed at Diakrina, he sighed.

"I perceive we are at a fork in the road. A choice must be made. But I cannot make it merely on this premonition of truth, wonderful as it seems. I must have hard facts. Your case will be tried, Madam. And though I confess to a growing and unexplained desire that all you say will be true, do not think it will influence my decisions. Even my desire must be explained."

Diakrina was bewildered. The Judge's countenance changed to one who was all business. It seemed she and her story were going to be put to some kind of trial. Even the people standing all around appeared to settle into some sense of routine as they took their places in chairs outside and behind the railed-in area in front of the Judge's bench. The ease with which this transition in the atmosphere of the Courtroom changed made Diakrina realize this had become suddenly a "business as usually" process.

She wanted to ask questions about what this trial meant, but she was apparently expected to understand. She was being taken in to a process that had been going on before she arrived, and which now continued with her as the object. She was puzzled as to what it all meant. One moment she was falling through the air, the next she was sharing her story and now, she was being told a trial was to commence in which the truthfulness of her story concerning the existence of the Light, and the integrity of she herself, would be examined.

If she seemed somewhat surprised and overwhelmed by it all, no one else did. Evidently the gentleman who had first protested was successful in setting himself up as one who would prosecute against her claims. He asked permission to approach the bench, and when it was given, took several others along and spent some time discussing with the Judge in a voice too low for Diakrina to make out. But soon he returned from the bench and took his place at what later proved to be the designated place for the prosecutor.

Diakrina wanted to ask the Judge if she needed to descend from the place where Strateia held her to some traditional place to make her defense. But there never seemed to be the right moment to inquire. Soon everything took on a certain form, everyone found their place, and then the Judge brought down his gavel.

"This court in now back in session," he articulated in a commanding voice. "We will suspend the former business, seeing as how the former defense's evidence presently lies under the pile of stones and rubble in the center of my Courtroom. Instead, we will consider the testimony of one Miss Diakrina and will try to determine if she indeed speaks the truth."

Then he paused and continued in a lower voice, "If it is determined she is speaking the truth, then it will be necessary for us to continue with proceedings to determine the implications this truth will have for this court. Many of our past verdicts may have to be rescinded."

The prosecutor stood to be recognized. "You may speak," said the Judge after raising one eyebrow at him for the interruption.

Diakrina now took special notice of this man whose voice had earlier caused her a start of undefined recognition. He was tall and slender, almost lanky, with dark eyes and a composed but somewhat drawn face. He moved with surprising grace, which one soon suspected to be acquired grace from some early childhood training—though he wore it like one wears a comfortable shoe. He was, to say the least, smooth and deliberate in his every action.

"Your Honor," he began.

No sooner had he intoned the words than Diakrina felt the same start of recognition but this time she knew where she had heard this voice before. "Sophidzo Logou!" she heard her mind shout. It was almost on her lips when she caught herself by clasping her hand over her mouth. He continued.

"As you are aware, I firmly deny the existence of this Light. I allow some have had an experience, which can be, of course, quite personal and powerful. But as to there being an objective reality to which these experiences can be correlated, this I most emphatically deny. The existence of this Light cannot be proven. And it is suspected it has been mythologized from men's experience of common light.

"As you know, your Honor, the case in process—and so rudely interrupted by Miss Diakrina—had at its center this very issue. So, I request your Honor combine these two cases so as to resolve this matter in a timely way and to bring my case also to a conclusion. And since I am prepared to prosecute against this notion, I request I be allowed to serve as the prosecutor in these immediate proceedings."

This last request struck Diakrina as strange as this had clearly already been determined. However, when the Judge responded, it became clear the prosecutor tended to grandstand and evidently felt he needed to state his case openly to make an impression.

"I believe we have already determined this last point," the Judge said in a tone showing his slight annoyance. "As to combining the two cases, this seems fair to me as it does not delay this immediate concern and will also have a clear application to the former case— which is yet unresolved—when a verdict is reached."

"Then," continued Sophidzo Logou, "if so much is going to be placed in the balances on the testimony of this Miss Diakrina, the prosecution—which intends to show her claims are mere fabrication and the most dangerous kind of delusion—will need every opportunity to examine this witness' claims. I would, therefore, request the court ask this witness to share her testimony in small, progressive sections and I be given the opportunity to cross examine her concerning each detail in her account before she is allowed to proceed to the next."

Diakrina motioned to the Judge for recognition.

"Your honor," she began, "if I am not mistaken, this man is the one I told of meeting in the Sanctuary of Communion. I believe you are," she turned to look at him and fixed her clear eyes on the back of his unturned head, "Sophidzo Logou?"

"I am," He answered, turning toward her. "And I might add, now that I have been addressed, your account of our last meeting was considerably slanted indeed. I have been in that sanctuary much longer than you, and I tell you there is no Light shining from any book."

"And," interrupted Diakrina, "according to you I never survived crossing the Bridge of Trust! Yet, as you can see, I am here."

"Madam, you must understand that I did not exactly say you had not survived," retorted Sophidzo Logou. "I merely pointed out . .

." But he got no farther because the Judge cleared his throat in a way which all knew meant, "Silence!"

"Miss Diakrina," the Judge began, "I must give way to Mr. Sophidzo Logou's request for it is a reasonable way to proceed. Therefore, we will ask you to give your testimony again and we will allow him to cross-examine you concerning each part. I assure you, I will allow no such double talk in these proceedings as you claim to have experienced before. And," he added as an afterthought, "I must ask you to come down here this time and give your testimony among us."

Diakrina was relieved she could allow Strateia to stop holding her in midair. At the Judge's request, Strateia flew forward slowly until she was even with Sophidzo Logou. On the left side, facing the Judge, were tables for the defense to use.

She was still about 10 feet in the air, still in the hands of Strateia, when she heard him whisper to her, "Little One, you need not rehearse it all again. Merely call for the evidence. The Light can vindicate itself. Because it is within you it will heed your call."

Diakrina was not sure exactly what Strateia meant, but she had learned to trust him. Then Strateia whispered again, "Start with the Light entrusted to you," and instantly Diakrina knew how she must proceed.

"Your honor," she said, "I am a witness to the Light I have found . . . or better put . . . has found me. I will call on this Light to display itself and we shall have objective evidence. There is no need for words to represent the reality when the reality will present itself here, now. Words are needed when it is absent. They are stilled in its presence."

When she finished speaking, Strateia slowly descended and placed her softly on the floor. When her feet touched the floor she held her hands to her breast and gave a quick prayer in a low whisper, "Living One, please manifest Your Light through me."

Instantly from deep within her came the swirling rainbow of Light she had received from the Great Book. It was a sphere about seven inches in diameter and it sprayed Light—almost as if it were a liquid—in straight lines into the air around Diakrina.

"This is the Lantern of Logos from the Book of Truth on the Altar of Communion."

Sophidzo Logou, who had taken a seat, jumped back to his feet. "Your Honor, this might be nothing but a cheap trick. I insist this Lantern of Logos must be . . ."

But he got no further. Suddenly, from overhead a soft illumination of intense Light shown over the whole of the Courtroom. Gasps were heard all around and eyes lifted toward the expanding ceiling.

When Diakrina looked up, the beauty of what she saw took her breath away. Through the opening, high above—the one through which she and Strateia had come—came the golden Light. It was, however, not behaving like light normally behaves, but almost like a liquid. I say "almost" because of some obvious differences.

This Light ran through the opening and then adhered to the underneath side of the towering cupola and spread out on its ceiling like an expanding star. It then ran down the slope of the great ceiling toward the outside walls, which were hidden from view by the upper level balconies. Soon the entire ceiling danced with flowing Light heard running like a mighty river of water! You might imagine Light would sound soft and less dense than real water. But Diakrina says this was not the case. It sounded like heavy, super-dense flowing liquid.

In any case, they could hear it filling up the upper balcony and then pouring over the edge of what had to be the top of the solid banister of that level. Soon the sound of a dense Light-falls (a confounding term Diakrina used) could be heard cascading down into and filling up the next balcony. The sound then multiplied as the Light flooded over this second level down to the third.

Diakrina could just see the top of the banister of the fifth level up. Everyone in the Courtroom had their eyes fixed on its top rail, waiting for the Light to pour into view. After what felt like a long time, it happened. Light flowed over the sides onto the level below, at first here and there; but soon in an unbroken golden cascade.

Mouths dropped open in disbelief as everyone could see a glorious river assaulting the fourth level. It became clear it would soon fill each level and then pour onto the floor where the onlookers stood. What would happen then? seemed to be the question on every face.

Every time the flood spilled over the next balcony, the sound of descending Light grew louder. By the time it reached the second level from the floor, an endless thunder of cascading Light drowned all other sounds.

The effect was indeed overwhelming. Diakrina said it was like being in a sealed tunnel with a speeding train bearing down on you. "Yet," she said, "there was no fear, at least for me. It felt as if peace itself was flowing toward me."

The incredible beauty and awe of seeing the cascading Light-falls, pouring one on top of the other, held everyone motionless. "There is no sight like it in this world," she informed me with dancing eyes as she told this part of the story. "It was beautiful beyond expression. Every color of the rainbow, and then some, sparkled from the surging surfaces of the pouring Light."

Soon the Light was thundering down onto the final level above them. When this level filled, it would certainly pour over the banister onto the floor and flood the Courtroom. The Judge was trying to say something, but no one could be heard over the thunderous Light-falls.

Diakrina spotted Sophidzo Logou running in a circle. He appeared to be screaming at the top of his voice, his face disfigured with mad panic. Suddenly, he ran at Diakrina and grabbed her, shouting in her face. Reading his lips, she knew he was shouting, "Stop it! Please, stop it now!" His frantic fear turned to crazed rage, and he shook Diakrina with an unheard scream: "I demand you stop it! Now!" Even with all this, Diakrina could feel nothing but peace.

Without warning, Strateia gripped Sophidzo Logou by the nap of his coat and tossed him like a squealing piglet halfway across the Courtroom. Sophidzo Logou landed against the Courtroom wall, hitting his head, and slumped unconscious to the floor. Just as he did, the Light poured over the banister and roared down upon him like an avalanche, burying him from sight.

When the Light hit the floor as golden liquid, it burst into vibrant unnamed colors and splashed rich liquescent hues in all directions. Light flashed in pulsating prisms of glorious splendor.

At first, some who were nearest the Light tried to get away from it, but it spread across the entire floor more quickly than they could find dry places. When it touched them, they stopped running and stood still, gazing at the floor and walls of pouring Light. Suddenly, the panic left their faces and they knelt down and splashed in the Light like children playing in a pool on a summer day.

A few still fought to keep from being touched by the torrent. Some of those who had been in Sophidzo Logou's company climbed up on top of tables screaming, though no one could hear them. From what Diakrina could lip-read, she was glad no one could hear, as they seemed to be cursing the Light with insane cruelty.

The Light soon flowed over the tabletops. One man, completely mad with fear and anger by this time, looked like a trapped puppy in a flood. When the Light touched his feet and began engulfing his legs, he screamed as if being eaten by acid. Diakrina thought this all quite strange.

By this time, she was standing, up to her waist, in the glorious illumination and could only feel strength and peace and glory flooding every cell of her body. But when she looked closely at those who were frantically and angrily cursing the Light, she could see it was indeed devouring them as if it were acid. Their legs, then torsos, and finally their heads disappeared as the Light dissolved them to nothing.

Yet, at the same time, all those embracing the Light were being transformed into more noble looking versions of themselves. The foolishness disappeared from their eyes. In its place, their countenances glowed with new strength and knowledge, and most of all, trust.

Yes, trust—for their faces now radiated with an absolute absence of suspicion or fear. They glowed with this golden Light, which now flashed from their eyes as gloriously unique colors.

Diakrina then spotted the Judge, standing with his back to the wall where a falling torrent of Light covered him. He seemed to be bathing with the most complete joy she had ever seen anyone embrace; laughing and celebrating with child-like glee.

Soon, the Light covered everyone and everything in the Courtroom. The scene is hard to imagine, for they were all under Light like we would think of being under water.

Their first response was to try to swim in the golden substance, but they could not. This was not because it was too thin or unsubstantial a substance—as I have said, it appeared denser than water—it was rather they were too unsubstantial. It passed through them like they were mere atmosphere in comparison to its density.

When the first level was full to the banister, the roar diminished as one Light-fall ceased. This continued with each level until the noise subsided enough to hear other sounds. Diakrina heard the Judge singing, like an enchanted child, as he breathed deeply of the Light.

Then, every eye was drawn upward toward the ceiling from where the Light had come. With astonished faces, each Light-bathed member of the Court slowly sank to his or her knees.

Following their gaze, Diakrina looked up and she, too, fell to her knees. "I saw the wonderful and terrible face of Light, Himself," she said. "Oh, the glory, wonder and mystery of His beauty. I saw hands with scars on them where they joined the wrist; hands of such beauty, reaching down to touch each of us. We all wept with joy and laughed like delighted children. But most of all we sang, and the Light mixed with our song and made it golden and silvery all at once."

When the scarred hands came to Diakrina, they held the small, swirling globe of Light she had first released into the Courtroom. The right hand gently pressed the sphere of Light into Diakrina's heart. Then she heard a whisper in her right ear:

"DO YOU SEE WHAT A GREAT FLAME CAN BE KINDLED BY A MERE SPARK, LITTLE WARRIOR?"

And then the hand lifted her chin upward and she felt a kiss of approval on her forehead making her flush with joy.

All this wonderful atmosphere continued for some time. Later,

Diakrina came to herself sitting in contented silence. Someone tried to stand up over by the wall where Sophidzo Logou had disappeared. She walked quickly over to him and was amazed to see it was indeed him—but, "Oh, how changed!"

She was still trying to take in this transformation when the Judge walked over to her and put his arm around her shoulders and also began to size up Sophidzo Logou. He broke into a wide smile and chuckled.

He looked at Diakrina and lifted his hand up and down in such a motion in the direction of Sophidzo Logou as if to say, "Look!" Sophidzo Logou looked back at them with a sheepish smile. But in spite of himself his face radiated joy.

Then the Judge, turning toward the rest of the Courtroom, raised his voice and shouted, "Case closed!"

Chapter Twelve

ESCAPE FROM SAPIENT CASTLE

No one who has not personally witnessed what Diakrina experienced in that Courtroom could fully imagine what it was like. Her term for it was, "being pierced by Light."

"Being pierced by Light," had truly changed Diakrina. Until the end of her life she always loved the colors in the rainbow and the beautiful paintings of the sunrise or sunset on the canvas of the sky. She said it took her back to those incredible moments in Sapient Castle. For at every level of her passage through the spirit of Sapient Castle, this Light had been the important element in all happening to her there.

One night as Diakrina sat out on a backyard deck, under an unusually clear sky, in which the stars appeared twice their normal size, she stared up into the celestial patterns with a look of peaceful delight on her face. Those around said nothing. Her gaze drew our attention upward to the sky, as well. Presently she broke the contented silence.

"It is much like the Dome of Reality, you know. If only we had eyes to see it accurately and understand the messages written there, it would speak to us."

She let her wish hang in the air for a moment and then added, "It's only by His Light that we see light. Only the rays of His Light can activate the eyes of our heart to the deeper beauties all around us."

She then related an amazing conversation she had with Sophidzo Logou in which she asked him about his astonishing transformation after the invasion of Light. His answer gave deep insight into their conversations in the Sanctuary. She related briefly his answer to her.

"Diakrina, what has changed is my perception. I have been freed from the lie of self-generated reality. My egocentric obsession had led me to invert reality and imagination. In another sense, I had inverted reality and art. I made philosophy my canvas and my egocentric desires my paint. I painted what I willed to be true, while denying any external reality not fitting my personal preferences. The result was my own imaginary reality took my mind captive while I denied actual reality.

"In the misuse of any art we are substituting pictures of life for life—pictures which can seduce us into self-deception. A picture—static or moving, whether mentally or physically represented—can invert reality. A picture can make the unreal seem real. At the same time, it has the power to make the real seem unreal. It often discredits what is and endorses as true and desirable things which can never actually exist. And these mirages can lure us into desolate places.

"In my misuse of art and imagination on the canvas of egocentric philosophy, I dreamed I was feasting at a banquet while I misused people and pleasures. Yet, always, I awakened starved and empty. I dreamed I was drinking cool, clear water while soaking in some forbidden pleasure, but I always awakened possessed of a raging thirst.

"Nonetheless, I was committed to the view of life and reality I was painting. With every awakening to what was truly real—the real hunger and thirst—I immediately fled back inside my imaginary construct. I refused to allow reality to invalidate my ego-centric-renderings.

"All this allowed me to be 'god' of my own creation. Within my own world, I made the laws or banished them. Or so I supposed.

"For you see, Diakrina," said Sophidzo Logou, "in the misuse of art and imagination as philosophy I weaved a myth concerning myself. I painted myself as healthy, whole and fulfilled. Yet, outside this dream world in which I had imprisoned my mind, I was actually sick, diseased and empty. Despite my pride and imagined self-sufficiency, my real life was increasingly becoming a nightmare.

"But, oh, the irony of it all! This imaginary world I had created did not remain my friend, nor I it's god. It became, instead, my ultimate tormentor. For truth and reality are stubborn things. They ultimately crashed in upon me and collapsed my illusory world. The winds of actuality blew away the fog in which I hid. As the myth-world I had formed fled away, it mocked me with demonic laughter. Outwardly, I tried to maintain my façade, but inwardly I huddled like a helpless child in the empty corner of what remained of my naked self.

"Then the Light invaded. It was, as someone has put it, a severe mercy. It exposed my inner ghetto and, for the first time, I could truly see the filthy corner into which I had painted myself. For the first time I could admit I needed grace: undeserved favor, undeserved help from outside and above myself. I also saw there is an infinite distance which lies between knowledge of God and love of God. Philosophy alone cannot open the door to reality. Love of God does.

"As you well know, Diakrina, the Light is that favor and help I needed. And the Light is not a something, but the ultimate Someone. He is what we need and He is what we are given. I will forever be grateful for His invasion by means of His undeserved love."

Diakrina discovered Sophidzo Logou was a real person who, like her, was traveling through the psychomorphic structure of Sapient Castle. And yet, he served to represent and illuminate the healing and transformation of a real aspect within Diakrina's deepest heart and mind: his transformation was also hers. She was being remade while he, too, was being remade. Their lives served to bring healing to each other within the matrix of Sapient Castle.

Diakrina could only imagine what part she might have represented in Sophidzo Logou's life. She said she hoped it was his inner desire to know the truth, which he kept constantly resisting, yet, ultimately, found by means of the Light.

She learned Sophidzo Logou was not his real name but was, instead, a descriptor of him when she first met him as the prisoner of illusion in the Sanctuary. His true name was Blaise Pascal, and he came to call the invasion of Light his "night of fire."

∞——∞

When the Light came pouring into the Courtroom that day, a significant change occurred in Sapient Castle. A threshold was crossed.

The spirit of the Castle, so to speak, came to life in regard to Diakrina, and perhaps Pascal as well. What Diakrina had experienced as separate levels—the Sanctuary with its Dome of Reality and the Shining Book of Truth and Light, the Library with its capacity for knowledge awakened by the Flame of Truth from the Lantern of Logos upon the Stone of Perception, and now the Courtroom saturated beyond dispute by the presence of the penetrating Light itself—all interpenetrated each other.

The Light, which removed obscurity from the Dome of Reality by means of its Truth, seemed to saturate the Library and Courtroom with the impact of the Great Story at realities center. This great impact now seemed to be working in a reverse direction.

Those in the Courtroom had the sensation of the room—still immersed in the glorious liquid Light—being slowly lifted into the Library above it. The Courtroom and Library remained distinct entities, yet they somehow mingled like two dimensions occupying the same space. The layout of each completed the other. Everything had its place, and the Light from the Stone of Perception dominated every feature of the combined space. The replication of the Dome of Reality filled the conjoined ceiling-copula of both the Library and the Courtroom.

These two rooms—Diakrina sometimes referred to them as the Library of Cognition and the Courtroom of Conscience—overlapped and mingled not only in space, but also in function. For while the Judge was deciding any case in the Courtroom, the faculty from the Library would surround him with many ancient books in their hands offering insights from these books informing and guiding the decisions of the Court.

The Judge also underwent a transformation similar to that of Meletao. When trying a case, the Judge and his bench would transmute into something like a Priest standing behind a great pulpit, and when he delivered his verdicts, it was always as this Priest.

When the Judge—now as Priest—stood to render a verdict, Meletao would take his place as Prince in the Chair of Focus facing the Stone. Together the Priest and Prince would declare the verdict in unison. When the verdict was true and accurate, the voice of the Stone would rumble a thundering, "So it is! Amen!"

At such moments something wonderful and very difficult to describe would take place. The Library and Courtroom—still distinct, yet intermingled—together with the blazing Stone and the resplendent chandelier, the stain-glassed windows, the rows of radiant books, the black marble columns, the oak table, the Courtroom furnishing, and all the inhabits of both great rooms—all would be shaken loose from unseen tethers and be pulled up into the Sanctuary above them.

The Sanctuary, however, was now much transformed from when Diakrina first saw it. No corner of it was dark. All was ablaze with dancing, golden Light from the Shining Book, splashing a rainbow of color off every facet of every object, and even the air itself.

Above it all, the Dome of Reality stretched from the north end of the Sanctuary across the expanse all the way to the south, covering the massive rows of seats, the great Chasm, the Bridge of Trust and the platform with its Shining Book.

This platform, you will remember, rested on the roof of the Great Portico. When the Library and Courtroom were pulled up into the Sanctuary, the two Porticos would rise with them—not displacing, but joining the platform and the Shining Book—and fill the space on the platform side of the Bridge of Trust. Rich foliage and fruits of every imaginable description blossomed within the crystal columns of both Porticos, and the aquamarine floor of the Great Portico mingled with the crimson floor of the Lesser Portico and became a swirling, living surface.

Together, in those precious moments, all the spirit levels of Sapient Castle would mingle with glistening splendor in this hallowed place of Communion. The Great Sanctuary seemed to swell beyond the confines of any indoor space, giving one the feeling of being lifted out into a vast living expanse full of Light and Life, where living creatures teemed with joy and plants grew at time-lapse speed.

When the Great Portico rose to join the Sanctuary, its grandest column—the one of indescribable clarity and clearness—dominated the area of the platform which held the Book of Truth and Light and the kneeling altar. The Book generated the column, giving it Life and Light. Anyone who approached the Book of Truth to kneel at the altar would pass through the surface of the column and enter its very substance.

Somehow Diakrina knew—though she never witnessed it—if anyone came with any mindset other than humbly seeking illumination from the Shining Book of Truth, they would not be able to pass in or get near the Book. Only those who came honestly seeking in teachable humility could pass in and discover its Light. This perhaps explains why some could look directly toward the Shining Book and claim not to see it at all, or claim it was merely an ordinary book.

Diakrina stared in wide-eyed amazement at all this, basking in the Light and the great sense of peace and joy filling the spirit of Sapient Castle. After some time—how long she could not tell— another strange sight unfolded before her. The Bridge of Trust, which was beyond and behind the Stone of Perception, began to expand and transform as if it were a living thing growing at accelerated speeds. Within just a few minutes, the narrow Bridge of Trust morphed into the enormous Tree Bridge, which lay across the great Chasm between the Garden and the Severed Lands. Diakrina watched as many people crossed over the Tree Bridge and knelt before the Book of Truth and Light.

As I've mentioned before, Diakrina would often lose her sense of time on this side of the Door of the Rose. At certain points in her adventures, time seemed to mean nothing at all. This was certainly true of her experience in the Sanctuary when the various spirit levels of Sapient Castle were healed of their severed condition and united into a wondrous whole. She never could place any sense of time constraints on her encounters there.

"We were lifted into a place beyond time," she said, trying to describe it. "Yet, nothing of time was left behind. It was simply no longer the small, narrow, linear hallway it had always seemed to be before. All was a limitless universe of a profoundly ordered and sequenced Now."

Suddenly, while Diakrina was only beginning to take in all happening around her, Strateia abruptly interrupted her wonder. "We must go, Little One. You have done well. The spirit of Sapient Castle is healed and communion is restored. The Light of the Lantern of Logos now burns on the Stone of Perception, and it is living in you. You can now complete your quest. But we must go, now. Time is short."

Diakrina's face pled with him for a bit more time to stay and experience the glories all around her, and she turned to look again at the unfolding, living drama. Suddenly the whole castle began to shake. Strateia looked upward for direction. Immediately his countenance changed to that of the warrior he was. He forcefully took hold of Diakrina's shoulders and turned her around toward him. Stern resolve registered in both his face and his voice.

"We cannot delay any longer! We must leave the Castle immediately! Anomos and his forces know we are here. They are attacking the castle with huge beast to try and collapse its walls. They have cut off every avenue of escape by now, but one. And we must use it before he can stop us." Then he added, "Make sure you have your shield and your sword in place. Be sure to secure the Atheos over your shoulder and under the shield and secure the shining page within your garment. The battle to regain the Tree Bridge begins now."

Strateia's urgency startled Diakrina back to full awareness of her quest. In the middle of all this indescribable drama of Light, she became instantly aware of the settling pressure of a cold dark presence.

"Yes, Strateia . . . yes, you are right," Diakrina blurted out as she embraced the force of his resolve. She quickly checked to make sure her sword, shield, crystal container and shining page were all secure.

"Follow me, Diakrina. And hurry!"

At that very moment the whole Castle shuddered as if struck by something massive; like an earthquake, but the source was not from beneath. Something gigantic had slammed into an outer wall of the

Castle. Diakrina felt the assault almost as if it had rattled some aspect of her own soul. The shudder of the Castle did not just go through her, it came from within her!

"Diakrina, it has begun in earnest!" shouted Strateia. "There is no time left. Follow me as fast as your legs can carry you." And with that he ran in the direction of the Porticos, and Diakrina scurried after him.

They ran past the Stone of Perception and toward the Tree Bridge, which had now replaced the narrow Bridge of Trust and lay across the great Chasm. Diakrina knew they were about to traverse more fully back again into the Severed Lands and leave this wondrous place behind.

When they reached the Tree Bridge, Strateia stopped to let Diakrina catch up. Then, stepping behind her, he quickly grabbed her by the belt and hoisting her up some 20 feet, placing her on the topside of the massive, felled tree. The moment her feet touched the top of the tree, he turned her loose and ran out over the Chasm toward the center of the Tree Bridge.

The gaping Chasm rushed up at Diakrina and made her suddenly dizzy. Even the enormous tree felt narrow, like a ribbon stretched across a canyon. She had the sensation of teetering on a tightrope as she hurried to follow Strateia.

As they passed along the top of the Tree Bridge, all the features of Sapient Castle faded, along with all the splendors of the Sanctuary. The Porticos, the columns, the Shining Book, the Library and Courtroom and their inhabitants . . . all melted away, leaving a dark, rolling sky, full of angry clouds carried on cold, damp winds. The jagged features of the Chasm walls leered at Diakrina, as the cold, misty wind bellowed a long, despondent howl. A rugged landscape materialized all around them. It seemed to be echoing omens of approaching evil. It took all the nerve Diakrina could muster to continue moving while this sinister world materialized and engulfed them.

But Strateia's urgent pace gave her no time to debate her fears. He continued at a giant's stride to the middle of the great Chasm, where he stopped and waited for Diakrina, who was running to join him.

"You must jump," Strateia shouted over the howl of the wind.

"I must what?"

"You must jump. It is the only way."

Diakrina took one look at the bottomless depth of the Chasm and stuttered in shock, "You are surely kidding me!"

"I am not!"

One more look at the Chasm and Diakrina lost it. "You are a master of the air, Strateia. Why should I jump? Can you not carry me to wherever it is we have to go?"

"Not we . . . you. I cannot enter the Chasm, Diakrina. It is the Chasm of Death, with no bottom which any created being can reach. It is a realm I am not able to enter or return from. It is forbidden to me."

"But what about me? If you can't enter it and return, how do you expect me to do so?"

Strateia spoke gently, yet his words penetrated Diakrina's understanding even through the howling winds around her.

"Remember, Diakrina, this is also the Bridge of Trust. Recall how you were never more secure than when you were on it. This Chasm can no longer threaten you, because the Living One has entered it and returned.

"He, who could not die, became one of you, taking on your mortality so He could taste death for you. This was so He could enter this Chasm in your stead, plumbing its depths and conquering it. The uncreated Creator took to Himself a created human nature. He became the Creator-creature who can carry the whole of creation within His uncreated Life while also being a creature.

"By your union with Him, Diakrina, not only has He conquered this Chasm, but you also, and all those of your entire race who entrust themselves to Him, have ascended with Him in conquest. He is the new and last Adam. All who are reborn through Him gain His power over this Chasm. By His descent into it, He embraced Adam's fall. His ascent back out from it has undone the curse. He put death to death by drowning it in His deathless, indestructible Life.

"Diakrina, this is the profound truth about your race. You are the only created beings in all creation who have conquered death and returned to life: first in the Person of the Living One—who is both uncreated and created—then in all of your kind who trust themselves into Him. Mankind is the weapon of weakness by which evil is being defeated. Those of you who trust the Living One are in covenant with Him. You are in Him, and He is in you. He made all that was yours, His, so He could abolish it. And He made all that is His, yours, so death is abolished. He has already taken you through the depths of this Chasm and brought you out the other side. In Him, you have already overcome the great Chasm!

"The Living One has blasted a breach through its darkness. It will never close as long as He offers His mercy to your world. It is through this breach you must now pass."

"Pass to where, Strateia?" shouted Diakrina against the howling wind.

"This breach of Light will take you back to the nine steps that led you into Thanatos' realm. There you must move quickly back through the nine-barriers of the stairway into Nekus—enacting a resurrection—and make your way to the Altar at the canyon mouth where you left the torch that is now your shield. I will meet you there to guide you to Lord Mazzaroth, whose help we will desperately need before this quest is finished."

"Strateia, I'm to go back into the realms of Thanatos with the Atheos? That doesn't make any sense! That is where Anomos wants it," she shouted. "It is in Nekus where he can keep it under his control. Why would we take it back into Nekus after going to so much trouble to get it out of there?"

"Because, Anomos is looking for you in every place in the Severed Lands but there!" shouted Strateia. "It is the one place he would never expect you to go. Besides," added Strateia, "he has always been rather blind to any form of resurrection.

You going back through the nine-walled stairs will be a path of resurrection from the realms of Thanatos. It is something he refuses to look at. He hates that place because it testifies to his defeat!"

"But Strateia, each of those nine-walls barred me from going back. They only allowed me to move toward Thanatos, not away from him. Moving back through is beyond my power."

"True. But you are not going in your own power. You now carry the Lantern of Logos. His Light has already blasted through those walls. You will find the walls no match for the Light now possessing you, and therefore, you now possess. Your possession of this Light is why we had to come to the Castle. Your possession of this Light will be your key to unlock the nine barriers of death."

The thought of jumping—deliberately JUMPING—into the Chasm and returning to the realms of Thanatos in Nekus Canyon seemed like insanity to Diakrina. Then something occurred to her.

"Isn't this the Tree Bridge we are trying to get to? If we are here already, isn't that enough? Why do I need to go anywhere?"

"In one true sense, you are already here, yes, but only in this realm. You must regain the Tree Bridge in the realm where the Immortal Fruit must be taken back across into the Garden. The fact you are here will make it possible for you to be there. The Tree Bridge invades every realm of reality. It is always the same: a finished, unconquerable work of the Living One. But this is not the time and place where you must cross."

Diakrina's head was spinning and her heart pounding. All of Strateia's words did not quell the panic rising up inside her at the thoughts of leaping into the dark, unfathomable depths of the Chasm. A shiver began down deep in her gut and rose up through her throat until she was visibly trembling all over and nearly too weak to stand. The cold howling of the wind didn't help!

She felt truly pathetic. She wanted to be courageous and strong. With all she had been through, surely she should be more courageous than this by now, she thought. Yet, here she was, nearly on the brink of collapsing under a wave of terror—a terror coiling itself around her insides and seeming to feed on an invisible root reaching down into the bottomless depths of the Chasm, itself.

Strateia went into action. Without warning He snatched Diakrina up and shot straight toward the sky, taking her breath away.

Just as suddenly they stopped in midair. As Diakrina's wits

cleared slightly, she realized she had felt something like a clinging vine being pulled out of her insides. Strateia had literally dragged her away from an invisible vine or root—or whatever it was—gripping her. She had felt it stretch taunt and finally snap loose as he whisked her into the air. Her whole body pulled free from its hold, at the last moment, before Strateia stopped.

Strateia seemed to know her thoughts. "That was no vine, Diakrina. You were being invaded by the squid-like tentacles of the darkness from the Chasm, seeking to pull the Lantern of Logos out of you. And it would have if I had not acted. Fear is always Anomos' calling card and the second of his deadly weapons."

Diakrina had now caught her breath. Knowing the answer, she asked it anyway: "And what is his first weapon?"

"Lies, Diakrina. Always lies! And the lies are what generate the unfounded, improper fears, he was intending to use to overwhelm you. Diakrina, you must choose to believe the truth no matter how you feel, or you will not be able to confront him.

"When you lose sight of the truth, it can make you become passively open to his lies. That is when the tentacles of fear slither quickly behind these lies to intwine themselves around your spirit and enslave you Those are the moments when you must embrace the truth by faith—by trusting what the Living One has told you no matter how you feel."

Diakrina realized how close she had come to failing in her quest just moments before.

"You have the Light, Diakrina. But it will do you no good—it cannot manifest through you—unless your will is actively trusting. You must consciously and intentionally trust Him. He continually empowers you to trust Him, but He refuses to by-pass your will: He channels His power through your will not around it."

Then as if quoting, he added, "It is the Living One who works in you. His work enables you to will and to act according to His purpose for you. He insists on working through your will, not against it. You must willingly choose to trust Him above all other thoughts, feelings or rationalizations trying to supplant His Reality. Will you do this,

Diakrina?"

Diakrina closed her eyes and took a deep breath. Then, after holding it for only a moment, with all the resolve she could find—and she was shocked how much she found—she answered, "I will!" Then reconsidering, she paused and shouted, with a resolve beyond what she thought she was capable, "I DO!"

"Good! We have only a moment. Reach inside, Diakrina, and take hold of the Lantern of Logos within you. Grip it in your left hand. Then unsheathe your sword into your right hand and hold out both ahead of you."

Diakrina reached her left hand up to her heart and instantly it was filled with the swirling rainbow of Light. She gripped the Light as hard as she could and found it to be tangibly firm even though it was still swirling in constant motion. Reaching with her right hand for her sword, she pulled it from its sheath with resolve. Then taking another deep breath, she took one last look at Strateia's face for courage and said, "I'm ready."

"Hold the Lantern and the sword straight up above your head with both hands," said Strateia with a clear, silver tone of command in his voice. Diakrina obeyed. Before she knew what had happened, Strateia had turned her upside down, and with a single hand threw her like a spear straight at the Tree Bridge far below.

As he threw her he shouted, "Keep the Lantern and sword firmly before you, Diakrina!"

As he released her, the swirling Light from her left hand expanded outward and completely engulfed her in its sphere. Yet it remained, as well, a swirling sphere of Light in her hand.

The Tree Bridge raced at her with incredible speed. She barely had time to consider what would happen when she collided with it. Besides, she trusted Strateia, and he had obviously aimed her directly at the Bridge's center. She couldn't help, however, closing her eyes and flinching as the impact approached.

But no impact came! Instead, she passed right through the Tree Bridge and into a corridor of Light—that was her best description of it—which streamed out ahead of her down into the Great Chasm.

Holding tightly to the Lantern and her sword, she opened her eyes wide and looked deep into the stream of Light before her.

She was plummeting at a speed constantly accelerating; a speed soon reaching the limits of her endurance. She felt she was being pushed to the speed of the Light, itself. This acceleration continued for several minutes until she felt she could hardly survive another moment. Just when she was sure she would be torn to pieces by the velocity, the acceleration gave way to the most beautiful calm and quiet as another dimension—another reality—materialized around her.

She appeared to be speeding through some densely filled portion of the universe. Stars and planets soared by at unimaginable speeds. She could only see them from a distance. This was because as she passed them, they would go by too quickly to be observed. The Light corridor stretched out before her like an illuminated tunnel through this universe. She could see down it like a tunnel, and also through its walls like a clear glass tube. The tunnel continued downward, but began arching to her right.

Then she saw Him. There, moving ahead of her, at what had to be many times the speed of Light, stood the most glorious Man she had ever seen. He was standing in the Light corridor looking back at her with a smile filling her with joy and courage.

He looked her straight in the eyes over the distance still separating them. His face then broke out in an even broader grin—a smile of utter delight—as He shook His head in a kind of playful expression of disbelief, as if to say, "Look at you. Who would have believed you would be trusting Me like this?"

He then turned, and beckoning with his hand, walked down the corridor and disappeared as if he had stepped into a cloud of pure Light. There, in the corridor before her, appeared crimson footprints exactly like those she had followed through Nekus Canyon.

Diakrina's heart pulled her in the direction of the footprints, as if to say, "Come quickly, perhaps I can catch up to Him!"

How she longed to do just that! But she was still falling, not walking, possibly at something greater than the speed of Light, and was unable to control her pace. She was content to know He was leading her.

Again, Diakrina could not tell how long she traveled through the Light corridor. It may have been only moments, or perhaps years. It did not matter, for it was a joyful journey. She gleefully chased the Source of the footprints and occasionally drew close enough to see a heel lifting from the last footprint made.

Then she heard His voice: "DIAKRINA, NEKUS CANYON AND THE FALLS ARE JUST AHEAD. WHEN YOUR FEET HIT THE STONE AT THE TOP OF THE STAIRS OF THANATOS, YOU MUST HAVE ALREADY JOINED THE LANTERN AND YOUR SWORD HANDLE TOGETHER IN BOTH YOUR HANDS SO THE HANDLE IS EMBEDDED IN THE LANTERN'S SWIRLING LIGHT. DO IT NOW."

Diakrina took the Lantern in her left and the sword handle in her right and pushed them together between her two hands. The handle of the sword sank into the sphere of swirling Light, as did her hands. The crimson blade of the sword glowed brightly and a halo of rainbow Light surrounded the blade.

You could still see the crimson light of the sword continue to pulse brightly within this halo. However, the rainbow-colored halo spun around and around until the blade was in a swirling tube of Light looking like a tornado with a sword blade at its center. The Light swirled faster and faster.

Diakrina heard a low rumbling like a whirlwind, but the pitch continued to rise with the swirling speed until it sounded, for a moment, more like a screaming whistle, and finally the pitch exceeded her ability to hear it at all. The Light raced around the sword so fast it no longer appeared to move but, rather, looked like a solid, clear tube of crystal with constantly pulsing colors flashing from the sword's tip.

Then she heard Him speak again: "BY THE LIGHT OF THE LANTERN POURING THROUGH YOUR SWORD YOU SHALL BE ABLE TO PIERCE THROUGH THE NINE BARRIERS OF THANATOS. FOLLOW MY FOOTPRINTS NO MATTER WHERE THEY LEAD, DO NOT TURN TO THE LEFT OR TO THE RIGHT NO MATTER WHICH DIRECTION MY FOOTPRINTS GO. FOLLOW NO MATTER WHAT TRIES TO HINDER YOU.

TRUST ME AND I WILL LEAD YOU BEYOND THANATOS' POWER."

He paused briefly, as though to collect her full attention. Then He said: "REMEMBER: NEITHER TO THE LEFT NOR TO THE RIGHT. FOLLOW MY FOOTSTEPS AT ALL COST! EVEN AT WHAT MAY SEEM LIKE THE COST OF YOUR LIFE!"

When the last word, "LIFE" was spoken, Diakrina felt a powerful decelerating force, like being in an airplane landed, and the jet thrust is reversed to stop the plane quickly. However, if you have experienced this, Diakrina says you should try to imagine it at 100 times the force.

"I have no idea how this decelerating force did not tear me apart," she said. "The sphere of Light around me—denser than water—must have exerted some kind of equal and opposite force keeping my body from disintegrating. But even then, the pressure was tremendous."

As Diakrina's fall decelerated, the universe through which she has been racing disappeared. Only the corridor of Light remained, surrounded now by darkness.

Slowly, Diakrina's deceleration brought her into sync with a different dimension. Little by little it became visible, like something coming into view that had been, at first, out of focus. Below her— far below her—Diakrina recognized the Falls of Nekus. Though everything beyond the sphere of Light was terribly dark, the sphere radiated enough illumination for her to identify the landscape.

The great Chasm gaped menacingly below her, with the second great falls plunging into it. The water poured silently down into a bottomless gorge and disappeared into inky blackness far beyond sight.

Farther back and above this, Diakrina could see the first falls. From it, gigantic thundering sounds echoed toward her. The corridor of Light stretched to the far side of the first falls, toward its very top, to where the courtyard and temple of Thanatos sat on the ledge against the eastern side of the canyon. From there the staircase, with the nine-barriers, ascended. Diakrina was being ushered back to the very spot from which she had taken her headlong plunge into the falls to escape Thanatos.

It occurred to Diakrina she would prefer to land on her feet instead of her head, and she tried to right herself, turning her feet toward the approaching ledge. She managed to do this just in time.

As her feet came over the edge of the ledge, about five feet up from its surface, the corridor of Light disappeared and Diakrina dropped straight down onto the cold, damp rocky floor of Nekus. As the Light vanished and she fell onto the ledge, His unmistakable voice whispered in her ear, "LOOK IMMEDIATELY FOR MY FOOTPRINTS! DANGER IS ON YOU!"

END OF
BOOK TWO

APPENDIX

Chapter Three B

THE TERRIBLE FREEDOM

As Diakrina turned to follow Strateia she was still boiling over with questions. "Strateia, I now understand love is supreme and rules the whole purpose of the Living One's creation. But what will bring mankind back into His love?"

"Trust, Little One," answered Strateia, turning and pausing once more. "And the Living One will make that possible—has made it possible in your time—by what He will do for your race. But because you are infected with the pride of Anomos, you must accept the Living One's help to reject the life of independence—a fool's dream anyway—and come back to full dependence on Him.

"He exemplified humility for you and put it on full display when He walked among you. Humility is full awareness of your total dependence upon God and your proper interdependence with others. Pride is a spirit seeking an impossible independence. Humility is the sanity to admit your need; first for the Living One and then, others.

"The supreme choice, which determines the continuance of the power of choice itself, is whether we will or will not love and trust the Eternal One. If we will not love and trust, He cannot help us, for we embrace death when we cut ourselves off from Him, who alone is the Source of Life. This death—separation from Him Who is Life—gives birth to corruption, or in your language, dying or aging. And dying, if allowed to run its full course, completes the separation to the point of no return."

"Do you mean if we will not choose to depend on the Living One, we lose the power to choose?"

"Yes, by increasing degrees. When one is separated from direct interaction with the Living One, one is dead to—separated from—the infinite possibilities and alternatives of His creativity. There is increasingly less to choose as you lose perception even of the alternatives still existing. From ignorance either of their existence or of their proper character, one misses possibility after glorious possibility."

Diakrina noticed how Strateia had changed from "we" to "you" in his answer. She later understood this was because his answer could not apply to himself, as he was not among those who had left the Great Dance.

"Is there ever a point where the power to choose becomes impossible?"

"Yes. If the severed branch is not grafted back into the tree, it will lose its very essence. And it is the same with one who is severed from Life. And a person without the power to choose is less than they were created to be. They have sunk below the level of true humanity."

"Do you mean one would cease to exist?"

"No, Little One. As I have said before, a moral being cannot cease to exist as you mean. But it can lose its ability to exercise the freedoms of its moral nature. Once all contact is lost between a person and the Living One, all possibility of freedom is lost. There are no real choices outside of Him."

"How is all contact lost?" asked Diakrina with concern.

"By the choices which embrace death."

Diakrina's mind raced. Then suddenly like a mental sunrise she saw it. "Death is separation from Him. When we left the Great Dance, we became dead in relation to the Living One. Death is a terrible freedom! It is freedom from Him. And to be free from Him is to be free from life, beauty, glory, splendor and ... freedom itself."

The responsibility of freedom had just laid its hand firmly on Diakrina's heart by means of a burst of sudden insight. "Freedom can give life or death. It can even kill itself—commit liberty suicide," she heard herself say in a whisper. "Not all freedom is good!"

"Your eyes grow very clear, Little One. But you must know freedom is neither good nor bad. Though it makes the moral possible, it is itself amoral—neutral. It is the frame only. The moral personality is the picture. What one does with freedom is either good or bad—tends to life or death.

"But there is one thing more you should understand. When you left the Great Dance, you would have been hopelessly and forever dead in relation to the Living One—just like Anomos—if it had not been for the other door which human nature possesses."

"What other door, Strateia?"

"The door of your material nature. It is an obscure and difficult door at best, but the Living One was determined to use it to reverse your straying from the Great Dance. Since your material nature is dependent on the immaterial spiritual nature for its existence, and your spiritual nature is dead in relation to the Living One and receives no renewal, your spiritual nature cannot keep your material nature—your body—alive for long. Thus, you begin moving toward physical death—the separation of your spirit from your body—the moment you are born.

"But like a cut branch, which can be grafted back in before it reaches a certain point of decay, your physical nature is a temporary window through which the Living One can reach your spirit. He uses that window as an opportunity to offer you a choice—a choice to submit to His cure and be brought back into the Great Dance."

"Are you saying," interrupted Diakrina, "we sons and daughters of Adam could see and hear the spiritual dimension before we left the Great Dance?"

"Of course. You could not have danced in it unless you could both see and hear."

"Then our present condition of not being able to perceive the deeper reality is . . . abnormal?"

"Yes, that is true. However, although you cannot perceive spiritual reality directly, you can still perceive the influence it has on material reality."

"You mean the activities of the spiritual dimension can sometimes be seen affecting the physical?"

Strateia gave a faint smile. "Little One, does the movement of your clothes manifest the reality of your body?"

Diakrina got the point. "You mean, then, life comes from the spiritual realm and the spiritual organizes and wears the physical much like a garment?"

"Something like that and yet, different from that. You see, the physical is more than a mere garment. It is able to mingle with spiritual reality. It would be much like your clothes becoming a living part of you. The spiritual is the foundation—the deeper reality, as you called it. The physical, however, can not only be acted upon by the spiritual, but can also be the channel through which one spirit can interact with another spirit, if both are clothed in the physical. And this is particularly important if a living spirit wishes to interact with a dead (severed) spirit."

"Then you are saying those of us dead to the Great Dance could only see those alive to the Great Dance if they were clothed in the physical?"

"Yes, for any clear perception. More importantly, you could only see the Eternal One if He were willing to clothe Himself in the material. In other words, He must enter through the side door, or you might say, He must show you Himself through the distorted glass of a physical body. It is a somewhat filtered revelation of Himself, but it became a necessary one."

Diakrina's heart was beating fast with suspense. "So, this is what the Living One did! He clothed Himself in a physical body to reach us!"

"Yes, that is part of the truth. But the whole is greater. He is not just clothed in human flesh; He actually became a man while remaining Himself without any loss. He is the God/Man. And even when He conquered death by walking out from among the dead, He kept His humanity and glorified it. He, the Son, will be a glorified human forever."

"Wow!" is all Diakrina could manage to utter as her mind was captivated by such a thought.

Strateia then turned again and began walking. "Come, Diakrina. We must continue to the south end of the Castle."

Diakrina fell in behind Strateia but still had a question she felt she must ask before this conversation came to an end.

"One thing puzzles me, Strateia. Anomos, like those he led in the dance of death, is severed from Life, too. Why is he not deformed and diminished like the others? Is he somehow different from the others? He even has a kind of strange beauty about him."

Strateia stopped at the edge of the circle and turned toward Diakrina. Then he stared off into the darkness beyond as though remembering a scene from the distant past.

"No, Little One, he is not different. He is the most deformed of all." Strateia paused and allowed the bewilderment on Diakrina's face to peak.

"You see, Diakrina, if you could have seen him before he chose to dance the dance of death, you would now shriek with horror at the contrast. He had been given splendid ability to reflect the beauty of the Eternal One. Of all the created beings, he had become most like the Creator. His beauty was dazzling even in the City. His music, beautiful beyond description, immersed and drenched us in the Glory of the Eternal. But when he forgot the Source and became enamored with himself, then he originated the dance of insanity and death."

"So," interjected Diakrina slowly, obviously still pondering this insight, "one must know the starting point before you can determined the degree of loss and deformity."

"That is truth, Little One. Yet there is another. You must also know the motive behind the use of what still remains. Anomos uses his 'beauty' to deceive and destroy. His appearance is like a gift of flowers, but he is a deadly serpent hidden in the bouquet—more dangerous and deadly because unseen and hidden within the alluring. In this he stoops to the lowest level in deformity, making the deadly appear pleasing and harmless: a complete reprobation."

"Re-pro-bation?" repeated Diakrina.

"It means the reversal of what was once right and true. It leads to the belief or appearance that things are the opposite of their real character. In other words, to call bitter, sweet, and darkness light; to teach nonsense as truth, and ridicule truth as nonsense; to substitute lust for love, the sensual for the beautiful, the unnatural for the natural, the philosophical for the personal, and the personal for the philosophical."

"Then," reasoned Diakrina, "reprobation is the ultimate manifestation of the rebellion of Anomos. Even after he separates a thing from the Living One he will not use it according to its created character. Is it because to do so would remind him of the Creator?"

"Your eyes are indeed growing clearer, Little One. Anomos is still trying to create a new reality. But since he is a created being, locked within the reality created by the Eternal One, his only method is the principle of opposition—reprobation.

"But there is one truth more to be understood as to why he does what he does. Anomos is trying to be independent. He chases the fantasy of an impossible aseity—a self-generated existence. In this sense, he wants to be like the Eternal One. So, he is caught between the need to be both totally different from the Eternal One, because he cannot be a similar, and yet totally like the Eternal One to reach his goal. He must rebel in order to be different, while at the same time he must counterfeit in order to appear to be like Him.

"This is all, of course, an obvious impossibility. It drives him in his reprobation to go the final step. He not only substitutes the bitter for the sweet, but he also tries to make the bitter seem sweet while remaining bitter. By this he feels he is like the Eternal One because he has made it appear the same. Yet he imagines himself independent from the Living One because, it is in essence, totally different."

"But how could he do that—make the bitter seem sweet while still being bitter?" asked Diakrina.

"He can only do this by corrupting the perceiver as well as the thing perceived. He must spread his reprobation to those who would taste the bitter. They must be altered to consider the bitter to be sweet even while it remains, in itself, bitter."

"But how does he do that?" repeated Diakrina, realizing the application would have everything to do with being able to resist Anomos and his schemes.

"He must sear their moral taste buds—destroy their proper sensibility, or cognizance, if you please. To do this, he gains a small foothold from which he applies pressure, getting them to surrender greater and greater control to him.

"For example, in your world the foothold of peer pressure may lure someone into using tobacco, even though they, at first, recoil against the coughing, nausea and general unpleasantness of the experience. Yet, as they acclimate to it, an obsessive need is created by the poisonous in the tobacco. Once the craving has its hold, they will build a destructive tolerance for it and will even tell you they enjoy it."

The glow in the flowers around them was fading slightly and everything already appeared less vibrant. "Strateia, is this circle of life going to stay here?"

"Not unless we stay here and defend it against the re-invasion of the Dead Swamp. But this is not a place of lasting strategic importance. We are to go on to the Castle."

"Then there is nothing we can do to keep the Dead Swamp out?"

"Not for now, Diakrina. But what we are called to do will ultimately release everything from the grip of death, including this place. Your efforts are better put into controlling a cause than into defending against a consequence."

Diakrina studied this thought for a moment and then asked, "But how do you know the difference?"

"The important things directly impact our Prime Directive in obeying the Living One's commands. Less important things may have momentary benefit, but they only incidentally relate to the Prime Directive.

"Such as this place here: it was valuable to conquer to give us the protection we needed for this moment. It incidentally relates to the Prime Directive through us. But it is not such a place as will continue to help us protect or conquer any other place. So, for now, we serve this place best by giving our efforts to the destruction of death. For, then, there will be no Dead Swamp to re-invade."

With that Strateia turned and walked again toward the Castle and motioned for Diakrina to follow.

∞———————————————————————∞

Return to **Chapter Four**

∞———————————————————————∞

Chapter Seven B

THE DANCE OF LIFE

Then a baby cried.

[The following is a continuation of the story Diakrina witnessed as it unfolded on the Dome of Truth while she knelt before the Shining Book.]

"What happened next," she said, "I now know to be a matter of history, as was everything else I had seen. But, nonetheless, I will tell it to you as I saw it illuminated on the Dome."

She watched this child, with immensity shining from His face, begin to grow. As He did, He danced the patterns that had been given through the covenant better and more beautifully than anyone had ever danced them (and well He could, for He had created the Dance, and the patterns were expressions of His own nature).

When He was fully grown, He stepped into the center of the covenant children and raised His voice. What came out was Speaking Music. Gloriously, He proclaimed the long-awaited day had arrived. Then with joyous grace, He danced the patterns as He had given them long ago, but with one wonderful difference: He now filled in many of the details which He formerly left out for simplicity. They had had centuries to learn the basic steps. Now the time had come to fill in the true intended content and beauty of the Dance.

Then, raising His voice, Speaking Music poured forth in a Song of Healing. Great crowds of those sick in heart and body, who could not dance the patterns because of their wounds, came from everywhere to be healed. And healed they were.

Soon many were leaping for joy and dancing with intense love the old patterns, which were now poured full with the beauty and meaning of the Living One's Song of Healing. Any who would willingly look could clearly see that the old patterns were indeed designed to hold this wonderful Song and its steps, which was now being revealed through the Living One's own example. You could see the former patterns were like well-constructed molds filled perfectly by the Song of Healing and the steps of joy the Song caused.

But among the leaders were those who mixed the patterns with the steps of Anomos. Secretly—so they supposed—in their hearts, they danced with Anomos. These leaders were out of step with the true patterns of the Dance they had been taught long ago. They mimicked Anomos, while claiming loudly they alone danced the true Dance.

They demanded everyone to follow them and forsake the instruction and Song of the Living One. Secretly, they were afraid they could not dance the new steps (though none ever failed who truly tried, for the Song would dance through them) and were fearful of losing what they considered their place of leadership in the Dance.

So they slandered the Song of the Living One. Some at first even tried to refute Him, but they only contradicted themselves when they tried. They were no match for the Song of Healing. When they came under its sound, it whispered to them that they, too, were in need of its healing touch; that they were no healthier than any of the others.

This their pride could not endure. So they slandered more and more the Living One and the Song of Healing which flowed from His Speaking Music. Yet, still greater numbers gathered around and danced in joy and freedom the magnificent new steps, which filled-in but did not replace the former patterns.

Soon even the simplest of those who danced to the Song of Healing danced more beautifully than any who followed the old, incomplete patterns. This made the leaders particularly jealous. They decided their cause was lost unless they could stop the Song (though if they had obeyed the Song of Healing, they would have found a better cause). They determined in order to do this they must silence the One from whom the Speaking Music came.

As the leaders laid their secret, murderous plans, the Living One gathered His joyous followers around Him and told them all about the leaders' plans and what they would do to Him. For though no one else recognized him, Anomos, in religious disguise, was seen often among these leaders. The Living One knew him well and also knew well his business with them.

Yet, the Living One's followers, even His closest friends whom He had entrusted with the Dance of Life, did not or would not believe it. He told them the leaders' evil plans were laid and that He Himself had a high reason for yielding to these plans. He had power to dance a single pattern that would trample them all under forever, but this He refused to do.

Instead He sang a dark, yet promising Song of how their treachery would be used to display a hidden pattern in the Dance of Life. This was to be the new theme around which all the rest of the Dance would gather. All in the Dance of Life would embrace this glorious New Creation when it was revealed by His death, and from it would come the Dance of Life with a power to bring healing to any in the bloody mob who would respond to the Song of Healing.

And just as He had said, they came. In the hour of darkness, when they danced most boldly the evil steps of Anomos, they came and gathered around Him, dancing their patterns of death.

Even now they were afraid of Him and His Song. They tried to slander Him but only trampled each other in their false patterns. So, finally, they accused Him of claiming to be who He was. And they, denying His claims, danced savagely in their rage the openly rebellious steps of the murderous Anomos. So explicitly did they now dance Anomos' steps that they danced openly in among his howling, bloody mob and asked them to help trample, kill and bury the Singer of the Song of Healing.

The sight was shocking, as their dance and the dance of Anomos' mob fit perfectly together. One could not help but see that Anomos had put much planning into it. Together they danced a most horrible dance of death—each knew well his part. They trampled the yielding Living One beneath their feet with slow cruelty. The hellish rage in their eyes and the cruel laughter from their curled lips sought for even one sign or sigh of weakness.

He never broke step with the patterns of the Song of Healing, even while they trampled Him. But this they could not see, for their rage blinded them to the glorious pattern He danced—one foretold in the beginning but never before seen. He embraced their cruelties with humble strength, as though He had some use for them.

What the mob could not hear, but somehow, Diakrina could—and she could clearly see those on the great blue were also responding to what she was hearing—was a most beautiful and haunting Song of Love coming from the Living One, even as they trampled Him. Diakrina remembers bitter tears streaming down her face all through this black scene, made even more moving by the pathos of the Song of Love. It felt as if she, too, were being trampled and mocked. The pain was so intense she could not consciously bear such torture. Mercifully, she blacked out.

When she came to herself, all was quiet among the followers of the Song of Healing. They sang and danced no more, but gathered in troubled groups and spoke softly in fear, while some wept.

Anomos and his mocking mob danced a solemn dance of defiant pride. A certain, cruel self-control enabled them to dance patterns of mock solemnity. But they could only hold rank for a few minutes at a time until they would fall in a heap of insane laughter, which was not in the least true laughter at all, but rather, relieved maniacal hatred—the celebration of true cowards. And then, as if they did not know what to do with themselves, they would start all over again with the steps of mocking solemnity.

The Living One lay trampled and dead with unspeakable wounds. The members of the Great Dance standing all around on the great blue bowed their heads in utter amazement, but not despair. Though they were uncertain as to what would or could happen next, that something wonderful surely would happen they could not doubt.

Each knew He would not have embraced this cruel death if it

did not befit the purpose of the Great Dance and the Song of Healing. All was designed to bring the dead and separated back to the Great Dance by way of what He had called the Dance of Life. Somehow they knew He was treading the steps of the Dance of Death backwards and undoing its curse.

Except for the mob, all was quiet until the sun saw this deed three times. Just as the sun spilled its rays for the third time upon the Living One, who was clearly dead, a glorious trumpet sounded far away over the horizon of the great blue. It started golden and soft. But it never took a breath as it steadily grew louder and louder until it seemed the whole of creation would surely shake until it crumbled.

A most beautiful angel, dressed in a garment of light with a golden sash around his waist and at his side a sword of gold with a crimson handle, came swiftly in flight down the center of the aisle which was formed among the dancers of the Great Dance. He did not stop at the edge of the bloody expanse, but flew without hesitation to where the Living One lay.

Standing in midair above the broken body, he raised a beautiful, yet terrible voice that shook the whole creation with these words: "NOW IS THE MYSTERY REVEALED. TEMPORAL ETERNAL DEATH IS SWALLOWED IN INFINITE ETERNAL LIFE. THE LIVING ONE, THE SPEAKING MUSIC AND THE SONG OF HEALING ARE RAISED IN VICTORY OVER THE FINAL ENEMY. LET THE DANCE OF LIFE BEGIN!"

The angel suddenly faded into obscurity as a blinding light exploded from under him. At the same moment, the Speaking Music erupted into the air drenching everything in a glorious Song of Healing. It sounded like a new song but actually it was the same Song of Healing mixed with the haunting Song of Love Diakrina had heard during the awful deed.

Previously, the Songs of Healing and Love had been played as if by a child with only a single note at a time being heard, like on a flute. But now it poured forth as from a full orchestra of Heavenly power and beauty. And there, in the middle of the blinding light, yes, the Source of the light itself, stood the Living One singing the New Song of Healing and Love in unspeakable glory.

He danced the New Pattern of His Dance of Life, first into the little circles of his followers. Jubilation began! He breathed on them and a new presence from His very Self settled within them. They expressed a new power and love by which they danced as none of their fallen race had ever been able. They sang the New Song of Healing and Love as they danced the Dance of Life in splendor.

For many days He danced visibly among them and showed them how they were to teach the Song of Healing and Love to all they met. Those who would begin to sing it would want, and would be able, to learn the Dance of Life and obey its glorious patterns of creative freedom.

Then He led them to the edge of the great blue. There He told them He was going Home to prepare places to receive them and all those to whom they would teach the Dance of Life. Yet, He told them He would be with them still, even while away, by living in them by the Gift of His own Spirit. They were to give this gift to any and all who chose to sing the Song of Healing and Love and dance the Dance of Life, for indeed, He is the Song of Healing and Love. Then He stepped across onto the blue expanse and the Great Dance began a welcome Home celebration as none could ever describe.

Diakrina watched with wonder as the followers of the Living One danced with grace and power. Indeed whenever you looked at any one of them, there with them was the Living One.

They danced like an invading army into the center of the bloody mob. They danced so gloriously and powerfully that Anomos ran around in cowardly fear and confusion while millions broke step with the dance of death and knelt down and sang the Song of Healing and Love, only to rise and join the Dance of Life. And when one would do so, there He would be, immediately with them. Then they would return to dance into the circles of their former fellows to reemerge on the other side of the circle with those who, like themselves, now sang the New Song and danced the Dance of Life.

Then Diakrina saw a most wonderful scene. After a time, some crossed over onto the great blue and were immediately with the Living One. She saw a vast multitude of shining people gathering around this Glorious One who had crushed death by dying. As they gathered in celebration, each became like a piece of an enormous living mirror that increasingly reflected His beauty. No one piece could reflect more than a single aspect of the Glorious One, and that imperfectly compared to His infinite Glory. Yet each continually grew in the clarity (I can only say clarity for there is no words to say what I really mean) of reflecting Him. All together, they formed a marvelous, ever expanding and deepening "mirror." And the Glorious One poured Himself upon them and through them in infinite Love.

Then leading them Personally, He took them to the great blue and into the Great Dance. And all was drenched in joy.

∞——∞

Return to **Chapter Eight**

∞——∞

END OF
APPENDIX

REVIEWS

"The Other Side of Reality is essential truth disguised as entertainment!"
— *David Russell, M.A., Founder & Director of Forever Young Counseling*
Billings, Montana

"The Other Side of Reality is like entering a school of philosophy and theology through the door of the imagination. Ingenious. This multi-dimensional journey into the depths of God is for ... the seeker of treasures. For years Gary Durham was my pastor. I sat spellbound as he established case after case for authenticity of the Word and the power of covenant fellowship with God. I would say he is a theological attorney who knows the Word at a level most of us would tremble to approach."
— *Pat McNab, Ph.D., Eagle's Glen Foundation, Divide, Colorado*

"I have worked and taught with Dr. Gary Durham in many different venues over the years. He is a creative thinker and a natural teacher. This wonderful story is a fresh example of his ability to share important principles through creating an entertaining and engaging story that will draw you into the characters, and before you know it, into new discoveries on your own journey."
— *Alan Scott, Former Senior Pastor, Trinity Church*
Colorado Springs, Colorado

"A riveting adventure story that bathes your mind and imagination in God's point of view. The high drama of this book took me captive much like The Lord Of The Rings. I can't wait to see this Trilogy become a movie."
— *Larry Ryan, Kingsway Foundation, Yukon, Oklahoma*

"An absolutely fascinating exploration of the deceptivity of the enemy of our souls and our ultimate victory over him in Christ! Knowing Dr. Durham as I do, I am not at all surprised at the depth, the coloring, the brilliance of his amazing insight into the reality of what we face in our spiritual journey. I highly recommend this read to anyone who seeks a broader understanding of *The Other Side of Reality*."
— *Dr. Steven Fletcher, District Superintendent Emeritus (and grateful friend), Church of the Nazarene*

"Gary Durham has written a sensational thriller that will keep readers on the edge of their seats."
— *Dr. Stan Toler, Bestselling Author & Speaker Oklahoma City, Oklahoma*

ABOUT THE AUTHOR

Gary L. Durham has been the Lead Pastor/Teacher of New Hope Fellowship, in Palm City, Florida for more than 20 years, and is distinguished for his captivating speaking and teaching. He is the Founder and Director of Veritas Resurgence, which focuses on educating believers through media and publishing. In the past he has served his denomination as a conference speaker, teacher, missionary and pastor and has taught in many different denominations.

He holds three earned degrees, including the Doctorate of Theology and has pursued a post-doctoral Ph.D. in Philosophy with a focus on Apologetics. He served for many years as theologian and master teacher for Freedom Ministries International, a pastoral training institute. He has been a speaker at C.S. Lewis Foundation events and a presenter at their academic forum at Oxford and Cambridge University.

In what he calls his "hobby life" he is an inventor, along with his brother Steve, and together they hold several patents worldwide in the field of electromagnetics and energy generation technology.

He has a daughter and son-in-law, Pastor David and Janet Russell, a son and daughter-in-law, Pastor Ryan and Colleen Durham, and four grandchildren, Gavin and Ethan Russell, as well as Kaia Grace and Ian Ryan Durham. He and his wife Sheryl of 52 years live in Stuart, Florida.

VERITAS RESURGENCE PUBLISHING